Deadly Friends

Through the watery haze, Getts could see that Doc had his knife out. He clamped his hand onto Doc's wrist, digging his nails into it as hard as he could. His lungs were screaming for air. He kicked toward the surface, struggling to get a breath, only to have Doc pull him down again. Desperately, he grabbed for the mouthpiece of Doc's regulator, yanking the hose from the tank. Doc had lost his air supply, but by now Getts was literally dying for air only four feet under the ocean surface. He let go of Doc's hand, kicked, and broke through the surface. He sucked in hard and was rewarded with a sweet rush of oxygen. Then it hit him.

Doc still has the knife!

He looked down to see Doc draw back his hand, the ten-inch blade glimmering in the underwater light, and now driving straight at him. . . .

NAVY SEALs
INSURRECTION RED

Mike Murray

A SIGNET BOOK

SIGNET
Published by New American Library, a division of
Penguin Putnam Inc., 375 Hudson Street,
New York, New York 10014, U.S.A.
Penguin Books Ltd, 27 Wrights Lane,
London W8 5TZ, England
Penguin Books Australia Ltd, Ringwood,
Victoria, Australia
Penguin Books Canada Ltd, 10 Alcorn Avenue,
Toronto, Ontario, Canada M4V 3B2
Penguin Books (N.Z.) Ltd, 182–190 Wairau Road,
Auckland 10, New Zealand

Penguin Books Ltd, Registered Offices:
Harmondsworth, Middlesex, England

Published by Signet, an imprint of New American Library,
a division of Penguin Putnam Inc.

First Printing, January 2000
10 9 8 7 6 5 4 3 2 1

To Brock, Murray, Michele, Kendel, Kolan and Kent

United Nations, New York

"Unan," Frederick P. Hazeltine said to the secretary general, "you said you were going to take care of that maniac two years ago. And he's still at it. I've been instructed by President Spalding to advise you that he is prepared to act without Security Council approval."

Unan Luumba stroked nervously at his beard, hardly more than a stubble, then at his mustache. Conscious of his shaking hands, he tried to turn toward his desk, away from the relatively young, portly man before him. Frederick Hazeltine intimidated the secretary general of the United Nations by a combination of the force of his intellect and his goddamn unvaried confidence that he spoke for the most powerful country in the world. Unan Luumba, born of humble origins in Zambia, Africa, had risen from eating grubs found in logs in the forest to dining in New York's most fashionable restaurants, and was now the prized guest of the world's most powerful and beautiful men and women. He shuddered at the haunting specter of returning to his homeland and to his former hand-to-mouth existence. Although he favored DiCanti handmade silk suits that fit his slim sixty-year-old body like a glove, in his soul of souls he sensed that the red dust of his mother country could still be found in his trouser cuffs. Hazeltine, by effortless contrast, wore off-the-rack suits that appeared rumpled even when fresh. The man felt no need to appear svelte—indeed he was plump at forty-seven—in order to work his will on the world. Damn the man. "Sanctions? Against his country? The people are already so poor that you would lose . . ."

"We have the grounds. You know that. Think about the Middle East going up in flames . . . or down, rather, in a pile of bodies if his filthy biological weapons are used," Hazeltine said, the pudgy fingers of his right hand moving lightly from side to side in order to make his point. Hazeltine's voice did not rise as he interrupted the older man who, in the diplomatic table of organization, outranked him. "The President has been more than patient." Hazeltine allowed his dark brown eyes, framed by heavy, black brows and lashes, to drift away from the diminutive African man, who squirmed in his chair.

"Of course he is a vile man, yes. But the weapons selling business is a thing of his past. He is hardly a threat to civilization. Nobody listens to him. He is unimportant."

"You are wrong. The President has sources of information that you do not, Unan," Hazeltine said.

My God, there he goes again. What nonsense. What insolence. "Mr. Hazeltine . . ."

"What happened to calling me Fred?"

"Okay, Fred. I think President Spalding is, forgive the characterization, 'obsessed' with this frightened little Serb. Krabac . . ."

"For your information William Spalding is not the kind of man who obsesses about anything. He is highly intelligent . . ."

"Yes, I know."

". . . as you know. Only small men become obsessed and I assure you that Bill Spalding is not a small man."

The secretary general detested conflict. His hands flopped uselessly in his lap. "I . . . we are doing everything that we can."

"That's just our point, Unan," the ambassador said.

God, he can be terrible. He looks through me, Luumba thought, he thinks circles around me, and he doesn't care about me or others like me in the world. What are we doing here, in this room, in this building, plotting? "Frederick." The secretary general used the American ambassador's first name only with difficulty; his training, education, and social customs were opposed to informality in this distinctly business setting. Americans pride themselves on being emotionally close to people who were almost strangers, he thought, to seem empathetic to casual friends, as though there were no such thing as a class system in their country. "We have been discussing the issue with the International Tribunal in The Hague. They are entirely familiar with General Krabac's history and they look forward to assisting us however they can."

Hazeltine allowed himself a whimsical smile as he moved gracefully to his feet, signaling, again out of rank, the end to their meeting. "Yes, well, that's very comforting, Unan. I know that you're doing the best you can." He held out his hand.

Chapter One

What guys like Peach think is that they can drink as much beer as they want without getting drunk. Since the massive man could bench-press 350 pounds, he figured he could cruise through a case of Bud without spilling a drop. He was only here because of his sister, a lady who helped run a wild animal farm for tourists south of Rogersboro, Tennessee, who was robbed at gunpoint, her trailer burned to the ground. Or so she said. Carleen Crosley Fisk never had much luck with men or saving money. She was forty-four, thirteen years older than Peach, and she looked every damn day of it. She smoked too much, drank too much, and women just couldn't hold the stuff the way men can, so Carleen looked lumpy everywhere she shouldn't. Her breasts sagged, too, and that bothered her. Her brows were always knit when she talked to him about her constant and latest problem, as if looking forlorn and glum would convince him that she was really sincere. She'd lost $2,000 in the robbery, she said, but he allowed that the figure was probably less and it was likely stolen by whoever Carleen was keeping house for at the time. Didn't figure, either, that the robber would take time out of his get-away schedule to set fire to Carleen's trailer. But, hell, he gave her $2,000 as a loan—she insisted they call it that—and saw that she got fixed up in a motel where she could cook for herself. He explained to her that he needed to report back to his place of business by 0100 hours Monday morning, and that it was a long drive back down I-75 to south Florida.

"God, you're a nice man, Glennie," she said, touching the palm of her hand to the side of his face. Long hours of exposure to sun had turned his skin dark and probably put some premature wrinkles in his face. Her rough, over-sized hand, which had been abraded by alligator hide and tiger fangs, felt strange to his sense of touch. She always said he was the handsomest man she'd ever known. When she said that, he thought about the notch on his ear, the scar on the bridge of his otherwise pretty straight nose, and the scar on the left side of his chin where battery acid had eaten the flesh. And the teeth she thought were so "beauti-ful and white" were plastic caps. Hell, you got to love a sister who doesn't see all that, he thought. "How come some nice girl never got her hands on you, little brother? You won't stand still long enough, that's why. Who was it you used to date from California? Joyce? Janice? Some-thing like that. I liked her."

"Jean. She liked you, too, Carleen," Peach said.

"Good looking, too, wasn't she?"

"Yep."

"So? What happened?"

"She got to know me, that's what happened," he said. He was opening the door of his Jeep 4x4 as his sister fol-lowed him close behind. As he turned, he saw that Car-leen's brow was knit again. Most girls hate freckles, and he guessed Carleen did, too, but he thought they looked good on her. Kind of kept her young. He felt sorry for his sister because she was her own worst enemy, never seeing the world the way it was, trusting everybody until they beat her up and robbed her, and still she forgave them. He wished she had just a little of the whipass he carried around with him. Yeah, she was just about a quart low on whipass.

"You can't tell me she left you," Carleen said. "I don't believe that."

"What woman in her right mind could bring herself to leave me? I don't think she wanted to go. What happened was her husband came and got her." He hadn't thought about Jean Scolaro for a month and didn't want to start again now. She was something special, and he would always miss her.

He was starting work on his third six-pack of Bud, forty

miles still inside the Georgia state line, when a red light lit up his rearview mirror. Had to be for him, the way the cruiser settled right down on his rear bumper. He let up on the gas pedal, eased the Jeep over to the right shoulder, and braked to a stop. He thought about hiding the beer but he hated sneaks and decided he'd do the best he could when the law got into his face. One thing he wasn't going to do was start an argument with a cop. He could see that the police cruiser was a sheriff's car, not state police. The deputy stayed in his car for a few minutes working the radio before stepping out to approach Peach's car. The cop stopped a half pace behind his door window. Out of the corner of his eye, using the outside sideview mirror, Peach could see that the deputy wore his Smokey Bear hat fastened in the back by a strap, the brim set low over his eyes to make him look intimidating. On his leather belt, Peach noted that he carried a mace canister, handcuffs, a bunch of keys, two ammunition pouches, and a holster that looked like a Glock model 22 or 23, a .40-caliber semiautomatic with a 10-round magazine. A black "crowd tamer" baton was stuck through a leather loop in the utility belt.

The deputy was a few years younger than Peach; big, buffed, but with some fat laid over his muscle system. He had tight curled red hair and green eyes, and a wide, flat face in the middle of which was a pug nose that Peach figured probably matched his dick. He never knew a short-nosed man who had a cock long enough to reach past his ring finger. Cops weren't any different. They might even be especially the same, he figured. Well, he'd keep that remark to himself just as long as he could. He breathed deep and placed his hands in plain sight on the steering wheel.

"Afternoon, sir," the deputy drawled, still behind Peach's left ear. "Nice day for a drive."

"Sure is," Peach said, wanting to say something else entirely.

"Where y' headed?" he said.

"Florida." Fuck him.

After a minute, the cop realized that was all Peach was

going to give up. "That an open can of beer I see beside you in the seat, sir?" he said.

"Not just beer. Heineken. Rest of that shit is what frogs and lizards drink. You ever see those ads on TV? Tells the whole story right there," Peach said. He looked into the backseat, where he'd been throwing the empty bottles. He thought that's what did it.

"Driver's license, please," the cop said firmly.

Peach produced his wallet, took out a driver's license that said his name was Gordon Everett, and handed it to the fuzz. "I know I wasn't speeding," he said, stupidly.

"No, sir, you weren't. When you went through the town of Adelle back there I saw you lift a beer to your mouth. I was sitting behind the bushes by entrance ramp number 133. Can't see me when I get in there. You'd have to turn around and look backwards." He almost beamed.

"And by that time you got me, huh," Peach said. He could see the deputy's name plate pinned over the right side pocket of his shirt. Schuyler.

"You sassin' me, mister?" the officer said.

"Me?" Peach said. "I don't believe in sass. Not giving it or taking it. I'm real easy, Deputy."

He looked at Peach's driver's license. "Gordon Everett? That right? Well, Gordon, you ain't very damn smart, now, are you? 'Cause I'm going to have to arrest you for having an opened alcoholic beverage while operating a vehicle. Step on out of the car please. . . ." The deputy moved a little to give Peach enough space to maneuver through the door.

Peach didn't move right away. "Stay calm, Deputy, but I carry a couple of pieces on me. KBI semiauto under my arm, here," he said, moving his left arm slightly but making sure to keep his hands on the wheel. "And a derringer in my pocket up here," he nodded toward his shirt pocket. "Knife, too," he said.

"Holy shit. Where's the knife?" the cop said, real alert now, tense as hell. He snatched his own gun from his holster and pointed it at Peach.

"Inside, left leg," Peach said, calm as he could with a Glock aimed at his head.

"Okay, buddy, get out of the car, real slow. Careful now or I'll blow your fucking head off. Do it . . . and get down on the ground. Down, right now!"

The sheriff's substation at the town of Adelle was a two-story building built sometime in the fifties, remodeled and painted a few times, now a soft ecru with green trim. There was an outer office that contained two desks near the north wall, several student chairs used for briefing shift changes, and a gun rack that stored shotguns and AR-15 rifles. The rack had a sturdy lock to keep it shut. Near the desks was a radio console filled with reasonably new VHF equipment. In a back room, where they took Peach, was a fingerprint setup, four cells operated manually and locked by key, and a mug-shot camera preset for processing prisoners. The smell of the place was familiar to Peach; gun oil, institutional cleaning fluids, armpit odors, and farts clung to walls that no amount of paint could cover up. He could see a small room off the main squad room that had weight-lifting equipment inside. The stuff had to be within easy reach for men who had a stake in dominating other men. To that extent, Peach and the cops had a similar interest.

"Name on your driver's license says Gordon Robin Everett," a desk sergeant said while Peach sat handcuffed to a chair that was sunk into a concrete slab. The sergeant's name tag said R. Hebert. He wore bifocals and was about ten years older than the other deputies standing around—there were two more besides Schuyler and Hebert—all watching him with interest. "But Florida DMV doesn't have an Everett license with your picture on it. Not even nearly like you. Want to clear that up for us, Mr. Everett?"

Peach could but of course he wouldn't. "Why, I can't believe that, sir," he said. His mouth was dry and he sure could have used a beer. Hair of the dog. "How about a drink of water?"

Sergeant Hebert gave him one of those real long looks, as though he were considering giving Peach either a glass

of water or a kick in the balls. Peach got these looks a lot.
At six feet, three inches tall, his hair cut short, Peach had
a set of muscles that allowed him to swim five miles non-
stop. He made his living bringing war to others. Somehow
that got that across to folks. If Sergeant Hebert knew what
else Peach was trained to do to anyone who opposed him,
Hebert might have just locked him right up and called for
the Feds, Peach thought. But he didn't. "Wesley," Hebert
said to one of his deputies, "get the man a drink."

"What were you doing with those guns?" Deputy
Schuyler asked.

"Well, I was taking them to Florida from Kentucky,"
Peach said.

"Buy 'em up there?" Sergeant Hebert said.

"Sure did," Peach said. "Garage sale."

"I don't suppose you got a receipt for 'em? Or a permit
to carry them?"

"No, like I say, I was just getting from one place to
another. Should have put them in the trunk, I guess." Peach
tried to sound as dumb as he was beginning to feel. Wasn't
too hard.

"You always carry knives strapped to your legs?" Hebert said.

"Sure do," Peach said. "Diving's a hobby of mine."

"We sent your prints to the FBI in Washington, Gordon.
May take a day or two but we'll find out for sure who you
are. We're in no big damn hurry because people who bullshit us don't get special attention. That's what you're doing,
isn't it, Everett?" Hebert said. "Bullshitting us?"

Peach knew a couple of things. One of them was that
the FBI wasn't going to come up with a damn thing on his
fingerprints. He also knew that any chance for escaping
from custody without hurting anyone had past. Unassisted,
that is. "I'd like to call my lawyer," he said.

Sergeant Hebert watched while his deputy handed Peach
a plastic bottle of drinking water. It was hard to manipulate
the bottle to his mouth with his hands still cuffed to the
chair, but the cops weren't about to take them off. Wise,
Peach thought.

"What's your lawyer's name?" Hebert asked.

"Bobby," he replied.

Hebert's jaw ratcheted a little tighter, but the name of Peach's lawyer was none of his damn business and he should remember that. "Okay," he said, "one call. Schuyler, put leg shackles on Mr. Everett, here, and bring the phone to him."

Peach was aware of how the deputies positioned themselves around him. Never more than one man came near him at a time, the others in a "ready" position, never allowing him to have his hands free unless they had attached leg shackles first, always keeping their firearms away from his hands. Not bad for counties. He kind of liked Hebert, liked the busted blood vessels that cris-crossed his nose, and the ears that looked like a dog had chewed them. Might even be fun drinking beer with the man, but Peach damn sure didn't trust him. Not at all.

Peach dialed long distance using a credit card number to place the call. There was no answer, but a machine picked up on the fourth ring. "You have reached the number you have dialed," a plain male voice said. "If you want to leave a message, wait for the beep." The beep sounded immediately and Peach started talking. "This is Gordon Everett," he said, knowing that using the name on his driver's license would say a lot about the fact that he had tip-toed into a puddle of doo-doo. "I'm afraid I got a little too thirsty for an ice-cold Heiny while I was driving and a very nice young policeman was kind enough to point out my mistake. I'm in the sheriff's jail at a place called Adelle, Georgia, and I would appreciate it if your law firm could bail me out right away."

At that moment someone picked up the telephone. "You are a dumb fuck," the voice said.

"My mother doesn't think so," he said.

"Your mother fucked the Seventh Fleet before it sailed," the voice replied.

"Mom has a strong work ethic," Peach said.

"Did the laws beat on you?"

"Not yet."

"Too bad," the voice said.

"I want to go home. I can't sleep without my pillow."

"So, pay the fine, you idiot."

"There is a complication. There is no fine because the laws have a problem with my name," Peach explained.

"The DMV fuck up again?"

"Yes. That's it exactly," Peach said. He could hear a sigh at the other end of the telephone.

"I'll talk to our divine leader. He will probably wisely recommend that you sit on your disgusting hemorrhoids for the entire weekend because the three of us are going to party our dicks to a nub. Do you understand that, sailor?"

"Yes, I do," Peach said. "But I'm begging for mercy."

"Are you begging for mercy just because you want to party with us, or because you are an oily gutted soggy sack of shit, completely incapable of thinking or acting for yourself?" he said.

"All of the above."

"All right. Stay where you are."

Doc was having too much fun so Peach just dropped the phone into its cradle. He and Peach had done service together before, so Peach knew how his mind worked. Or didn't work. Doc was bigger than a midget, whatever minimum size you had to be for their outfit, but Peach knew that he had balls big enough to carry around in a wheelbarrow. He was left handed so naturally he figured he was smarter than anyone else. And he more than loved women. He prostrated on their footfalls. Often Peach's bloodhound nose had been thrown off the scent of perfectly viable ladies because Doc, in his juvenile eagerness to find erotic pleasure, had slobbered all over the spoor. Peach only hoped that he found Adelle, Georgia, before a lady crossed his line of vision.

Sergeant Hebert was looking at him with his eyes half-crossed. "That was your lawyer?" he asked.

"Answering service. They're trying to get hold of him, now."

The guy Peach had to get hold of was his skipper, Lieutenant Robert Getts. Of course, like Peach, that wasn't his real name. They were a new unit, called Mob 4, shorthand for Mobile 4, and Peach was the only one who had known Getts before, known him more than he maybe should have. He didn't know Grumpy, but he was a SEAL, too, so they all had a common experience of demo training and covert ops before Mob 4 was put together for "special" missions.

It was Saturday night and there wasn't a jail in the Western world that wasn't getting filled up near midnight. Alcohol has a terrible, terrible effect on amateurs. So Peach was meeting and greeting new friends as they were hauled in, almost all drunk, some beat up, most of them poor. Hell, if they had money they would have bailed themselves out. Pretty good share of them were crop pickers, half were Latinos or black. Peach could sleep anywhere. He had slept on the deck of a ship with ice cold seawater sloshing over him; he had slept in a snow-covered foxhole, on a pile of rubble of bricks and mortar, in trucks, airplanes, trees, concrete. He'd no sooner start sawing logs than they'd bring in a new guy who would step on his face a couple of times before collapsing on his own good square of unused cell floor. When Peach awoke again at 0300 hours in the morning, all four cells were full of I-75 pilgrims. Anybody who didn't wake up when this latest piece of walking garbage was put into his cell must have been dead.

The man stunk. Bad. He smelled like somebody had poured an entire bottle of sour booze over his head, which, Peach later found out, was exactly what had happened. You wouldn't ask a guy like that to take a breathalyser test because why waste everybody's time? He smelled like he'd puked on himself, only worse. You can only achieve that kind of stench by rolling around in the guts of animals killed in a slaughterhouse and having the stink blow-dried onto your body. It's the kind of odor that's so bad, if you're within fifty meters you want to gnaw through the concrete walls of the cell to escape. Naturally, you can't do that without doing a lot of damage to your teeth. So Peach's fellow inmates groaned as one and cowered even closer to the inner wall, away from the new arrival.

Despite his vile face, unwashed body, filthy clothing, and

sickening smell, Peach was glad to see Bobby Getts. He didn't rush up and kiss him, though.

The jailer locked the door behind him as quickly as possible and almost ran down the aisle near the cells to get back to the relatively sweet-smelling squad room.

"Hello, darling," Peach said, pursing his lips toward his unit commander.

"Go fuck yourself," Getts replied, not smiling.

Getts, Peach, and the others in SEAL 6 had often used disguises in the past. Peach had once dressed himself in the costume of a Chinese juggler and entertained an audience in Macau without the soldiers who were frantically searching for him seeing through his heavy makeup. SEALs had used the uniforms of other country's military, as well as street people, firemen, businessmen, to name just a few. Whatever it took to do the job. SEALs like Mob 4 had access to the best disguises and papers the government could produce.

The other SEALs believed the scuttlebutt that Bobby Getts got a commission from ROTC at Stanford and his claim that he got an academic scholarship to go there. But if he was really so damn smart, Peach figured, he wouldn't have volunteered for the SEALs. Especially SEAL 6. Bobby was a shade under six feet—Peach thought it bothered Getts that he wasn't "tall"—but he was as hard as a dried boat painter. Peach thought every guy in his unit could probably kick Robert's ass, but most folks would have to dedicate their lives to the job in order to get it done. Except him. Peach was tougher than donkey dick. Getts was three years younger than Peach but probably spent his time better. While Peach drank to wretched excess and chased dick-huggers, Bobby did things like study German, Arabic, and Italian, and took graduate courses by correspondence. Also, he was the official leader of his unit and the U.S. Navy paid him more than Peach, a chief gunner's mate, which is something that Peach never admitted bothered him. He was kind of proud of Bobby because he even went to the trouble of wearing caps on his front teeth. The man was as good as his word. If you were lucky enough to be one of the people to whom Getts gave his word, you owned something awful damned valuable. That was a big fucking asset in their business, Peach thought. He loved the guy. Fact is, Peach figured they'd give their lives for each other. Couldn't survive any other way.

He saw Getts wink a cruddy eye in his direction and Peach said "Howdy, stranger. We don't smell many like you in these here parts."

Getts opened up his mouth like he was going to respond but instead he kind of gagged. He pointed to his mouth. "You can't talk?" Peach said. "Or you want me to shut up?"

Getts kind of hummed, started gyrating his hips. He couldn't sing but he was a fair dancer—Peach had seen him dance with Lydia well enough to make other people clap when they were through—and Peach got the picture that Getts thought he was in the Casbah doing a cobra tango. The thought was interrupted when Getts opened his mouth wide, reached inside with his thumb and forefinger, and started to work on a molar in the back of his jaw where his wisdom teeth used to be. Peach was interested. He'd never seen anybody do this, not even Getts.

Something came loose back there and Getts gently pulled an object out of his mouth. It was a tooth. Wrapped around the tooth, which was really only an emplacement, was a fine piece of filament. Bobby slowly started pulling. Up came the filament and on the end of that was tied a length of DOD CODE: M456, stock number 1375-028-5-168, commonly referred to as det cord.

Simply put, it goes boom.

Attached to the det cord came the coup de grâce, a small plastic bag with a little something inside.

Getts burped. "Ah, much better." He pointed to the plastic bag and said "C-4."

"Bless you, my brother, for I have sinned, yet verily you are paying the price. For this you will spend a fortnight in the arms of my fourteen-year-old sister who loves filthy SEALs," Peach said, heartfelt.

"You don't have a fourteen-year-old sister," Getts said.

"No, but if I did she would be all yours. I swear it."

"What the hell is wrong with him? He sick?" a bald man with snaggly teeth said. He and others, now awake, eyed Bobby with rightful suspicion, though still not curious enough to fight their way past his smell for a closer look.

"No. He's a magician," Peach said.

Time is always of the essence when escaping from jail, so Peach wasted none opening up the baggie that contained the white, putty-like material that was a mixture of RDX (cyclonite), polyisobutylene, diethylhexyl, and a shot of motor oil. The texture was similar to the caulk you could buy at your local hardware store for installing windows. In their case they were going to use it to open doors. Getts didn't waste words asking how Peach got into the current mess, but there was a good reason to get him out. If the local Mounties held on to him long enough, they would find out more things about him than they should know and, by extension, about Mob 4. And if those items ever surfaced publicly, Mob 4 would be all through serving its country clandestinely. So neither of them talked while Peach packed the cell door keyhole with C-4 and then wrapped det cord around the wad. Meanwhile, Getts dropped his trousers and scummy looking underpants to expose not only his family's jewels but six inches of M670 safety fuse. He didn't wince a bit when he pulled the taped fuse from his leg, bringing with it a bunch of hair from a very sensitive place.

Getts placed the fuse securely onto the end of the det cord. Now all that was needed was a match. "Got a light?" he asked. Peach didn't. He asked the bald headed guy if he had one. "Don't smoke," he said. "Not even dope. Never did." But luckily for them and the tobacco companies, other folks in the cell did.

"Stay back," Getts said in a commanding voice. "Cover your face." The kind of mini-charge they'd put together would expend itself inside the lock chamber of the door, but small pieces could possibly escape from the keyhole and ding somebody. Peach made sure his cellmates stayed on one side or the other of the blast line. They were all wide awake now, some a little nervous, but mostly real interested in what was going to happen next. Any blow struck against authority seemed to turn them on.

"Where's Doc and Grumpy?" Peach asked Getts, meaning Jake Gathers and Truman Lynch, the rest of their team.

"Outside," Getts said. "They'll go on the bang. Okay, let's do it."

So he touched it off. The fuse burned at a rate of about forty seconds per foot, so it didn't take long for it to burn down to the det cord. Det cord burns at 21,000 feet per second, so the C-4 went off instantly. Kabloom. There was a slight concussive movement of air, a noise like a big firecracker, and the door swung open.

Peach knew exactly what would happen then. At the sound of the explosion, his two swim partners outside would pull balaclava scarves over their faces and rush quickly inside the sheriff's office. They had practiced takeovers like this in SEAL 6 hundreds of times, maybe a thousand. They could do it in their sleep—and sometimes did—and they always knew what each team member was doing. The secret to success in the antiterrorist hostage rescue business was timing and precision, all of which equals surprise. And that only comes from practice. Practice and more practice, and when you finally have it down cold, even more practice. That way you surprise the other guys, and not your own. By the time Getts and Peach entered the squad room, Doc and Grumpy were shackling the two on-duty deputies to the very chair Peach had been attached to hours before. He noticed that none of them carried a weapon. It was a good thing, he thought—they didn't want to hurt anyone and, besides, they didn't need them anyway. They secured the deputies' mouths with duct tape, then took away their guns. They would be as good as new in a couple hours, with nothing more than bruises and red faces. The SEALs retrieved Peach's personal belongings, including the keys to his 4x4.

"I apologize about the inconvenience, Officers," Getts said in a pleasant enough tone. "We just couldn't let this

sorry sack of shit stay here too long. If he's away from his
mommy more than a couple of days, he gets colic.''

Getts removed all of the money from Peach's wallet and
dropped it near the deputies. "This ought to pay for what
we broke.''

Chapter Two

During the six months that Mob 4 had been together, they always hung out at a place called the Conch. It was a fly-blown food and booze dive that had three walls and, when the bar was closed for the night, rattan curtains that unrolled behind a sliding iron scissor gate. The house specialty was anything caught in the Gulf of Mexico that day and sold to Slick, the guy who owned the Conch. Slick served whatever came to his mind. You could get any meal at any time. Spaghetti served for breakfast, sometimes whether you wanted it or not, or sushi at all hours. He served beer both in bottles and draft, booze of any label, and soda from a coin-operated machine that stood next to an ancient jukebox. Slick's creaking tables and cedar benches came from Sears' patio department, complete with holes for umbrellas. In their campaign to secure total male bonding, Doc, Peach, Grumpy, and Getts had torn up their share of bars, but were very careful not to wreck the Conch. It was already falling apart and didn't need their help. They were currently celebrating Peach's escape from the clink by drinking pre-dinner rum shooters and eating hors d'oeuvres straight from the can, with nothing else planned for the night. Getts had had a lot on his mind for the past few weeks, but Crosley's bust-out served to clarify his thinking.

His recent birthday reminded him that it was about time to make a decision whether or not to stay in the Navy. After all, he had a degree from Stanford in Social Psychology, plus forty hours of graduate study applicable toward an advanced degree, and that didn't count the twelve units of foreign language he had accrued at the Monterey language service schools in California. It wasn't that he could step out of the Navy and open a SocialPsych store, of course, but with more academic work he could look forward to a reasonably satisfying career teaching at the university level. Or, with the MS, he could at least expect to find something in personnel at any one of a number of major corporations, maybe even one with overseas potential. Counseling was also a possibility, although the idea of giving advice to other people seemed pretentious to him. Giving orders, on the other hand, was an entirely different story.

Money wasn't the dominating factor in considering Getts's future, luckily for him. His father, an investment banker, had been on KAL Flight 007 when it was shot down near Sakhalin Island in the USSR. Getts was only thirteen years old at the time and he took it hard. In retrospect, it was the Russians killing his father that made Getts want to enter the armed forces. In any case, his father invested very well during his life, and he had taken out a large amount of insurance on himself. So much so that Getts and his mother probably couldn't spend it all if they tried. He always got a hell of a kick out of his mother, Lucille. Everyone called her Buzzy. Once, when Getts was nine years old, he told her he needed $5 because he was going to hitchhike to Los Angeles to visit his uncle Joe. His mother thought about it for a minute and then said it sounded like a good idea. She'd hitchhike with him, she said. They packed a single bag and took a city bus out from the West Hills in Portland, Oregon, to Barber Boulevard where it crossed I-5. They got out there and started thumbing. Twelve hundred miles over two days. As they passed through Salinas, he and his mother ate stuffed artichokes and garlic bread. Nothing ever tasted so good to Getts before or since. When his mother died, he thought, the world was going to stop turning on its axis.

He had played water polo for as long as he could remember, including at Stanford, where the team was rated in the top ten every year he was there. The Navy SEALs was a natural choice for him after ROTC. It was a lot tougher than he thought it was going to be when he volunteered, but there was no way to prepare oneself, either mentally or physically, for the shock that your mind and body got when you started BUD training. But if it was tough, it was just as exhilarating. He loved jumping out of airplanes, locking out of submarines, playing with explosives—all the stuff a nutcase likes, he loved. It was hard to be a SEAL and not be cocky, hard not to swagger, to feel superior. Because the fact of life was that SEALs were the elite of elite forces, and SEAL 6 was somewhere above even that.

Every minute of his military life was exciting. They traveled all over the world, swam in waters from the Gulf of Alaska to the Florida Keys to the Gulf of Aden to Truk Lagoon. They spent weeks in Europe, months in the UK training with the SAS, went on missions in South America and Africa. And they played hard. Sometimes a smidge too hard.

Like when he first saw Lydia. She was sitting right here in the Conch with a nothing of a guy and another couple. Getts had to meet her, had to impress her by saying something really cool, but naturally when you're under pressure to impress someone your mind invariably goes blank.

Then he thought of the perfect thing. He reached into Grumpy's plate of spaghetti and took hold of a noodle. Then he sucked it into his nose partway and let it hang there. "What the fuck are you doing?" Grumpy said.

"That girl over there in the blue sweatshirt. I'm going to attract her attention," he said.

Grumpy thought about it for a minute then said, "Well, if you really want to impress her, put one in the other side, too."

So he did, sucking one up his right nostril. He looked over at the girl but she wasn't looking at him. Bummer. Meantime, he ate calamari broiled in butter sauce and knocked down rum shooters. Somebody at a table next to them, a woman, put her hand over her mouth and ran outside. She went around the corner but the Conch's walls are real thin and soon they could all hear her stomach turning inside out. "It's not working. She's not looking over here," Grumpy said.

So Grumpy put the other end of the spaghetti noodle in his mouth and sucked it out of Getts's nose. Two more people ran out of the Conch, leaving their food right there on the table. "That do it?" Getts asked Peach, not wanting to look at her himself. He was trying to be cool. But he could never compare to Peach. Peach was wearing a baseball hat backwards, a sleeveless sweatshirt ripped at the neck with "Certain Death" lettered on the front. He was wearing dark glasses, too. Talk about cool. The rest of Mob 4 looked ratty next to him. "Nope," he said.

"Let's go see a movie," Doc said, bored with the whole charade. It sounded good to Getts. There was only one movie house in Pamino Beach and he always tried to make it a point to see every film that got there. He also wasn't making much progress with the lady across the room. As they stood up to go, Peach grabbed a handful of raw fish floating around in soy sauce and green mustard and stuffed them into the pocket of his shorts. "I'll get the bill, Skipper," he said but Getts pushed him away and paid for it himself.

SEALs get $175 a month dive pay, $225 parachute, and between $55 and $110 per month pro pay. But Getts still had more money than his swim buddies. SEALs don't stand much on rank, the object being to identify with one another so thoroughly they were interchangeable teammates when push came to shove. They only called him Skipper when they wanted something, Getts accused them. The others were already outside, a streak of soy sauce running down Peach's leg like he'd been hit in an artery. Getts couldn't help but notice on the way out that everybody in the place was looking at him. Everyone except the one he wanted.

But he thought his hard work was not wasted, because she called. That was five months ago. He had seen Lydia on almost all of his off-duty days ever since.

And he still got to do all these fun things with guys that seemed to him like the greatest guys in the world. They shared food, danger, their deepest secrets, and pain. Lots of pain. Getts had been having a hell of a time asking himself if he wanted to give that all up and go back to a classroom or a corporate office. But cracking Peach out of the Georgia jail made the decision for him. He realized then that setting up the operation, pulling it off—in this rare case without hurting anyone—and doing it all like nobody else in the world could do it, felt too good to leave. And it was still kickass fun.

So tonight, Getts was feeling great, and he made up his mind to make the Navy a long-term proposition. Sure, there were times when you had to put up with some buttheads that sent orders down from the Pentagon or USSOC (U.S. Special Operations Command) to the deputy chief of naval operations for plans, policy and ops, or from NCA (National Command Authority), all of whom they answered to.

Although it was a bureaucratic nightmare, Getts was still glad his orders came from the Top. The U.S. Navy to this day does not admit that SEAL 6 exists. Well, it does. And Getts's special unit, Mob 4, damn sure exists. But they had some sharp brass in that chain of command that saved the unit from most of the mass monkey fucks that plagued every other unit in the Navy from time to time. The Navy was an honorable calling and as long as it was holding his interest, Getts couldn't imagine doing anything else.

The meeting took place not in the oval office, but in one of the many small, private, and secure conference rooms scattered within the White House. Room L-212 was below ground level, and therefore had no windows. It was a generic conference room, containing a network of the main building's telephone system, a fancy coffee urn with White House cups and saucers, recessed lighting, a projection screen, and a dark mahogany table that would seat eighteen. For this meeting, however, there were only three people present. Frederick P. Hazeltine maintained his usual slouched position in one of the Leatherette swivel chairs, his mop of black hair hanging petulantly below one eye, his four-in-hand tie slightly askew, giving him the appearance of an upwardly bound car salesman. In a chair next to Hazeltine was sixty-six-year-old Roger Demerit, the National Security Council advisor. Demerit still had a full head of snow-white hair that matched his bushy eyebrows. His face was heavily lined, from too many hours spent under the sun at the helm of his twenty-two-foot racing sloop named *Ruthless,* after his wife, he would say. Demerit was a hero of the Cold War, an Ivy League–bred CIA man, the kind of man of whom the Agency was most proud. Following Yale law school, he quickly marched through the ranks of the Company doing jobs from intel estimates and data analysis to serving as a field agent in three countries, before being appointed to the trusted and esteemed job of station chief in Berlin during the "savage sixties." Back then, the USSR believed that America's strength was being sapped by the Vietnam War—with the concentration of strategic military men and materials assigned to Asia, America's willpower and intelligence activities would necessarily be weakened in Europe. Almost single-handedly, Roger Demerit built a modestly effective intelligence-gathering capability in Western Europe into an aggressive powerhouse of agents, who penetrated not only the USSR but the inner circles of the KGB itself. Demerit was responsible for turning and controlling Colonel Rudolf Kozinsky, running him well into the 1980s, when it was clear to many, and certainly Demerit, that the USSR had lost its capability of striking a mortal military blow against the West.

Kozinsky was eventually caught by the KGB counterintelligence division of the First Chief Directorate. He was interrogated for twenty days, then thrown alive into an oven. The event seemed to affect Demerit personally. Soon afterward, he quit government service and turned to the practice of civil law with Hillings, Willard, Seagate and Freidkin in Washington, D.C. Roger Demerit kept a very low profile, enjoying his private life spending time with his wife and three grandchildren, but was never farther away from the ear of the President than his desk telephone. His reputation for honesty was without equal, and his insights into world affairs almost prescient.

When President William Spalding called upon him to serve his first administration as National Security Council director, Roger Demerit accepted with only minor reservations. As much as he had savored the cloister of his work and family, a part of him had missed the intrigue of international gamesmanship. He was, he supposed, a spook at heart. And he thought he could bring something unique to this young president who had no experience and little knowledge of things military, and was an admitted neophyte in the foreign policy arena. Demerit could do more than simply give honest advice—he could actively guide William Spalding as only an older, well-experienced man could steer a younger one. One administration later, he found, to his surprise, that the young president had come to enjoy not only the trappings of power, but the wielding of it as well. Heady stuff for a man who had his finger on the trigger of the world's most advanced and powerful army.

Demerit shifted in his chair, reaching to adjust a stocking under the rich, blue serge material of his suit. He hated wearing garters, but there were times like this when he could not stand the distraction of hiking up a sagging sock. He glanced at Fred Hazeltine who cared not in the least about his own appearance and was busy echoing the dark thoughts and mendacious words of his college classmate, Bill Spalding.

"I don't understand your reluctance, Roger," Hazeltine said without looking directly at the National Security Council director. "The President has been the very personification of patience in this matter. Right? Or have I somehow misunderstood the issue?"

Demerit looked up at the President. "Bill" Spalding, as he preferred to be called, was well over six feet, expanding slightly at the middle despite his well-publicized early morning jogs around Washington. His face remained youthful, unlined, an easy smile forming often under his rather bulbous nose, the only detraction from his otherwise handsome face. The President had stopped pacing the room and allowed himself to sink into a chair opposite his ambassador to the UN and his NSC advisor. He regarded the older man with impatience and, Demerit thought, some antipathy. "Well," Demerit said, "I don't know what more we can do. You said yourself, Mr. President, that the international community doesn't love our trade sanctions as much as we enjoy using them."

"Now, what the hell does that mean, Roger?" the President said.

"It means just what I said. Somebody gets out of line and we hit 'em with trade restrictions. Period. Hell, it works. I won't argue that. Better sanctions than a war any day," Demerit said.

"Well, I'm not going to waste my time defending trade sanctions," the President said.

"No, sir. You shouldn't. In fact, I think we ought to continue to squeeze Serbia even harder. Sooner or later they're going to have to throw Vadim Krabac out, and when they do we'll be there to catch him."

"For Christ's sake, Roger," the President groaned. "I'm not going to wait for what the Serbs may or may not decide to do."

"Roger," Hazeltine leaned forward in his chair, "would you be kind enough to explain to us what happens to the rest of the Middle East and the Western nations while we rock back and forth on the White House porch? General Krabac is not only guilty of murdering thousands of innocent Muslims . . ."

"Hundreds . . . ," Demerit interjected.

". . . and assorted other groups during an illegal war in Croatia, but is the largest dealer in biological and chemical weapons in the world. We're still on the same page there, aren't we, Roger?"

"In the first place I think we should refer to the man as Minister Krabac," Demerit said. "He's an elected official of a sovereign nation, after all."

The President regarded Roger Demerit with stoney silence. Hazeltine did not blink. "Minister, my ass. He's a monster! If we don't stop him from spreading that deadly shit around the world to people like Hussein, more innocent people will die. Generations of them will be genetically poisoned. Not just Kurds, Roger. Americans. Can you live with that?"

"We have no verification that he's involved in biological weapons trading," Demerit said, slumping deeper into his chair.

"I said he is," Spalding said.

Demerit admitted silently to himself that Hazeltine might be right about Krabac being a heinous war criminal. But he suspected the President's intense hatred of the man stemmed from something different altogether. The disagreement was really about what to do with Krabac. The President hadn't said it yet, but Demerit could feel it coming. He had been in the business of guessing what the other man's intentions were too long to miss the subtleties of this setting—a maximum gathering of power and a minimum amount of witnesses.

"So what do you think we should do?" Demerit said.

"We take the son of a bitch out."

So there it was. Demerit shuddered, not at the thought of taking a life—hell, he had some experience of his own with that—but at the way the President said it. Like he was invincible. Like it was *his* courage that would be on the line. Yes, the draft dodger from down south was proving he could bite the bullet with the best of them. How in the name of God, Demerit thought, could it come to a place in this nation's history that a morally dysfunctional man could rise to the rank of commander in chief? "You mean kill him, Mr. President?"

"That's exactly right."

"Assassination," Demerit said.

"You've never heard the word before? Are you telling me that after all your years in this business you've never given an order to have someone killed? Is that what you're telling us, Roger?" the President said.

"There is a law against assassination. Executive Order 12-333 says . . ."

"It's a presidential order and I'm the president, so I can *damn* well change any order I want."

Demerit felt his chest contracting, a numbness spreading in his fingertips. "Like hell you can."

"Like hell I *can't*! I just have, and you'll carry it out, Demerit, because I'm your commander in chief. Now, let's get it done."

The President stormed out of the room.

Hazeltine started to rise. "Stay a minute, Fred," Demerit said. As though he had been expecting it, Hazeltine sat down again, his head resting wearily against the back of the overstuffed fake leather chair.

"What's on the President's mind?" Demerit asked the diplomat.

"That's obvious, Roger. You've heard it all."

"I don't think so. This is all bullshit. Krabac is a fourth-rate player in Eastern Europe, not on the world stage. He isn't Moammar Kadaffi or Saddam Hussein or another Adolf Hitler. He's a nobody," Demerit said.

"He's a threat to world peace," Hazeltine said, still avoiding eye contact with the older man.

"You don't believe that and neither do I. Krabac called your friend, the President, some nasty names. That's what happened. He publicly said that Spalding was the most superficial leader the West has ever had. Spalding is embarrassed, and that's it, isn't it?" the NSC director said.

"Nonsense." Hazeltine rose from his chair. Still avoiding looking Demerit in the eye, he said, "Bill Spalding isn't that kind of man."

"He's exactly that kind of man," Demerit shot back.

"Then quit, goddamn it, Roger! If you don't approve of the President's decisions, have the good grace to resign your office."

"I think about that every day of my life, Freddy, but I'm afraid that if I did that, he'd appoint someone like you to replace me. No, I'd rather have him fire me so I could tell everybody why."

This time their eyes met. "Never mind, Roger. I'll take care of it myself."

*   *   *

Structurally, Mob 4 was an experimental team, an autonomous unit that trained and executed missions often apart, but not always independent of, the larger SEAL teams. Mob 4 used force multipliers in com gear, delivery systems, firepower, and experimental war hardware. Like the new "smart shooter," the objective individual combat weapon (OICW) that fired two kinds of rounds: a 5.56mm round good for two thousand yards with dead accuracy in the lower barrel, and a 20mm high-explosive round through the top barrel from a 6-shot magazine. It had a fire control and sight system, optics selector, and a 20mm fuse control. When the weapon finally goes into mass production, its estimated cost will be more than $15,000 each. SEALs had them right after they were engineered. Mob 4 and SEAL 6 planned to give them a real field test. With enough ammunition, the four of them could whip the ass of an entire battalion.

Marines have recon teams whose job is to scout for operational landing areas and takeovers (like oil platforms at sea) and they are usually comprised of four-man teams. Getts's unit was equipped, trained, and prepared to do force recon work, but as a part of SEAL 6, which specialized in antiterrorist and hostage rescue missions, they did exactly that work. These assignments typically required a larger unit capability—but a honed tac unit, like Mob 4, could get into a target area clandestinely and neutralize an individual or a small group, and be out before the shit hit the fan. They were sprinters. With the firepower, communications, and transportation provided by the larger SEAL unit, a Mob 4 group could theoretically make the dash into the fire zone and deal with the target directly. Or, if required, they could stand off and execute the target mission from a distance of three thousand yards or more, roughly the maximum effective range of a sniping rifle. Mob 4 duty was a two-year gig, and Getts and his buddies were enjoying the hell out of the simple tranquility of their social warm-up at Pamino Beach. Someday, when their present tour was accomplished, they would be reassigned to a

SEAL platoon either back at Coronado in the west or Dam Neck on the east coast.

Getts was not only the commissioned officer in charge of training (OIC), but he was also in charge of leading Mob 4 into the infernos of combat. To do that, he dreamed up every kind of mission he could think of there in Florida and the surrounding waters until Peach, Grumpy, and Doc couldn't stand the sound of his voice or the sight of his face. On the high side, he worked right along with them— a true leader, he was always going first.

Sometimes, being a leader wasn't fun. Once, they had a problem attaching limpet mines to the hull of an aircraft carrier. The carrier keel was deep in the pitch black, cold water, and damn near touching the bottom of the harbor. The team went down using rebreathing apparatuses to avoid sending telltale bubbles to the surface. No lights were permitted—everything had to be done by feel. They swam in pairs with four simulated RE-603V limpets in each swim team. The limpet was specially designed to break the back of large ships, and it was imperative that each mine be placed precisely under the keel, in this case at twenty-foot intervals.

Mission time was scheduled for thirty-six minutes. The team finished with five minutes to spare. Peach was Getts's swim buddy, while Doc and Grumpy worked together. Getts hand-signaled Peach to head for shore, and using the extra time, he checked the other charges by feeling his way down the giant ship's keel. A sickening feeling hit his gut when he found that the explosive devices were not where they were supposed to be. Back on shore at 0341 hours, he waited until he had Grumpy alone while Peach and Doc were cleaning equipment and setting up for debriefing. Getts was so mad he was almost shaking.

"Talk to me, Grumpy, and watch you say the right fucking thing before I send your ass back to the Creek." He was referring to Little Creek, where SEAL 6, the father team, was based.

Grumpy's eyes dropped for a heartbeat, then he looked

Getts square in the eye. "I didn't get down to the keel," he said.

"I know that, mister. You slapped the fucking limpet thirty feet down and ran your ass out. Mission zero. Understand what I'm saying? You blew the whole thing for Mob 4. We failed because you failed. Why?"

"Sir," he said, "I got claustrophobia. I don't know why. It just hit me and I panicked."

SEALS were constantly tested and retested for claustrophobia. It could prove absolutely fatal for men who worked down deep, often in the dark, confined to places where the sun never shines and where goblins and ghosts are worse than anything you ever dreamed of as a kid. The fact that they were constantly checked for symptoms made Getts surprised that Grumpy admitted to it so frankly. But it took damn near a superman never to feel its effects. Getts had felt sudden panic, too, but he had always managed to beat it back and deal with it. Those who worked the SEAL trade had just one tenet—the mission cannot fail, for any reason. "Ever had it before?" Getts asked him.

"No, sir. Well, yeah, a little bit, but I could always handle it. I just couldn't tonight."

"Tell me—can you handle it now?" Getts said.

"Yes, sir."

"Okay, put your mask back on. You and I are going down again. We're going to do the mission over again and this time we're going to do it right," he said.

Grumpy's face hardened and for a moment there was something in his eyes that made Getts feel cold. Whatever it was, Grumpy better learn to stuff it because Getts didn't want him any other way.

"Yes, sir," he said.

The two men slipped back into the black waters, which seemed even blacker now. They paused at the thirty-foot mark on the hull to retrieve the limpets they had left there, and then descended straight down the side of cold steel. From their position underwater, they could hear the sounds of machinery inside the ship, even music from the berthing area. Then, as they sank even deeper, the sound of life inside faded away until there was only the muted noise of bilge pumps, turbine rotations, and the occasional clank as steel hammered against steel. Getts saw an apparition; a ghost swimming toward him, eerily white and three times the size of a man. Then it was gone. He knew it was an illusion brought on by a combination of tension, oxygen deprivation, and a medication he took that almost no one else knew about outside the team. He was shaken for a moment but he had had experience with these apparitions before. Grumpy would have his own devils to worry about as well, Getts knew. But he had better damn well whip his problem, because the rest of the unit couldn't carry it for him.

Grumpy and Getts surfaced at 0416. They did not speak as they cleaned their equipment, showered, then met Peach and Doc for transport back to Pamino Beach.

That was then—this was now. On Tuesday night following the bust-out, Getts notified the folks up the line that they were going to do another exercise, this one in the Gulf. They made provisions for obtaining emergency medical assistance if needed, and Getts delivered his pre-mission briefing. It would be a shallow dive, he said, and they would "chart" the beach for an imaginary troop landing that morning. After the "landing," they would take positions to hit a target—in this case an enemy commander—after the main force arrived. Each of them took along a wrist compass, depth gauge, face mask, fins, a flare, a slate writing board, a knife, and a snorkel, and strapped semiautomatic pistols to their thighs. Getts carried a MP5N submachine gun, and all of the team packed .45s instead of the favored weapon of the SEALs, the 9mm. Grumpy carried a Chicom TY56-Zs, effective up to three hundred yards, Doc took an M-14 with a folding stock, while Peach packed an M88 .50-cal sniping rifle with a high-powered night vision spotting scope designed to hit a target at three thousand yards. But their imaginary enemy general officer would come into their range at closer to fifteen hundred yards. Dead meat for Peach's M88.

The unit plan sheet called for a night combat recon target

access with Getts, the OIC, to swim in to the beach first, reconnoiter the assigned area, determine the starting point of the recon, and read the baseline bearing. In a Mob 4 team operation such as this, he would also do the work of a "pacer," normally a swim buddy with whom Getts would operate to arrive at the RAB, or right angle bearing. The pacer would signal the team on the boat with his flashlight whether or not it was safe to swim in. If something was wrong, he would send a different signal and swim out to meet the pickup boat. It was a routine operation for SEALs. Getts and his swimmers had done it a hundred times. But they would never finish this one.

Chapter Three

Every member of a SEAL team has more than one specialty. Among other things, Truman Lynch, or "Doc" as he was called, was also the team medical specialist. He did a thirty-week course at Special Operations Technicians Training at the Naval Special Warfare Center (NSPECWARCTR), Coronado. He could treat burns, gunshot wounds, trauma, and illnesses unique to underwater diving. He used to tell the guys that if they pissed him off in any little way, he'd just let them bleed to death. Doc had a medical bag that he towed underwater when Mob 4 swam toward a target. The Navy did a damn good job of making a medic out of him, and he felt as well qualified to treat some battle injuries as a surgeon. The SEALs had dynamite med-evac systems in place for their people and never, ever in the history of the UDTs or the SEALs had they left one of their own on the battlefield, alive or dead.

Tonight Mob 4 was working out of a Mark V insertion and extraction craft, a nifty, fast, and well-armed critter that could roll the team into the water and pick them up again without stopping.

At zero-dark-thirty, they throttled back the Mark V boat from forty knots and moved out onto the sled. The sled was attached to the power boat, and it put the swimmers closer to the water before they got the hand signal to roll in. The team extracted the same way, from the water to the sled. They practiced executing those maneuvers at fifteen knots so that the boat was never a sitting enemy target. With Getts already on shore, they were now all watching for his light when the boat skipper gave the word. "Come back on board."

"Huh?" Doc said. Even though it was only a training operation, the adrenaline was already pumping and the team wanted to go, go, go.

"Orders to abort the mission," he said.

They could see another crew member flashing a light shoreward for Getts. It would be a recall. The Mark V throttled up to twenty-five knots while it prepared to loiter in the area until Getts could swim out. "What the hell's going on?" Doc said as he climbed up the side of the Mark V lifting his gear, which weighed almost a hundred pounds out of water.

The boat skipper, a Navy JG, shrugged. "Signal from NCA," he said.

National Command Authority. The junk room phrase to explain all orders that nobody understands or knows anything about. In point of fact, no SEAL team took on a real mission unless the order came directly from NCA, Spec Ops Command. The National Command Authority starts with the President. On the way down from there are a hell of a lot of people who, for any reason, can issue an order to someone like Mob 4 or to a missile launch crew, an aircraft crew, or anybody else who wears a uniform. But a unit like Mob 4 got most of its orders from USSOC (U.S. Special Operations Command) which was in the NCA chain of command.

"What do you think's happening?" Doc asked Peach as they sat on the deck of the boat detaching pieces of equipment from their bodies.

"I'll tell you what the hell amazes me," Grumpy jumped in, "that anybody in the NC-fucking-A is up this early in the morning to give an order. It just blows my mind."

They waited about thirty minutes for Getts to swim out from shore, figuring he could make almost a half mile towing his tanks and gear, then they moved carefully toward shore. Five more minutes and they saw his light. Slowing, they maneuvered to put the sled right by him for the pickup.

"The hell's going on?" Getts said when he was on deck, removing his equipment. Nobody knew.

The team used hand-pumped fresh water to clean the seawater from their equipment on the way home. "We thought you might know," Grumpy said. "It's like, you're an officer and sooner or later you're bound to know something that we don't know."

Getts didn't find anything funny about that. He was concerned about why Mob 4 got called off an operation it had been preparing for weeks. "Who took the stand-down signal?" Getts asked the boat skipper.

"I did," he said. The boat skipper was still on his six-month probation so he didn't have his Budweiser—the SEAL insignia—yet, but he looked good to the team. They had worked with him before and he did what the hell he had to do and didn't run his mouth when he wasn't asked. That was important in their business. He was about twenty-four years old and like most of them, kept his hair cut short and stayed in solid physical shape. "Came through from SpecOps," he said.

"Was that it?" Getts said. "No further orders?"

"No, sir," the boat skipper said. "Just to stand by."

Forty minutes later, the Mark V dropped the team off at the small Navy pier at Pamino Beach. At the end of the pier was a building that looked like a boat shack, but it was made with reinforced concrete, hardened steel doors, and air-conditioning to accommodate stores of bango toys like demolition charges, cable and chain cutters, plus Amatol, HBX-1 and -3, Pentolite, Petn, RDX, Tetryl, and of course, det cord. They also kept grenades in the shack, everything from flash-bangs to antipersonnel fragmentation devices. If war broke out in southern Florida, Mob 4 would make a very good account of itself. The reason they kept all that jazz there was so that they would be able to stage out of Pamino Beach and hook up with any SEAL or Navy unit to which they were assigned.

It was midday before they got their gear properly cleaned up and stowed away. They took apart regulators and changed the carbon dioxide absorption canisters, even though they didn't need it. "Peach," Doc said, "I didn't see you drinking water when we got ashore." Peach didn't seem to like the taste of water so Doc had to watch him close.

"Well, I did," he said.

"How much?" Doc asked.

"I don't know," he said, "quite a bit."

"Let me see you drink some more," Doc said.

Doc passed him a clear plastic bottle full of filtered drinking water and watched while Peach tipped it up and drank. Damn if the boy didn't act like he was taking medicine. He rolled his eyes, mouth twisted. "Pretty bad, huh?" Doc said. Peach didn't answer, but he did finish the bottle. It was dangerous to become dehydrated, but it was damn easy when swimming, especially in seawater.

"We getting orders, Bobby?" Peach asked Getts.

The skipper shrugged. "That's what it sounds like."

"When?"

"I'm a humble servant of my government. I don't read fucking minds," Getts said.

"I hate it when you yell at me." Peach pretended to cry.

"Then don't piss me off."

They decided to wait for further orders at home. The Navy provided them with special housing allowances so the team could live in modest but adequate places at Pamino Beach. They had come across an old beach house built in the late forties with a wide front porch, two big dormers facing the ocean, three bedrooms, a den—which they converted to a fourth sleeping area—and an oversized kitchen. The place rented for $2,000 a month, which was a stretch for the team, but they made a deal with the real estate office so that they could do certain maintenance projects in exchange for a $500 reduction in rent. They took the responsibility of cleaning the old place up pretty seriously, and in the months they had been there they had reshingled the roof, painted the house inside and out, replaced most of the front steps to the porch, erected some outer wall lap boards, and installed a big Kelvin refrigerator. The team also bought the biggest portable barbecue set they could find at an outdoor store in Naples. They went a little nuts with it, as it cost over a thousand bucks, but they barbecued about every night, and nobody, not even Slick down at the Conch, had a better seafood menu than Mob 4.

Every afternoon before dinnertime, they would send one of the team out the front door with flippers and a snorkel in one hand, and a Hawaiian sling in the other. The others started the pit fire. They drank ice-cold white wine instead of water, something the Navy sure as hell didn't want them to do, but as they ran, swam, and lifted so much, they could have easily tripled their booze intake and never missed a beat. That's how they felt about it, anyway.

While Bobby was out in the surf catching the team's dinner, Grumpy was making the biggest bowl of coleslaw ever seen east of the Mississippi. Peach was taking a nap. When the telephone suddenly rang, Doc ran to grab it.

"Hi, Doc," a female voice said. "Can little Bobby come out and play?"

"He's catching dinner. Why don't you come over and help us eat it?" Doc said, recognizing the voice.

"That's very nice. Okay if I bring a girlfriend?" she said.

"Who?"

"What do you care? You should be grateful that another woman even wants to meet you guys."

"She's a dog, huh?" Doc said.

"Her name is Viv Archer, and she's very attractive," Lydia said.

"Probably works in a library," Doc said.

"She works at the phone company. What are you saying?"

"Nothing. If you say she's a winner, we love her."

"That's better. What time are you serving?" she said.

"Five minutes ago." After Doc hung up the telephone, he tried to think of what Vivian Archer might look like. Had they ever seen her with Lydia before? Well, who cares. It wasn't like they were going to get married after dinner. Too bad Bobby couldn't drop dead and leave the rest of the team with Lydia. She wasn't beautiful in the movie star sense, but she sure was sexy. Lydia had dark hair, almost black, and big brown eyes. She had beautiful teeth when she smiled, and she smiled a lot. She had told the guys that she was a quarter Cherokee, which accounted for her skin tone. She was one of those people who could take a short walk on the beach and come back looking like she'd been out there all summer. And she could stop a floor show when she danced. Everybody thought Getts was lucky beyond belief. She had gone for the guy like a falling rock when he stuck the damn spaghetti up his nose. That day she had worn rock-washed jeans, a plain white short-sleeved blouse, and a seashell necklace tied high around her neck. She had on a pair of white canvas deck shoes and wore no socks. Her jeans were not too tight, but Lydia had one of those athletic-looking bodies that no clothes on earth could hide. Doc was sure the others' mouths watered when she looked at them and smiled. She made eye contact with all of them without blinking first.

They'd all been nosing spaghetti ever since.

Doc never forgot her first phone call. "Hi," a female voice said. "This is Lydia Brooks. I'm calling for Bobby Getts. Is he there?"

Doc didn't know about anybody else, but he could form mental images of people just by hearing their voice. He'd been fooled before, but this one sounded sure-fire gorgeous to him. Her voice was confident, open, healthy, seductive. A lot of being sexy was attitude, and this woman, he thought, had it in spades. "Sorry," he said. "He's dead."

"Dead?" she said. "Are you sure?"

"Pretty sure."

"But I saw him two days ago at the Conch," she said.

She must have got their number from Slick. "Oh, *that* Bobby. He's out with his boyfriend."

"You mean he's gay?" she said.

"Yeah. Him and Peach," Doc said.

"Who is this?" she said.

"Lydia, if you tell me where you are, I could meet you there in ten minutes. Then I can explain about Bobby. Won't take long, then we could . . ."

"Would you give him my telephone number?"

That's how Lydia came into their lives.

It wasn't like the team had never had ladies at their place before. Matter of fact, one was almost always there. Some they even had to throw out and threaten to keep them away. It's safe to say that a surprising variety of women were drawn to Navy SEALs. Mob 4 always had a lot of fun, because having a good time was the most important thing in the world for them. And they looked good with their clothes off. They didn't necessarily spend a lot of money, but they spent every bit they had. But something about Lydia coming over made the swimmers set the table a little fancier than usual. Maybe it was Bobby and the spaghetti hanging out of his nose that they were trying to make up for. So they jerked a sheet off of Doc's bed and spread it on the table, put fresh candles into old wine bottles, and used some good flatware that Grumpy had originally bought for his parents' wedding anniversary. Their dishes were army issue. Salvation army, that is. But they had as many wineglasses as most hotels and they served everything in them, including coffee and tea.

When Bobby came back with a few choice snappers, the team got busy cooking. They used real melted butter, fresh diced cloves of garlic, salt, pepper, sherry, and Old Boston fish seasoning to baste the fish. They went with an Eric Clapton CD, and were looking pretty mellow and relaxed when Lydia showed up with her friend.

"Hello. Anybody home?" They had never put a ringer on the front door, and opted instead for a ship's brass bell that Lydia always clanged in case one of them was in skivvies. There was no way to ring that bell quietly, and the whole neighborhood knew when anybody came to the house. Bobby answered the door while the rest of them stood around and tried to look disinterested. Hell, it didn't hurt to start things off civilized. Bobby kissed Lydia, then Lydia introduced Vivian to each of the team.

"We can offer you almost anything you'd like to drink," Bobby said to Vivian. "Scotch, bourbon, gin, vodka, wine . . ." They both chose white wine. Vivian Archer was a couple of years older than Lydia, maybe even more, and she certainly wasn't as sexy, but she had a real presence. She had blond hair that didn't have luster, and it was maybe a little long. She had a habit of pushing at the sides of her hair to keep it out of her eyes and mouth, then she would kind of give up until she had to move it again to see. But Doc still thought Vivian would look good enough in a swimsuit.

It was March, and southern Florida was still experiencing heavy afternoon rains. A ten-minute downpour hit them hard enough to make them all stand on the front porch, making small talk while watching the ocean level rise. The water didn't drown out their barbecue, though, and it didn't take long for the snapper to cook. On their second glass of wine, they went inside to eat.

In a suave gesture, Bobby lifted his glass to toast the ladies. "To the most glamorous women in Florida. I give you Lydia and Vivian."

Nice thing to say, Grumpy thought, and the evening settled into a cozy atmosphere of wine, food, and laughter.

But a telephone call would cause their world to come unglued. It put an end to all the fun. And it would prove to become deadly.

Chapter Four

"Getts," Bobby said into the phone. He listened for a few seconds without saying anything, then put the phone back down in the cradle.

"So?" Peach asked, expecting some kind of communication to explain today's stand-down.

"Bad connection," Getts lied. "I'm going to call them back." Bobby pulled on a pair of canvas shoes and shoved his wallet into a back pocket. "I'll use the liquor store phone."

A few doors down was Helm Street, the main drag through Pamino Beach that was lined with a couple of restaurants, a bait shop, a bicycle rental shop, souvenir stores, boat sales and parts dealerships, and, most important to the team, a liquor store. The rest of the guys knew, of course, that there was nothing wrong with the telephone connection. Rather than install a secure line into their house, a pay telephone call to a designated number would link them up with whomever they needed to talk with for the first phase of receiving orders. As the com man in the unit, Getts also had several radios—VHF and UHF—two of which uplinked to satellites if need be. But nobody liked to send anything into the ether if it could be avoided. So Bobby went out the front door, leaving the rest of the team to finish dinner.

The air went out of the conversation while Getts was gone. It was the SEALs' fault, naturally, because they knew that something was going to happen in connection with their unit, probably immediately upon Getts's return, so they were preoccupied and didn't work too hard at maintaining small talk.

Bobby was back in fifteen minutes. He sat at the table and looked at his cold fish, apparently not hungry anymore. They didn't ask him in front of their guests what the phone call was all about. Lydia looked up at Vivian, then at the men. "I guess you guys have something to do . . ."

"Not until later," Bobby said, but it was halfhearted.

"Well, I think you want to get at it," she said and nodded at Vivian. Lydia got up from the table, put her arms around Getts's neck, and gave him a kiss. "Thanks, sailor," she said.

"Make sure you come again," Grumpy said, meaning it.

"I'll take you home. I'm really sorry about that call," Bobby said to Lydia. "I'll make it up to you."

"You stay here. We've got our car," she said, then kissed Doc on the cheek, then Grumpy and Peach. "Good grits. Thanks, everybody."

The telephone directions ordered Getts to bring only one man with him to a designated meeting spot in Miami; Chief Gunner's Mate Glenn Crosley. Getts would have preferred taking the whole team, but security would have been difficult to maintain with that number. Short of that, he would have preferred going alone. But the directions were precise: he was to come only with Peach. He reckoned that it wouldn't make any difference in the end, because when SEALs finished planning a mission, everyone knew everyone else's job down to the last round in a magazine. All of the map references to punch into GPSs, com frequencies, support resources—all of it was shared, then gone over ad nauseam. In addition to a lock-blade knife, Getts carried to the meeting in Miami a 9mm PPKS in his belt, while Peach packed a Springfield Armory ultra-compact .45 semi-auto, his personal "city" weapon. They seldom went anywhere without a piece. It wasn't that they were paranoid, it's just that they didn't trust anyone. When you practice the art of eliminating folks with guns and explosives sixteen

hours a day, six days a week, you begin to believe they
might be trying to return the favor.

Getts and Peach drove down over one hundred miles of
Highway 41 through the Everglades, straight to Highway 1
in Miami. They had been directed to meet a contact at
Biscayne Yacht Club and to make sure they were not followed. Theirs was not to wonder why, so Getts left Highway 1 at SW 17th, then doubled back south on SW 24th,
making a series of hairpin turns while watching their rear.
They stopped at a curb a couple of times, as though they
were checking a map, but nothing that looked like a tail
showed up. Convinced they were clean, Getts got onto SW
22nd, crossed over Highway 1 to South Bayshore, and
made a right turn into the Biscayne Yacht Club entrance.

They stopped at the gate and gave the guard the name
Perez, and told him he and Peach were guests of Mr. John
Barry. The guard checked his sheet and confirmed that they
were expected. The guard gave them a parking pass to put
on their dashboard and directions to the slips. After only
one wrong turn, they found the designated pier and parked
the car.

"Who is this guy, Bobby?" Peach asked.

Getts shrugged. "I'll tell you that in about ten minutes."

It was a CAVU day (ceiling and visibility unlimited),
about a five-knot breeze, just enough to keep them comfortable and make the rigging on the boats clang atop their
masts. Biscayne was a pretty big marina and accommodated
boats of all sizes, from sixteen footers kept on racks ashore,
to 80s rigged for blue-water sailing, to power boats that
looked like well-appointed apartments on water. At the
shore end of the pier was a gate constructed of cyclone
fencing, topped with two strands of barbed wire to discour-
age anyone from jumping over. The gate itself was accessible by correct manipulation of five buttons that would
release the locking mechanism. Getts's contact had not
given him the numbers, and they wouldn't embarrass themselves by asking anyone to let them in, so Peach ran up
the side of the fencing, went over the top of the barbed

wire without getting a nick, and, dropping down the other side, opened the door for Getts.

The boat they were looking for was the *Raffish*, and they found her tied up halfway down the pier. She was a forty-two-foot Morgan, a pretty boat with a blue fiberglass hull, and a twelve-foot beam that would get you wherever you wanted to go in comfort as long as you weren't in a hurry to get there. Getts couldn't help but notice a face at a cabin porthole as they neared the boat. They expected whoever it was to show themselves in the lazaret. They waited. Finally, Getts called out, "Yo! Anybody on board?" Almost at once, a man appeared in the hatchway. He was about five-foot-seven and balding, and had combed the fringe from one side of his head over the top in a vain effort to cover his scalp. He wore an ill-kempt beard that made the man appear to be older than he probably was. Wire-rimmed glasses perched on his wrinkled nose, as though the glasses were an irritation. He blinked his eyes like a bear emerging from a dark cave after winter. A close look at his eyes and surrounding features caused Getts to think he might have been in his late thirties. It was hard to get by the beard for an accurate guess, and Getts was transfixed by the strands of hair radiating from ear to ear. "Mr. Perez?" the man said.

"Yeah. Jim Perez. This is Carl Chase," Getts said, still following his telephone directions.

"Hmmm. I'm John Barry. I understand you want to buy a boat," he said, following his end of the identification procedure.

"Actually, I'm just looking," Getts responded.

"Do you have a price range, Mr. Perez?" John Barry said.

"Yes, but I'm going to keep that to myself." That was the end of the script. Barry's chest seemed to collapse. The man had been more nervous than the SEALs realized.

"Let me show you around," he said, stepping back to give them room to board. They followed John Barry through the center hatchway, down the steps, and into the boat's galley. "Maybe there is something in particular you'd like to see first," he said. "The engine, perhaps?"

What the hell was all this about? Getts wondered. He knew they didn't actually want to buy the boat, so why the grand tour? "It's a Perkins diesel," Getts said, "with a ninety-gallon fuel tank, and I can tell you at least six ways to sabotage it."

"Yes, well, you'd know more about that than I," Barry replied. Getts and Peach waited. The boat was nice to look at and was well built. It had an aluminum main spar and was cutter rigged. It had depth sounding gear, wind speed and direction sensing equipment, and half-inch lines for heavy weather. She'd roll like a pig, though, and Getts could think of a lot of other boats he would rather sail into a gale. Below decks, she had an outmoded loran and a decent VHF radio system. The stove was propane and she probably had a refrigerator that used the same gas for cooling. There was one particular item in the galley that held Getts's interest. It was a government-made titanium briefcase with a wrist cuff that required a key to open. Getts and Peach looked at each other. "I think we should get down to business," John Barry said.

"May I see your identification, Mr. Barry?" Getts said.

"What? Why?" he said.

"Well, sir, all these signs and countersigns are just fine, but so far you're only a voice on the phone and a guy with a boat. We need to know who we're dealing with," he said.

"This is a highly classified assignment I'm going to give you men. It comes from the highest possible source and your commander wants absolute deniability," John Barry said.

Nobody who does grunt work likes the word "deniability." It suggests that *it's your ass, not mine.* Peach took a seat on a padded bench facing the dining table in the main cabin and waited for Getts to continue. "I appreciate that, Mr. Barry. We're used to working under those conditions, but our orders come from National Command Authority. Like NSWDG or USSOC. I'll have to know that you represent one of those agencies."

John Barry's face began coloring as frustration crept from his neckline upward. He angrily pulled a plastic I.D. case from a coat pocket and handed it to Getts. It had an eagle on it, all right, along with John Barry's photograph, with L.L.D. after his name. No military rank, or any civilian office that Getts recognized. He passed the I.D. card to Peach, who barely glanced at it and tossed it to Mr. Barry. "Sorry, Mr. Barry, that won't hardly do it."

"Wait a minute, Lieutenant," he said, licking his lips. He had wanted to control the tenor of the meeting, but it wasn't going the way he wanted. "Look, this is really an important operation. Really. Why don't you let me brief you on what it is and give you the mission folders? Then you can authenticate through USSOC."

Much later, after the world had begun to burn around them, Getts would look back on that moment and say with absolute certainty that he should have gotten them out of it right then and there. It was the wrong setup with the wrong guy, representing the wrong people. The way John Barry put it to Getts in the cabin of the Morgan sounded reasonable, but they should have gone by the book. Instead, Getts heard himself say, "Okay, I guess we can do that."

"Good," John Barry said. What followed sounded to Getts like a prepared speech. "General Vadim Krabac is not only a fugitive war criminal, but an ongoing threat to the United States and its allies around the world. It is the expressed opinion of the government of the United States that all other diplomatic efforts have failed, and that he should be removed by force from his present location in Bosnia and delivered to responsible authorities. General Krabac would then be transported to The Hague, Netherlands, where he will stand trial for war crimes. It has been determined that Mob 4 is capable of this assignment, and you are so ordered to carry out this objective." Mr. John Barry had a good memory. He referred to his notes only once. Getts would have bet that he had once been a trial attorney in another life. Maybe still was.

So it was a simple kidnap—a tag and bag assignment. "Who did you say originated the order?" Getts said.

"You men of the SEALs . . ."

"We're just part of the SEALs," Getts interrupted.

". . . have been chosen by the highest level of command to carry out this vital mission."

"And just who is this highest level of command?" Getts said.

"I am not at liberty to pass on that information, Lieutenant," Barry said.

"No disrespect intended, Mr. Barry, but you're not an overwhelming source of useful information, are you?" Getts said.

"I've told you all you need to know. The rest of it is in this folder." Barry slid the mission folder across the salon table toward the two Mob 4 warriors. A quick perusal of the folder contents revealed several photographs of the mission's target, General Krabac, and photographs of a large villa in which he was expected to be when the mission was executed. The villa appeared in aerial photos as well as clandestine pictures taken from various locations on land. Did we have a man inside? Getts wondered. There were also com frequencies contained for each form of support aircraft, sea force and intelligence briefs, and times for each leg of the mission, but the subordinate parts of the plan's execution were left to the team itself. Peach studied the material with interest as it was passed to him by Getts. He looked at his skipper and slowly nodded.

Everything looked right. But Getts was still uneasy. "That's it?" he said.

"Vadim Krabac will be in a private villa located on the Adriatic coast south of the city of Zga for two days on the tenth and eleventh day of next month, according to reliable intelligence sources. . . ."

"Excuse me, Mr. Barry," Getts said. "What 'reliable' intelligence sources would those be?"

"I am not in the intelligence gathering or analysis business, Lieutenant, but you can be assured that if I tell you our sources are reliable, they are," Mr. Barry said.

A bell should have gone off again for Getts, but he was in his reasonable mode. After all, he thought, intelligence from Bosnia-Herzegovina wasn't nearly as hard to come by as places like Iraq, Iran, or North Korea. The CIA or DIA would be able to gather top-quality HUMINT (human intelligence) with relative ease. It sounded to Getts as though they had at least one asset well placed in the government structure inside Bosnia. And he could accept that Mr. John Barry wouldn't know the name of that source.

That would prove to be another fatal mistake on his part.

But Getts was in a box. SEALs, like other military personnel, do not pick and choose their assignments. Getts and Peach thus had no grounds upon which to refuse to launch, short of resigning from the SEALs and potentially from the Navy.

"Okay, let's just take it one step at a time," he said, spreading out the files so they could both take another look. He and Peach spent the next hour poring through the mission package, studying it and asking Mr. John Barry questions as they examined the material. Barry could answer almost none of them. "I'm not military," he said. "You know what all that stuff means. Sorry."

In what Getts later regarded as his long series of mental mistakes, kicked off by overcoming skepticism at the outset, he didn't question Barry's ignorance. By then, he didn't give a shit about Mr. Barry. He was an inexhaustible source of exactly zero information, making Getts's headache worse. "Okay, Mr. Barry," he said, "I'll make contact with my boss and if he says go, we go."

Mr. Barry offered his hand. When Getts took it, he was surprised at how strong it was, despite how short Barry's fingers were. Peach took another look at the man's little feet and nose. He was sure John Barry must have a short dick.

Chapter Five

The Conch was full of fishermen, surfers, divers, sun-
bathers, tourists, and others who just appreciated bad food.
Most of them were loud and drunk. But there was an empty
seat next to Grumpy at the bar, and John Barry slid into
it trying to look inconspicuous. "You're Grumpy, aren't
you?" the civilian said to the SEAL.

Everybody at the Conch and Pampino Beach knew him
by that name, but Grumpy sure as hell didn't know the
pasty-face man who ordered a Manhattan—yes, a Manhattan—from Slick.

"You a tax collector or something?" Grumpy said.

"Of course not. Never mind, I know you're kidding," he
said. "My name is John Barry." Barry passed the SEAL
his card.

Grumpy leaned over and whispered into his ear, "You
don't know how fucking relieved I am to hear it. Just what
do you do, John?"

"I think that's need to know, to use a term of your trade.
What *is* important is your mission. I'm the person who gave
your boss, Robert Getts, and his associate, Peach, their mission orders."

Grumpy drained his Budweiser and regarded John Barry
for a long moment. He knew the name Barry because Getts
had briefed the team and included all of the details, like
who brought the bad news.

"Can we go someplace to talk?" John Barry said.

Grumpy shrugged. "What's wrong with right here? Nobody can hear, and if they did they wouldn't give a shit.
Hey, Slick, give me another Bud."

It seemed to Grumpy that John Barry pulled his head, perched on a skinny neck, down into his summer suit until his shirt collar disappeared. It was like talking to a turtle. "So. What brings you all the way down from . . . where the fuck did you come from, John?"

"Washington," John Barry said in a hushed whisper.

"Ah," Grumpy said, his voice pitched theatrically lower to match the civilian's.

"I have an additional order. It's only for you," John Barry said, ignoring his drink.

"Order? You got the wrong guy, John John. The man you want is Getts. He's the boss. I just sweep up," Grumpy said.

"Sweep up?"

"Yeah. Ever hear of a 7188 street sweeper? Twelve-gauge, 8-round magazine, fully automatic shotgun." Grumpy began to giggle. "That's how I sweep up, John." Grumpy leaned over his glass, a menacing look in his eyes.

John Barry watched the SEAL with his mouth slightly open. "I see," he said.

Grumpy's laughter broke out loud and he reached out a large hand for John Barry's shoulder. He squeezed until the civilian winced. "Oh, God, that's funny. Isn't it, John John? I love my work. And if you don't love your work, you won't do it worth a fuck." Grumpy put back his head and howled. "Shit, John, I'm sorry," he said, suddenly sober and deeply focused on John Barry. All signs of humor vanished from his face. "You said you had an order. For me?"

"Yes. *Only* for you," John Barry said.

"Okay. What is it?"

The civilian hesitated, then surged ahead, his voice very low, his eyes darting nervously about the bar. "We, uh, don't want the prisoner to, uh, come back. We want you to make sure of that."

"That so?"

"Yes."

"Well, what do you want to happen to him, John?"

Grumpy said, his teeth flashing under a bloodthirsty grin that spread quickly across his face.

John Barry shuddered. "We want, well . . . let's say there might be some shooting. The general might get hit."

"And die?"

"Yes."

"You want me to kill him?"

"Yes. It's imperative."

"Imperative." Grumpy was grinning evilly, greatly amused.

John Barry, on the other hand, was not.

"I'll bet I'm not supposed to tell the team. Right?"

John Barry nodded emphatically. "That's right. It's very secret. Strictly need to know."

"See that woman over there?" Grumpy nodded at a distant part of the Conch. John Barry's eyes tried to follow the SEAL's eyes.

There were several women in the room. "Which one?" he said, peering through his bifocal glasses.

"The one with the pearl necklace. Blond hair. She has about forty million bucks and a Filipino pimp. Can you beat that? She'll suck your cock for ten dollars. Do you want her to do you, John? She'll do it right back there in the head."

Grumpy calmly lit a cigarette and blew the smoke into John Barry's face.

"Weird," John Barry said.

"Weird?" Grumpy opened his eyes wide. "Is that what you said? Weird? What's weird? Don't you like to get your dick sucked?"

John Barry's jaw worked a few times before he could force a sound out. "Yes," he croaked.

"Yes?" Grumpy slapped John Barry on the back. "Oh, you mean it's weird that she has so much money. Yeah, I think about that a lot, John John. Forty mil. Think about how many cocks you'd have to suck to make forty million dollars."

Grumpy blew perfect smoke rings into the tepid atmosphere of the Conch. John Barry scarcely moved, his breath shallow.

"Let's see, where were we?" Grumpy smiled pleasantly at the Washington man.

The civilian swallowed hard. "Look, Grumpy. There is a price on Krabac's head. A very large reward. Did you know that?"

Grumpy moved his head slowly from side to side. "I thought there was a law against that kind of thing, John."

"It's, uh, a technicality. The money comes from discretionary intelligence funds. No questions asked. Ever." John Barry managed to gulp down his drink. "We made a mistake with Saddam Hussein. A very big mistake. And we don't want to make another one with Krabac. He's got to be eliminated from the world stage, and that's why we're sending a crack SEAL team after him."

Sweat stood out markedly on the civilian's forehead. He reached inside his pocket and withdrew a fat envelope, which he pushed furtively into Grumpy's hand. "There is a great amount of money in there. More than you could ever save in the Navy. And all you're doing is following orders. That's all."

John Barry rose from his bar stool and, trying with difficulty to smile, nodded his head toward Grumpy, then hastily withdrew from the bar.

Grumpy slowly opened the flap of the envelope and peered inside. What he saw made his heart race.

Chapter Six

According to the mission folders, Mob 4 had fourteen days to execute the assignment. In their business, it wasn't much lead time. There were hundreds of details to set up from selecting BDUs (battle dress uniforms), to weapons, explosives if needed, E&E (Escape and Evasion) plans, high-speed boats, long- and short-range WX reports, NVG (night vision equipment), coordination with theater commanders, mission planning, and last but not least, rehearsal. If, for example, their mission was to liberate a hijacked airplane with hostages aboard, the team would borrow an identical aircraft for carefully choreographed practice runs of forced entry into the plane, each time improving their technique for clandestine entry, shortening the exposure time, until they could do it blindfolded. If their mission was a hostage rescue from a building, they would obtain detailed floor plans to all parts of the building, noting all entrances, exits, and windows, and the roof and wall composition. The team would practice getting inside silently and quickly, and being deadly. But the first thing Getts had to do before they started any mission was to confirm the order from JSOC.

Again, he used a public telephone to place a long distance call. That number put him through to Joint Special Operations Command. He asked the DO to put him through to Colonel Arnold R. Talent, U.S. Army. He knew the Chief of S-4 personally. If anybody had knowledge of their mission, he would.

"Colonel Talent," a gravel voice came on the telephone. Talent was Ranger qualified, an ex–Delta Force executive officer and a task force leader in Desert Storm. He called himself a black Irishman—dark hair, big smile, and a love for single-grain scotch whiskey. He'd played football for UCLA, not, he said, because he was any good, but because running into people at high speed was his idea of fun. Getts had never heard any man say he didn't like Arnie Talent, and Talent had never broken his word. A man's word in SpecWar business was as important as the next breath he took. You can't lead men in battle if you lie to them.

"Lieutenant Getts, Mob 4," Getts said.

"Right, Bobby. I hear you," he said. Colonel Talent had said a lot in those five words. First, he told Getts that he recognized his voice and could confirm his identity. Second, he knew it wasn't a social call and that his rank and position in JSOC were at issue. And third, he was prepared, within limits, to "do business" over an unsecured telephone.

"Sir, can you vouch for Mr. John Barry?" Getts asked.

The brief hesitation might have seemed longer in the SEAL's imagination than in fact before Colonel Talent said, "White House."

"Yes, sir. That's my understanding. Unless you say otherwise, sir, Mob 4 is prepared to assist Mr. Barry in his needs." Getts waited.

Again, there was a slight pause before Colonel Talent gave a response. "You can accept Mr. Barry at face value. He is at the top of NCA."

Getts let out his breath, hardly realizing that he had been virtually holding it since Colonel Talent came on the line. He was always, *always,* pumped when his team got a "go" order. He could never remember an assignment that he wasn't keen to execute and to distinguish himself and his team among fellow SEALs. But while this one shouldn't have been any different, it was the first he had some inner whisper of mortal danger. Getts realized before hanging up the telephone that he had hoped, somewhere in the far recesses of his heart, that Colonel Talent would countermand the bureaucrat known to him as John Barry. "Aye, aye, sir," Getts said, and hung up.

So it was go. According to the mission folders, they had rock cliffs to scale in order to get to the mansion where Krabac would be found. Peach, Doc, and Grumpy assured him that they had climbing training, but he had never seen them do it. The easy way would have been to take their word for it. It would cost them two days to find out how good they really were at it, but Getts decided that the time must be taken.

On Getts's order, the team flew in a C-130 to Little Creek, picked up climbing gear, then proceeded in the same aircraft to Bangor, Maine. From there, they drove down the coast to an area that was similar in height and degree of technical difficulty to that which they would face in Bosnia. They waited four hours until it was dark, then geared up. When they were ready, Getts started first. The climb was to be about one hundred eighty feet. As he found handholds, Getts pounded in pitons, attached carabiners, and strung rope. He was about forty feet high when he felt a tap on his leg.

"Hey, Skipper," Doc said, "why don't you let me have a shot?"

As Getts looked down at a smiling Doc, he could see that Peach and Grumpy had also begun to climb. "Okay," he said, personally damn glad that one of the team with superior ability had stepped up, unasked.

Doc took over the lead. It became clear that he was going to be Getts's first man up. He had strong hands, was light-footed, and found handholds without seeming to look for them. He literally walked up the sheer face of the granite Maine walls, pausing to jam in pitons (hammering them in would have been more secure, but the noise level was unacceptable) so that the rest of the team could ascend behind him at his speed.

Peach and Grumpy made the ascent behind them, smoothly and efficiently. But something bothered Getts. Heavy gear, including weapons, ammunition, and camo equipment, remained at beach level while the team climbed the cliff. Getts talked to Peach about it when they were returning to the Creek in the C-130. "You're the exec in this unit," Getts said. "I don't ever want to see you pull that kind of shit again."

"Sorry, sir. Didn't seem to make sense to pack all that gear up a cliff when we were planning to come right back down," Peach said nonchalantly.

"Everything we do, every minute of our training, simulates combat. Got that, Peach?"

"Aye aye, sir," he said and turned his head away. Getts was aware that Peach was a proud man, and he was finding him to be exceptionally competent in all the ways of a warrior. He wouldn't have been assigned to Mob 4 if he wasn't. But errors in judgment made Getts wonder about Peach at times. His confidence bordered on arrogance. There had to be a balance of both in a good SEAL.

Grumpy, on the other hand, hadn't spoken ten words all day. Getts made a point to sit beside him in the C-130 as they were heading south. "Good work today, man," he said to Grumpy.

"Think I'm doin' okay, huh, Coach?" Grumpy said. "Am I gonna get in the game?" Grumpy was wearing a wide grin but Getts couldn't find the humor in his cold eyes.

Back in Florida, the team loaded up their gear, including OICW weapons. They had a few hours before they had to drive to McDill Air Force Base, and Getts wanted to see Lydia. This was another first. The team never told anyone that they were preparing to leave. Not for an exercise, and especially not for a real shooting mission. Never. But this time Getts wanted to say something to a woman who, he realized, had come to mean much to him. Too much for his own good, maybe. She was home when he called, studying law books for her county sheriff's final exam. But she said she was glad to have the interruption. Her apartment was only a few blocks from the SEAL's house, so they agreed to meet on the beach halfway between.

She was wearing a short-sleeve orange cotton shirt and Navy blue shorts when she appeared, jogging toward Getts on the wet sand with a pair of sandals in one hand. They kissed before speaking but her smile faded slowly as she regarded his eyes. "What's up? You haven't been around for days," she said.

"You know, Navy stuff."

"Ah. Did you miss me?" Lydia said, her smile now back, lighting up her already luminous face.

"Sure."

"Are you starting to take me for granted, Bobby?"

"I think I am." And it was a warm, comfortable feeling. And a new one for him. "How did you know I've been gone? Did you call?"

"Yep. I didn't leave messages because I didn't want you to think I was one of those cloying types."

He put his arms around her and kissed her again. This time it was a long, slurpy kiss that made his toes curl into the sand. She pulled away and said "Want to go to my place, sailor?"

His heart was already pounding, but that made it jump up a few beats per minute. What a waste. "I can't, Lydia."

"Got your period?" she mocked him.

"Worse. We're leaving town," he said, touching her face delicately with his fingers.

"More training?" she said. He gave himself away by hesitating with his answer, because she just said, "Oh."

"Yeah, just more routine stuff." But she knew better. He was no good at lying to her. He'd have to practice up.

"When do you leave?" she said.

He shrugged, helplessly. "Half hour. Soon as I get back to the house, we go."

She pulled back, her eyes falling to the sand. "Okay. Well . . ." When he leaned forward for one more kiss, he could feel her tears against his cheek. He had never been in love before. It was the kind of feeling that whispered *This is it, dummy.*

They said good-bye. He watched her turn and walk back whence she had just come, less happy this time.

Chapter Seven

The mission folders informed the team that their operation was code named "Redbird." Code names are chosen randomly, by computer. No pattern, no intelligent thought behind it. The higher echelons of government felt a hell of a lot safer if nobody with a brain was involved in their decisions.

This Redbird carried with it a lot of juice. Mob 4 had all of the U.S. Navy SEAL support and other services, as well. The first thing they did was move to Norfolk Naval Air Station, just up the street from the Little Creek U.S. Navy Amphibious Base, where east coast SEAL teams 2, 4, and 8 were stationed. At Norfolk, they had secure land lines and access to aircraft. They were going to the Adriatic and needed at least three types of planes to complete the assignment. First, they'd need one to get there mucho pronto. Getts found out how much suction Redbird had when he asked for, and received with no questions asked, a C-141 for a fast hop to Naples, where Mob 4 would liaise with COMNAVSURFLANT (Commander Naval Surface Atlantic) Ships for support.

Getts continued their planning while airborne, and during the days and nights they were at HQLANTFLT, holed up in a secure room that measured fifty by forty. Most of Mob 4's gear had arrived by then, including an IBS (inflatable boat small); parachute equipment, including steerable chutes, release assemblies, reserve chutes, timers for HALO jumping, and altimeters; as well as weapons. Getts, Doc, and Grumpy would ordinarily carry the H&K MP-5 submachine gun while Peach packed an extra piece. He favored the HK PSG-1 sniper rifle that used a NATO 7.62 round. It had an effective range of over eight hundred meters with a magnified ambient-light night scope.

It is the bible, the mantra, of SEAL teams to put out massive firepower packed into the ferocity of a focused attack, then withdraw. The enemy is not only to be intimidated but destroyed in the process. This time, Mob 4 was going out with the OICW.

It was a fucking cannon, held snugly in the arms of an expert. With an infrared sensor for night vision, it could red dot a day or night target with an electronic fire control system. It used a laser range finder that would translate precise range information to the HE round's detonating fuse. The "under" barrel fired a 5.56mm kinetic energy round over one thousand meters with the same precise accuracy. And it weighed less than a fully equipped M16 system. And Mob 4 was going to unleash this baby on Bosnia. Ooooh, ahhhhhh.

Each man also carried two knives and auto-loading handguns in leg-strapped holsters. Finally, they would take along an Ithaca M-37 12-gauge pump shotgun with a magazine capacity of 9 rounds. Instead of shot loads, they would carry a supply of four-ounce lead slugs, perfect for taking doors off hinges and generally tearing great, big holes in things.

Each SEAL would carry over 150 pounds of equipment that included night vision glasses, a flashlight, light sticks, and a rubber radio earpiece and lip mike. Peach made sure they carried several kinds of grenades, including flashbangs; an M-79 grenade launcher; CS (tear gas); GPSs; radios; compact combat medical kits; and ammunition. Lots of ammunition.

Getts put Doc in charge of the climbing and swim gear, such as fins, wet suits, and snorkels, in case their rubber boat deflated. They would also carry an assortment of M3 pull-release booby traps, clothespin initiators, and a couple MK1 MOD 1 combination booby traps.

Grumpy coordinated all of their comfreqs with SOC (Special Operations Command), including fall-back or emergency plan bands (EPBs). The OpsPlan Getts devised called for a HALO jump seven miles offshore, inserting with an IBS with an ultra-quiet motor. The team would climb a cliff approximately eighty-five feet high to access the villa. Detailed terrain photographs in their mission folders showed that the cliff climb shouldn't be tough, made even easier by their state-of-the-art equipment. Mob 4 would have two days of MREs (meal, ready to eat).

Nobody in COMLANTFLT (Commander Atlantic Fleet) knew what Mob 4 was doing, of course, only that Navy support would be provided when and if the team asked for it. They would jump from a C-130 Hercules from twelve thousand feet, low enough so that they wouldn't have to deal with oxygen in the descent, and high enough to not attract attention from interested parties on shore. They would open their chutes at one thousand feet, drop out of harnesses at ten feet (hopefully) above the water, inflate the boat, collect their gear, and navigate to shore.

To get out with their prisoner, they would rappel down the same cliff they came up, use the IBS to stand offshore a distance of between one thousand and fifteen hundred yards, at which time a CH-46 Sea Knight would pick them up. The CH-46 is a big six-ton assault chopper with a rear ramp which would open as it approached the team's position. The chopper crew would drop a caving ladder from the ramp. The team would grab hold of the ladder as the big bird moved overhead and climb upward to the ship. If the rotor wash didn't blow them off the ladder.

With two days and five hours left before Mob 4 jumped off, Peach pulled a bottle of rum out of his gear and opened it. "Sugar, anyone?" he asked. They found cups and Peach gave each man a couple inches. It was the first drink of alcohol any of them had had for two weeks and, harkening back to Navy tradition, they were long overdue. Everybody had a drink but Bobby. Alcohol could set off his depression, they all knew, and he was walking on edge as it was.

"What about resistance?" Grumpy asked, looking in Bobby's direction. "We gonna ask them to please put down their pieces and their prayer shawls or do we use our boom sticks?"

"Like always, Grumpy. You know that," Bobby said.

"Yeah. Well, just checking. Doesn't hurt to make sure, huh?"

"No sense in carrying all that ammunition if we're going to just talk to them," Doc said.

"Okay, I just want to get that straight," Grumpy said, his eyes still locked on Getts.

"We're not picking a fight," Getts said, "but we have to settle it quick if there is one."

Getts produced aerial photos of the villa. He Scotch taped these to a wall. In addition there were drawings that he had sketched himself. It was a floor plan of the villa based on information provided in the mission folders, presumably gathered by the DIA (Defense Intelligence Agency). The grounds of the villa were large but not vast, approximately five hundred feet deep by eight hundred feet wide. On the south side of the grounds was the sea cliff, which dropped about eighty-five feet to beach level. At the top of the cliff was a short path that led to a grand gazebo constructed of wood, and one hundred feet beyond that was a curving driveway that serviced a courtyard and continued from west to east, rounding the villa, and eventually linking to a main road that led to the city of Mostar.

The one-hundred-year-old stone-walled building was built in a large U shape with a six-car garage comprising the east side of the villa, over which were three small apartments originally designed to accommodate domestic servants. Large picture windows fronted the lower level of the north section of the mansion, behind which was a library, a living room, a conference room with double doors at each end, and an extensive receiving area with a wide, winding staircase accessing the second floor. Here was a master suite and adjoining bedrooms on either side. The master suite had a fireplace and two bathrooms. On the west side of the building at ground level was a large dining room, a den, and a kitchen with a substantial pantry. Above, accessible by still another stairway to the second floor, were two more guest rooms and a small solarium.

On the northwest corner of the grounds was a guest house where security personnel could be billeted during VIP visits. Getts came up with a wrinkle to the plan that the SEALs liked a lot. It simplified the time they'd have to spend watching the villa and put the initiative into their own hands. The team had an L72447-0090 Infra-red System (IRS) with a heat sensing monitor that could reproduce from a distance of two hundred yards. The team would time their ascent up the cliff to arrive at 0100 hours local time, allow two hours to verify security personnel patterns, and wait until most, if not all, persons inside the villa had gone to bed for the night. Continuous sweeps with the IRS would tell the commandos what everybody was doing at all times.

The guesswork came in two areas; (1) the size and effectiveness of the security force (although the briefing books said there would unlikely be more than ten, lightly armed with automatic weapons) and (2) the room in which Vadim Krabac would sleep. Getts had to assume that they could handle anything that the security people could throw at them, and that Krabac would occupy the master suite on the second floor. Other conferees would no doubt sleep in the adjoining bedrooms and in the special guest rooms on the second floor of the west wing.

For the jump, the team would tape condoms over the barrels of their weapons to keep out seawater. The IRS equipment came in a rubberized container, as did SEAL assault radios. Earpieces and lip mikes were marginally affected by water immersion, so they were placed inside heavy duty Ziplock bags until ready for use when the team got ashore.

"How about the vehicles, Skipper?" Doc said.

"Leave them," Getts said. "Grumpy, we need traps laid for the security folks to trip when we go out. You do that." Grumpy nodded his understanding. He would rig trip wires and booby traps from the grounds to the point of egress so that when the team went down the cliffs, any pursuers would spend their time watching where they stepped instead of where the team was going.

The team discussed ambient light intensifiers. These were glasses that could intensify any light at all—starlight, moonlight, streetlight—100,000 times, turning night into day. The downside was that when the glasses were removed, the user had destroyed his night vision. Mob 4 decided that they were far better trained for all phases of night fighting than any enemy they were likely to meet, and because the OICW had built-in fire-control systems that functioned perfectly at night, they passed. The less they had to carry out the door of an airplane, the better.

"Peach," Getts said, "you're the entryman. You know our man is upstairs and you know the room. I'm right behind you shooting left." A well-trained entryman was an absolute must in house combat. He must be tough, have fast reflexes, be decisive and, above all, determined. Getts knew that nothing short of a bullet in his heart would stop Peach from getting to their target.

"Grumpy, you're the link. I want you just inside the door near the base of the staircase. Got it?"

"Aye, aye," he said. Getts took a second look at Grumpy. For whatever reason, he seemed distracted. Not nervous, not scared, but as if his head was somewhere else.

"How do you feel, Grumpy?" Getts asked.

"Wonderful, wonderful. Why? Anything wrong, Skipper?" he said.

"No." Getts regarded him for a long moment. The link man, like each team member, had a vital function. He relayed communications and CombatSit (combat situation) to the men or man outside, who was dealing with whatever enemy forces were outside of the house. "I want you to put a harness on Krabac. Whoever grabs him from upstairs, and that'll probably be Peach, throws him to you at the base of the stairs. Then you suit him up while we cover your back. Got it?"

"Rahja," Grumpy said.

Getts turned to Doc. "Doc, you've got everything outside

when we're inside. We'll be out in four minutes. Can you deal with it?"

"I can fight off a horny officer's wife for four minutes," Doc said.

"There's an idea," Peach said. "Unzip your fly when the Serbs mount a charge. When they see that little weenie of yours, they'll laugh so hard they'll fall off the cliff."

"Yeah? Well I'll bet my unit is so big you couldn't get your fat lips around it. Want to prove I'm a liar?"

"Shut up," Getts said. "I know I don't have to tell you but I'm going to do it again, anyway. Snap shooting and bursts . . ." Mob 4 men groaned. It was like telling a veteran pugilist to keep his left hand up. Snap shooting, mastered to a man by Mob 4, involved using only the foresight of the weapon and firing with both eyes open. It's a favorite SEAL technique because the enemy doesn't obligingly stand around and wait for you to take a nice, long aim from a comfortable prone position.

"After we're out, Doc will destroy the IRS, and go down the rope to the beach first. Then Peach, with Krabac in the harness, then Grumpy. I'll give covering fire if we need it, then follow Grumpy." Navy SEAL teams have found that descending ropes from helos or from cliffs can be quickly and efficiently done using heavy leather gloves to slow their speed downward. If they time it right, their hands feel hot but not burned.

All through their briefing, each man made notes, not on just what his assignment was, but what everybody was supposed to do. If there were any team casualties, the mission still had to go on.

They calculated time. At 0100, Mob 4 would neutralize any animals and their handlers that might patrol the grounds and study movement inside using IRS. They would use two men to reconnoiter the grounds looking for motion sensors, heat detectors, and the like. Getts thought a first-rate security system at this location was unlikely, because the villa was not under the control of the military. And their Intel reported nothing to the contrary. At 0300, the team would silently approach the building and use picks on the main and side door locks. If the locks were too sophisticated, they would either shoot the hinges with the Ithaca gun or pack them with C-4 and blow them with quick igniters.

Getts would give the team exactly sixty seconds to try picking, 180 seconds to blow the locks if picking failed. At 0304 they had to be inside. Twenty seconds later they would be into the main suite, waking Vadim Krabac from a dream into a living nightmare. He would be pulled from his bed and not be given the time it takes to dress.

Chapter Eight

They went over the plans again and again, smoothing out small wrinkles, considering minor and major alternatives if events turned out differently than they anticipated. And they always did. Intelligence, sometimes an oxymoron, could be wrong about the security people on duty. There could be trucks full of them. They might have placed automatic weapons on the perimeter. They might have foot patrols near the cliffs. They might have boats in the water, or radar in the villa or next door, or a mile down the road.

"What if Krabac's not there?" Doc asked.

Getts shrugged. "We go home. We're not there to invade the Balkans." No, Getts thought, but they'd be doing their little share to move history along. The Intel folder told them that Balkan was a Turkish word for mountains. Couldn't be more descriptive of the place they were going. The region used to be the center of old Europe, a thousand years and more before Christ. Lots of kingdoms came and went under the Balkan sun: Thracian, Macedonian, Roman, and Byzantine empires flourished and faded. Later, the Balkan empires became part of the Serbian kingdom, then Bulgaria, then subjugated to the Ottoman Empire under the Turks—a four-thousand-year-long history of fighting and killing. Empires and their armies dissolved, but the implacable mountains and rivers remained. Now, it was the U.S. Navy SEALs' turn to invade from the air and the sea.

Getts watched while Peach emptied the bottle of rum equally into the three cups. He lifted his canteen cup of water in toast. "Death to our enemies, life and love among brothers." They drank.

There was one more swallow left in their glasses. "To pussy," Peach toasted with a shrug. They finished the liquor and the stuff felt warm in their guts.

"Secretary General Luumba calling for Ambassador Hazeltine," the distinctly Afro-European female voice said to Irene Bailey, Frederick P. Hazeltine's personal assistant. There would be no avoiding the call this time. It had been prearranged after three embarrassing calls were not returned by the United States representative.

"Please hold," Irene said to the caller, "Mr. Hazeltine is expecting the call." After several moments allowing for interested parties to pick up their extensions, Hazeltine spoke warmly, ever so affectionately, into the telephone. "Unan? Fred here. How are you, my friend?"

"I'm fine, Fred. And you? How is Thelma?"

"I feel like a million bucks. Thelma wants me to join her health club but I don't need it. Glass of wine with dinner and my heart will run forever. Sorry about the delay we had getting together on the phone, Unan," Hazeltine said.

"My fault, of course," the secretary general replied courteously but disingenuously. They both were very aware that Hazeltine had been avoiding him. "Well, since we have survived the work of more important business, I can report to you progress in the Vadim Krabac matter."

The American ambassador did not respond.

Unan Luumba continued. "I have been in touch with Krabac personally. He has a message to pass on to President Spalding."

"President Spalding does not accept messages from the likes of General Krabac."

"I can understand that, Fred, but in this case I think you will want to pass the information on to your President. Mr. Krabac is prepared to present himself to The Hague court within a matter of weeks. It seems he intends to run for public office and wishes to have this war crimes issue behind him. Apparently, he is confident that the court will find the charges against him without merit."

"He already holds public office. Why should we care

about his future elections? Elections in that country are farces, anyway."

"Yes, well, they are still an improvement over the old regime, eh? The point here, I think, Fred, is that a solution to Mr. Spalding's anxieties would seem to be at hand."

"Hmmm."

"Is that a yes, Fred? When can you get back to me on this? I think it is fortunate that Mr. Krabac feels that time is of the essence in view of the fact that you, too, have insisted that we move forward."

"Of course I'll get back to you," Hazeltine said.

"And that will be?" Luumba said.

"Soon."

Zulu time in Bosnia-Herzegovina was Greenwich plus one. Mob 4 received a Met briefing from Fleet that said cloud cover at the target area for 0001 Zulu 11 Apr was six thousand scattered, winds 290 at five knots, sea swells four feet, barometer 30.10 and steady. No moon. Conditions could then be expected to deteriorate to five-foot swells, overcast at two thousand, barometer likely to fall by 1300 hrs., winds 30 at fifteen knots gusting to 25, water temperature 68°.

Getts wasn't reassured about the Met data, but if they did their work right they should be well out to sea by 0400 and extracted within an hour later.

So at 2030 hours the team loaded their gear aboard a C-130 Hercules turbo-prop, the workhorse of the Army and SPECOPS units everywhere. Four Allison engines, rated over 4,000 each, pulled the Herc along at a cruising speed of 350 mph and could carry 35,000 pounds of cargo. With only Mob 4 aboard, with its relatively small cargo, they would hardly register on the big plane's weight and balance log. The team checked and rechecked their gear, secured it down for the flight, politely rejecting the loadmaster's offer to help stow it. That way, when they got the jump light everything would be in place and ready to go where they could find it.

The C-130 was off the ground at Naples at 2200 hours and climbed to thirteen thousand feet to clear the Apen-

nines Mountains. While the aircrew went on oxygen at that
altitude, the SEALs didn't. They were in superb physical
shape, so hypoxia at that height was not a factor for them.
When they left the airplane, it would be at twelve thousand
feet, not an oxygen deprivation consideration. Thirty-six
minutes after wheels up, they passed over Foggia and
crossed the coastline of the Adriatic Sea.

The plan called for the aircraft to fly an ovate pattern
on a mean course of 55° magnetic as though the flight were
destined for Dubrovnik. Approximately twenty-five nauti-
cal miles from the coast of Bosnia-Herzegovina the aircraft
would swing north by northwest, and pass over the east
end of the Korculanski Kanal. At 0030 hours Mob 4 would
free-fall from twelve thousand feet, and open chutes at one
thousand feet, landing in the ocean approximately nine ki-
lometers off shore. The distance from their POD (point of
departure) to the operations area was only 520 miles round
trip if flown direct.

Each SEAL had made hundreds of parachute jumps, almost a third of them HALO or HAHO. High Altitude Low
Opening done at night without the moon, over unknown
terrain, was the hairiest of all. They often jumped at thirty
thousand feet or higher, which called for oxygen equipment
and thermal body protection. They would free-fall until
they reached an altitude of one thousand feet, then either
pull the ripcord manually, or let an altimeter automatically
open it for them at a preselected height. When the ground
was nothing but a black, blurry mass rushing up at you at
more than one hundred miles per hour, it took balls to wait
just ten hundred feet from the deck to pull. Tonight they
were going with auto-openers. The same devices were
attached to a cargo bundle that included their IBS, com
gear and weapons, and other goodies that they would need
on shore.

The C-130 rattled its way through the inky skies while
each of the SEALs continued to review his assigned check-
lists. "Hey, Peach," Grumpy said. "Tape your gear."

Peach regarded Grumpy. "I did."

Every man taped his own gear to prevent equipment from rattling and giving away their position at night.

"I can hear you. Rattled like a fucking tin can getting aboard," Grumpy said.

Peach again regarded Grumpy darkly, wondering if the man was imagining things, losing his nerve, or if something else was on his mind. It was no time to start a personal beef, so he said, "Okay. You do it." Peach rose, approached Grumpy, and held out a roll of tape.

Grumpy turned his head away. "Forget it."

"You sure, buddy? I couldn't hear shit, but hey, if you can, maybe they can."

When Grumpy did not respond, Peach just shrugged his shoulders and resumed his seat near Getts. The two SEALs exchanged quick glances. Grumpy turned to double-check his gear.

Doc moved from his seat to one next to Peach. "He's a tough motherfucker, you know," Doc whispered, rubbing his hand along the seam of a cargo pocket on his jump suit.

"Who?" Peach said.

"Grumpy. You don't have to worry about him."

Peach knew that Grumpy was tough. Hell, they were all tough. Why did Doc have to tell him about Grumpy? "Why, should I worry?" Peach asked. Strange, but Peach *was* worried about him. He couldn't put his finger on it, but Grumpy seemed different. Cold. And crazy. Ah, hell, weren't they all?

"No, you shouldn't," Doc said. "He's just high strung. Intense, you know." Doc's eyes seemed almost imploring. Peach just attributed it all to PJJ—pre-jump jumps.

Getts looked up at Peach. "Okay, let's hack," he said. Each man pulled the stem on his wristwatch. "On my count it's zero-zero-six. Ready . . . hack." Each man started the second and minute hands of his watch to correspond exactly with the others in the unit. Ten minutes later, the C-130's loadmaster appeared. Getts nodded to him that they were ready. "Nine minutes to jump. Let's do the check. Stand up."

As TL (team leader), Getts designated himself jump master, and it was his responsibility to check every man's equipment. To make absolutely sure there were no mistakes, however, each man would also check his teammates' gear again. Getts made sure each of their composite jump helmets was fastened. Risers were checked for equal length, and they removed the cloth cover from the canopy release, checked for foreign matter, then placed the cover under the lower lip of the release assembly. Quick checks assured there were no twisted straps and that the quick release assembly was functioning properly. Leg straps had to be free of twists and they insured that the lugs were correctly inserted into the quick release assembly. They returned the safety clip in each rig and looked over their waistbands, making sure they were secured to the adjuster with a quick release.

Instead of wearing jump boots Mob 4 elected to use a special heavy-duty fabric hiking shoe made by Nike. They worked for almost everything they had to do, including water jumps where they could fit oversized swim fins over the shoes. Lastly, they made sure that each man had a fixed-blade knife secured to his leg within easy grasp, in case the quick release assembly failed or they otherwise became fouled in the parachute rigging and had to cut their way out.

"Hey, Bobby," Peach whispered into the com radio. "You take your pills?"

Getts nodded that he had.

"Too bad. You're a hell of a lot meaner when you forget to take 'em."

The a/c intercom crackled in his right ear. "Pilot to jump master."

"Jump master, go ahead," he said into the aircraft's crew mike.

"Coming up on your LZ, three minutes," the pilot said.

"Roger, open your door," Getts said. There was first the howl of air rushing by the plane's fuselage as it slowed from three hundred plus knots to jump speed, which was approximately 125 knots, just above the aircraft's stall speed. Then there was a grinding shriek as hydraulic motors forced open the aft ramp of the large aircraft, wind licking by its thin skin, screaming around the minute angles created by the changing configuration of the plane's empennage. Communication by electronic means would be difficult inside what sounded like a raging hurricane. Instead, Mob 4 would operate on hand signals from now until they were in the IBS. Getts tapped Peach's chemical light, then snapped the semirigid plastic. Chemicals inside the small tube glowed a bright green. Doc immediately snapped Grumpy's, then Grumpy activated Getts's. As they fell through space, each man would track the man in front of him, keeping him in sight by the green glow on his back.

Their cargo pack was moved into position on the ramp by the loadmaster who, simultaneous with the jump, would launch the cargo pack attached to Getts's waist into space with a fifty-foot tether made of ultralight weight line. Standing in the blackness of the night, howling wind grabbing at every inch of their bodies, Getts could feel his gut start to tighten. It was this way on every night jump, because the slightest miscue, any failure in equipment, any wrong guess on their part, meant certain death. Jumping out of airplanes for sport is just that: sport. But going out at night in full combat gear over uncharted terrain, well, that's a different ball of wax altogether. Getts's heart pounded faster as the seconds ticked by.

He raised his hand, pointing. He moved near the abyss of the yawning blackness spreading below him. He looked briefly away from the red jump signal light on the bulkhead of the Hercules, toward his team. They appeared, with faces blackened, clad in strange, bulky equipment, like monsters from the very depths of hell. When he looked back at the jump light it was green. He made another hand signal and the four of them stepped to the outer edge of the ramp, did a half-pirouette, and dropped off into the night.

After the initial shock blast of propeller wash and wind hitting them at 125 knots, everything became quiet until they began to pick up downward speed. Getts and his men positioned their bodies to fall as slowly as possible for best steering, and so that when their chutes deployed, the opening shock would be minimized.

As Getts reached terminal velocity at 139 mph, he could feel the intense cold wave. He knew that the uncomfortable iciness he experienced at twelve thousand feet would warm rapidly at the rate of about 4.5° F for each one thousand feet of altitude. Before opening, the air would seem uncomfortably warm because of his insulated uniform.

Even though there was no moon, as he fell through the scattered cloud layer he could pick out the outlines of the islands around Korculanski Kanal—Otok Hvar to the north and Poluotok Peljesac peninsula to the south. Getts airfoiled his body slightly toward a spot in the ocean that he thought would be close to the LZ. He felt a slight tug of the cargo tether as his body shifted direction. As he got closer to the surface of the ocean, the islands disappeared from his vision. Suddenly he felt and heard the opening of his chute, and had the familiar sensation of being pulled upward.

Getts quickly removed his swim fins from their fastenings at his waist, pulled them on over his shoes, then turned his quick release box to the unlocked position and removed the safety clip. At what Getts judged to be about a hundred feet above the black water below, he maneuvered into the wind and put his fingers on the releases but did not apply pressure just yet. What seemed like an instant later he could feel his feet touch water, and he released the left side of his chute by pulling down smartly on the release.

Getts's parachute collapsed as he released the remaining Capewell release, then hit the quick release box, freeing his leg straps and removing the harness. The water was cool but not shocking. After training in fifty-degree water at Coronado, it takes arctic water to make any impression on a SEAL. The others in Mob 4 were down and out of their harnesses and Getts could already feel the presence of Doc swimming ahead of him.

Their chemical lights continued to show their relative positions, and within two minutes, they circled their floating supply source. Without speaking, they unsnapped the flaps and pulled the compressed air lanyards that inflated the cargo float. All of their gear, including the IBS outboard motor, was inside. Quickly they pulled themselves into the boat, began donning their battle vests, camo hats, and balaclava masks, and unpacking the weapons and ammunition. Grumpy and Peach positioned the outboard on the back of the IBS, attached the fuel line, and on the third pull, started the engine. Mob 4 headed east toward shore.

The team had put precise coordinates into their GPSs and were confident of their accuracy within a square yard. Grumpy steered the IBS by watching the bearing and track arrows on his display. Getts sat forward on the port bow, only glancing at his GPS, focusing on spotting landmarks of any kind on the dim shore. Without the advantage of night vision glasses, they could only see an outline of the sheer cliffs that rose up from shore, and he saw lights from buildings or street lamps beyond the cliff tops.

Getts eventually spotted a face-shaped pattern of rocks that had shown up in an Intel photo that featured a prominent "nose" toward the sea. He was then sure that they were right on target. Grumpy's eyes met Getts as though he had seen it, too, because he nodded and steered for the beach directly below the "nose." They removed their flippers, leaving them in the bottom of the boat, and Peach and Getts placed the climbing gear within reach, checking that no lines were tangled and harnesses were secure. Getts quickly inventoried their sixty-meter 11mm core-heated Sterling climbing ropes, the CMI Ultra 8 belay devices tested to six thousand pounds, constant angle cams with five-thousand-pound ratings, steel pin gate carabiners, and pitons. Getts was glad he had taken the time to ask Doc about potential climbing snafus. Intel advised that the cliffs should be easily scaled hand-gripped, but they had all of the necessary gear just in case the game was different than advertised.

About one-quarter mile out from shore, the SEALs cut the quiet running outboard motor and sat bobbing in a mild sea, listening. They listened for voices, machinery—anything. When they heard nothing but the sound of surf,

Getts gave a hand signal. They each picked up an oar and began paddling silently toward the beach. Within fifteen minutes they were ashore. The beach was composed of coarse rock, about twenty yards wide at mean tide. They silently unloaded the IBS and secured the boat to rocks while Doc readied himself to lead the climb.

The wall was not vertical, probably eighty degrees, and the rock was hard and rugged, without handholds and cracks as they'd expected. Doc gave the signal that he was ready, then began to climb. They watched the ramparts through night sighting techniques (looking just above or to the side of the object of interest), guns ready should anyone hear or see Doc as he climbed. They noted his progress with fleeting glances until, eighteen minutes after he started, he had reached the top. For several minutes they waited for his all-clear signal while he scanned the grounds of the villa. Then the rest of the team began to ascend.

When they reached the top, all seemed quiet. The time was 0051. They were right on the mark.

Doc set up his infrared scanning gear, and as he swept the grounds from west to east, Getts watched the imaging screen. In the supposedly empty guest house, about four hundred meters distant, at least three human forms, two supine, one moving about, showed up on screen. There was also a third heat-emitting source within the house that was smaller, inert at the moment, that might have been a dog. They would keep an eye on that. Moving slowly east, they kept the main house in their left quarter quadrant. There appeared to be no heat sources on the main level of the west wing, but, again, supine images were emitting from upstairs. The exact number was difficult to estimate because of their relative angles, but Getts raised five fingers and Peach and Doc nodded their agreement.

Behind the main house was a second building that looked newly constructed. Getts estimated it to be approximately fifteen hundred square feet. The building could not be penetrated with IRS. Getts didn't like this development but there was nothing he could do now but proceed with his plans.

Doc continued the sweep to the right and noted a single heat source in the center of the mansion house which appeared to be coals in a fireplace. Upstairs, the IRS showed one, possibly two heat sources in the area where the master suite was located, both perhaps on a single bed. Continuing, the garage on ground level revealed two sources showing heat. By their imprint, they seemed to suggest automobiles. Upstairs, where Intel folders said the domestic quarters were, showed two more sources, also supine.

Using hand signals, Getts motioned to Peach and Grumpy that they would begin their reconnoiter, Doc staying put to hold the team's perimeter which was soon to become their escape route. Peach gripped the Ithaca shotgun tightly at his side.

In a crouch, moving silently using heel falls to deaden the impact of their steps, Getts moved toward the west wing of the manor house and Peach angled to the right, while Grumpy moved behind both men to provide cover. If they were detected by motion sensors, they would either retreat to the perimeter and draw the enemy into an ambush, or they would aggressively attack the objective, blow the doors, and seize their prisoner. That decision would be made by Getts on the spot, estimating the capacity of the enemy force against them. If he thought they could put the Serbs down, it would be fast and nasty. If he thought their force was superior to Mob 4, it would only take them a few minutes longer.

The air smelled musty, like dead vegetation mixed with burnt coal. There were fingerlets of ivy vines creeping up from the damp, black earth into the ancient rock that comprised the walls of the villa. What had once been scattered sky conditions had now turned to overcast, blocking even faint starlight. They froze at the sound of a dog barking. Then a second dog began to bark.

Without hesitating, Getts realized two things—there were no special sensors located in the main house, because they had reached the center of the courtyard without electronic detection, and after they took out the dogs they would be committed to action. They would have, however, plenty of time to penetrate the main house before the absence of the dogs aroused their handlers.

Peach now moved to Getts's side as he turned in the direction of the guest cottage. "Skipper. Dogs," he said. Getts turned his head in time to see two rottweilers come burning around the corner of the manor house. They were moving at top speed, eyes fixed upon Peach and Getts, mouths open and slathering to do what they had been trained to do. An arm or leg caught inside the jaws of these specially bred attack dogs would be ripped to shreds. Getts pointed his OICW at the lead dog, and depressed the trigger that fired the 5.56mm round. The lead dog's head went down into the ground and he took two somersaults before coming to rest in a bloody mass. The second dog took hits in the chest and went down sideways, without a sound. Their silenced weapons allowed no noise except for the clack of the mechanisms levering back and forward, and the very faint burp of subsonic rounds leaving the muzzles of their OICWs. Getts doubted if anyone inside either building heard the reports.

For several beats Grumpy was in and then out of Getts's vision. Then he heard a muffled click and a simultaneous thud. Getts looked around and immediately found Grumpy. He could see that he was injured. Getts hurried to his side and saw something out of a bad dream. Grumpy had stepped into a well-concealed trap, manufactured in Eastern Europe to kill groundhogs but, in this case, set to catch a man. It contained a powerful spring that set loose two pointed steel rods, bent to plunge inward on a foot or an animal's head. The steel rods had penetrated Grumpy's right foot to the bone, possibly even breaking it, and the pain must have been incredible. He uttered not a single sound.

Getts lay down his weapon and, using all of his strength, pried open the terrible, bloody jaws of the trap. Without Getts asking, Grumpy made a hand signal that he was not disabled.

Well, he wasn't okay, but there was really nothing the others could do for him at this point of the operation. His foot was already bound in his boot and while there was plenty of blood around the wound, there did not seem to be an artery cut. Getts had to assume Grumpy knew what his own capacity to move was. "Go," he whispered into his lip mike.

Doc, watching them move from his vantage point, understood that the team was now committed to action. Getts spoke to him into his lip mike. "Call Redbird. We're going in." Doc turned to his UHF radio and broadcast the code to begin the extraction. One way or another, Mob 4 would be in and out of the villa and away from the beach within thirty minutes.

"Redbird, this is Redbird One. Over," Doc said into his mike as he operated the Push to Talk button on the radio. No response. "Redbird, this is Redbird One, do you read? Over."

"Roger, Redbird One, this is Redbird. Go ahead," the radio crackled in Doc's earphones. The response came from Task Force 81.2 patrolling thirty miles west of Zga. Their CS (Command Ship) was an FFG-31, a guided missile frigate. With it were five DDGs, strike destroyers and an LHD, an amphibious assault vessel. On board the missile frigate was a Charlie-Hotel-46, the Sea Knight heli, that would be their primary source of extraction.

Doc started the wheels turning for egress. "Stand by for sea extraction, map section Blue twenty-two. Pickup at thirty minutes on the mark. Ready, mark. Over."

"Roger, Redbird One, understand you are on the way out. Extraction at Blue two-two on your mark. Be advised sea conditions at three and building, wind ten at fifteen knots, gusting to twenty, swells five to six."

"Roger, got your weather advisement. Redbird One, out." Doc said.

Peach ran from his place near Getts to the west door that led into the dining room. With blood seeping steadily from his shoe, Grumpy was already working on the lock. He shook his head. No good.

The three SEALs silently moved to the main door that led into a foyer. Beyond was the living room and the winding staircase to the upper floors. Again Grumpy tried his picks on the locks of the large steel-reinforced doors. He shook his head once more. Okay, so it wasn't going to be a silent entrance.

Getts nodded to Peach. The big SEAL placed his Ithaca shotgun approximately six inches from the lock, used about a five-degree deflection to avoid blowback, and pulled the trigger.

The sound seemed especially loud in the otherwise quiet of the night. The lock plate sagged inward. He quickly pumped another round into the chamber and pulled the trigger again. This time the bolt tore away completely and the door swung inward. Getts, Peach, and Grumpy were through the door on the run, Grumpy limping but keeping up a fast pace, quickly taking up his position inside the great hall. While Grumpy covered their flank, Getts and Peach began to move quickly up the massive stairs, their OICWs in fire position. So far, no sign of people. But the team knew they were there. "Go," Getts said into his lip mike.

With the shooters at the top of the stairs, Grumpy caught movement out of the corner of his eye on his left, near a door that should have led into the dining room. In a crouch, he whirled, bringing the OICW into fire position.

Three men were in the doorway moving toward him. They were armed. He tapped his trigger twice. Their technique was poor, all of them crowded into the small frame made by the doorway. He couldn't miss. The first two went down, dead or wounded, and the third man leaped sideways, still in the dining room but no longer showing himself. Grumpy quickly scanned 360 degrees, shifted his position, and waited.

There were two suites at the top of the stairs—Getts had only figured on one. "Peach," Getts said over his lip mike, then only had to nod his head. Peach kicked open the door, and Getts moved rapidly inside. He swept the room with his OICW. Nobody. Peach, still at the door, saw a figure emerge from the far end of the long balcony. He snap fired.

The man, in uniform and armed with a French FN CA (5.56), dropped to the carpeted floor, dead.

The balustrade was heavy and ornate. A thick oriental carpet ran the entire length of the balcony that gave access to the room. Getts tried the doorknob, finding that it turned freely. He used his shoulder to pop the door open fast. Peach moved inside while Getts slipped in behind him, covering side and rear. There was somebody in bed. They swung their OICWs into position as Getts reached the bed in two steps, pulling the covers down to expose two women, one young, one middle aged. Getts couldn't have cared less who they were. He and Peach left them alone and bolted from the room. Their target would have to be next door.

Peach tried the doorknob. Locked. He nodded to Getts, then kicked the door of the master suit. At first it moved, but did not give in. He kicked a second time while Getts put a shoulder to it and the door flew inward. The commandos jumped inside, keeping low, maintaining firing positions. The man they saw was Vadim Krabac. No doubt about it, it was the same man they had seen a hundred times in photos in the Intel folders. He was wearing a pair of pajama bottoms, but was shirtless. Krabac was in his middle fifties, and the hair on his chest, heavy and matted, was turning from black to gray. He had a Stalin-type mustache that was neatly groomed, and his eyes twinkled like a kindly man. They knew he was anything but. He had become fatty around the middle, and the skin on his chest was beginning to sag. He was larger than he looked in his pictures, Getts thought, and the SEAL leader figured he was an inch or so over six feet tall. His hair had started to recede, but it was still thick and curly. He had a high, broad forehead and prominent nose that looked a lot like one Getts had seen on a bust of Constantine. His chin wasn't large but it was firm. His face didn't have a lot of wrinkles—women probably found him handsome.

He was out of bed; he'd probably gotten up when he first heard the SEALs blow the main door downstairs. He had a pistol in his hand. Getts couldn't tell what kind it was because Krabac dropped it as soon as he saw the

OICWs pointed at him. He stood by a window that he had opened but figured he couldn't make it through in time. Getts looked into his eyes and saw a complete lack of fear. He didn't blink excessively; his chin didn't quiver. His hands were large and he let them fall easily to his side as he waited for the SEALs to make a move. So this, Getts thought, is an enemy of our country. The peddler of mass destruction. The mass murderer of his own people.

Out of training and instinct Getts and Peach quickly searched the room, including an armoire and the bathroom. No one was in the bathroom, but a lady was hidden, shivering, in the armoire. She screamed and clamped her hands over her mouth in utter fright. The lady looked to be in her early forties but, outside of being a bit plump, she was pleasant to look at. She wore pink short pants with lace trim and an equally short top that she was half out of. Her hair was entirely blond and entirely out of a bottle. Getts didn't waste time trying to tell her not to be alarmed. Once he saw that she was unarmed, he left her in the armoire and turned back to Krabac.

"Do you understand English?" Getts said to him.

"Yes, I speak," he replied in a heavy accent.

"You're a prisoner and you are coming with us," Getts said.

Krabac made no move to comply with Getts's order. "You are here to kill me," he said.

"No. You will be safe with us," Getts said, waving his weapon toward the door.

"It is known. *Lei mi ucciderà,*" he said, lapsing into Italian.

"I give you my word as an officer in the United States Navy. I guarantee you safe conduct. I insist you come with me."

Peach grabbed the general in his vise-like grip and jerked him toward the door. The time for talking was over. Getts led the way from whence they had come, along the balcony toward the head of the stairs. They could hear gunfire but it was light and sporadic. As they started down the stairs, pushing Krabac ahead of them, they could see Grumpy holding his position, commanding the entrance from the west side of the house and the two doorways to the north and east.

There was no need to speak as Getts and Peach took up positions near the blown main door. Getts was about to hand-signal for Peach, Grumpy, and the general to follow him to the cliff when he saw two armored personnel carriers pulled up at the west wing of the house. Military troops quickly disgorged from the vehicles. Getts turned to Grumpy and pushed Krabac into the SEAL's arms. "Take him. We'll cover."

Getts and Peach immediately took cover behind a waist-high concrete balustrade and began to lay down a withering suppression fire, their OICWs on full automatic, but their disciplined trigger fingers squeezing off exactly three rounds with each mini-burst.

Grumpy, limping badly but holding General Krabac firmly in one hand, made off at a trot toward the cliff, where Doc began putting out a stream of covering fire.

The automatic arms fire the SEALs were beginning to take from the Serbs was, Getts thought, from FN CAL (5.56) rifles, a French weapon considerably better than the AK-47s and Vz58s that they had expected. The heaviest damage, however, was dished out by the SEALs, expert marksmen who hit their targets with every trigger pull. Getts and Peach watched while one of the PCs with a 30mm gun mount began turning toward them.

"Take the gun," Getts said to Peach as he slid another magazine into his weapon. With his weapon recharged, Getts intensified his fire on soldiers who were using the PC for cover. He could see the effects of Doc's rounds, which kept the enemy troops' heads down.

So far Peach was the only one who had put his weapon on 20mm to take on the PC's 30mm gun. The OICW has a built-in computer/laser chip in the sighting system, enabling the shooter to lay the infrared sight on a target and, within a hundredth of a second, the range finder to arm the 20mm airburst round with the coordinates for the correct detonation time. Whenever they pulled a trigger, some-body dropped.

Peach, now using his laser sighting system and automatic fuse control, took careful aim on the two-inch-wide visual slot on the personnel carrier and squeezed off a 20mm HE round. The round caught a piece of armor on its way to the slot. It exploded and the enemy 30mm gun fell silent. But Peach knew he had not dealt a killing blow. He aimed again, and squeezed off a second round. This time the HE round passed cleanly through the eye slit and exploded inside the PC. An explosion of fire and smoke told the SEALs that the folks inside the 30mm were out of business and out of this world.

"Good shot, Peach, baby," Getts said.

Then, suddenly, Getts was blown backward by a heavy blow to his chest. He lay on his back, sucking for air without success. He struggled to rise but was unable to move. He didn't know what hit him.

From his position at the perimeter, Doc did. "Some prick's got a Dragunov," he said into his lip mike. "Behind the big pine tree." Doc swung his OICW toward the bole of tree and began firing. Peach turned toward the same target and, looking through his magnified gun sight, picked out the distinctive details of the Russian-made SVD Dragunov sniper rifle. The gun fired a 7.62 round from a 10-round magazine and mounted a 10×10 scope atop the barrel, deadly at nine hundred meters. Peach knew the sniper had to be taken out, and fast. He and Doc concentrated their fire on the Serb shooter, laying down a stream on both sides of the tree. After several seconds of intensive fire coming his way, the sniper made the mistake of attempting to run for better cover. He made it only two steps before Doc and Peach cut him down.

"Changing out," Peach said, reaching for yet another 5.56 magazine. At that moment Grumpy rolled into a fire-fight position next to Getts. He squeezed off several bursts of suppressing fire then bent over to look at Getts. The Navy lieutenant was pushing himself up with both arms.

There was no blood. "Getts?" Grumpy said into his lip mike.

"I'm okay," Getts responded. He was still gasping but recovering fast. The round he took had hit him square in the solar plexus, but had not penetrated the Kevlar vest they all wore. "Let's get the fuck out."

"They're rolling in another PC," Peach announced into his lip mike.

"Roger that." Doc's voice came on line. "Two more on the east side."

Just about the time that Getts was ready to admit that their Intel was right on the money, for a change, all hell broke loose. They heard the sound of more vehicles moving into position. They heard voices shouting, commands being given. And worse, there were more troops, a lot more of them, in the building behind the mansion. While the SEALs were disposing of equipment they couldn't take with them, they started taking heavy fire from both corners of the house. The enemy didn't have night vision equipment, but their firepower was immense and sooner or later they were going to hit something. Unlike the SEALs', their rounds were not smokeless, so the team could see them clearly with their infrared sights. They took their time, aimed carefully, and hit what they aimed at. Mob 4 couldn't afford to get into a protracted firefight, because ammunition was limited and they had a Navy task force waiting for them off shore. They had to haul ass, but first they had to suppress the Serb fire. The four of them went right to work and kept at it for about eight minutes, squeezing off a burst, resighting, then squeezing again.

If you're on the other side of that kind of accurate firepower, you suddenly realize how close you are to God. Or Allah. When the guy next to you catches a kinetic energy round through his left eye and the guy on your other side takes one through the skull, the message is that it ain't just luck. You want to put your head down, keep it down, and start crawling your ass backward. Apart from guys looking to be martyrs, it didn't take the Serbs long to have second thoughts about charging whoever was out there.

"On two, for the ropes," Getts said. "One, two . . ." The three SEALs moved at once on the count. They forayed in a fire-team configuration, each man covering a flank as they kept low moving quickly across the open grounds of the front of the villa, passing the gazebo and then sprinting the remaining twenty meters to where Doc was maintaining covering fire. At that moment the ground started to open up around them as yet another series of 30mm cannon fire tore into their position. Getts would descend last and keep the PC occupied while the others went down.

"Where's Krabac?" he said, switching his weapon over to 20mm HE fire.

For a fleeting moment nobody spoke. Then Grumpy said, "He's dead."

"What? How?" Getts demanded.

"He had a hide-out," Grumpy said, meaning that the prisoner had had a pistol on him that they had not found. "It was him or me, Bobby."

The Serbs had taken heavy casualties and they were losing their enthusiasm for heroics. Fire was now coming at the SEALs from very discreet, well-protected places of fire. "Okay," Getts relented, "get out."

Peach, leading the way down, was followed soon after by Grumpy, then Doc. Doc set the short-detonation fuses that would melt the IR equipment and render it useless to the enemy. It was too bulky to carry in a fast retreat. Then he swung his legs over the side of the cliff and, using nothing but thick leather gloves, jumped over the side of the rocks. When he got to the bottom his gloves were almost smoking.

Getts, aiming at the PC's turret, fired off all six rounds of air-burst 20mm HE at the gun. The 30mm went silent. Getts then vaulted over the side of the cliff.

When Getts reached the bottom of the cliff, the team had already pulled the IBS out of cover, Grumpy pulling the lanyard to start the motor. Getts took two steps toward the boat, then stopped. There, in the rocks, was Krabac. Getts stepped over to the body. He looked closely, then rolled him over.

"Bobby, it's going hot," Getts heard Peach say in his ear.

No sooner did he get the words out of his mouth than a firefight broke out anew. Serbs at the top of the cliff began firing down at them. The SEALs returned withering fire from their OICWs, causing the Serbs to pull back long enough for Getts to leap onto the boat. "Cease fire," Getts said. No point in giving the enemy muzzle flashes to aim at.

He turned to Grumpy at the tiller. "Tell me what happened," he said.

"Say how?" Grumpy said, his eyes raised above Getts's.

"Tell me how the prisoner died," Getts said.

Grumpy shrugged. "He had a hide-out. He pulled, I fired. That's it."

Grumpy was clearly in great pain. Doc withdrew a syringe from his med kit and pulled off the plastic covering cap with his teeth. "Ready?" he said to Grumpy. It was not practical to remove the SEAL's shoe first. Grumpy nodded. Doc accurately but forcefully stabbed the number 22 needle through Grumpy's composite sole and into his flesh. It took almost a full minute to pump enough Lidocaine into Grumpy's foot to ease the pain.

"Where did he have it?" Getts said.

"The fuck do I know, sir. Maybe in his waistband. I wasn't going to take the time to ask him," Grumpy said.

"Steer one-ninety," Peach said to Grumpy, referring to his GPS for navigation. "Never mind, I'll take it." Peach took over the tiller from Grumpy's grasp.

"You shot him in the back of the head," Getts said to Grumpy.

The reaction among the others was electric. Their heads snapped around to regard Grumpy. He looked back at them. Peach and Getts removed their Balaclava masks. Grumpy did not. "Maybe he caught a Serb round," he said.

"No wound in the front, Grumpy. Just one hole. Execution style."

"It was there. You just didn't see it," Grumpy said, avoiding Getts's eyes.

"You're about fifteen seconds away from being charged with homicide, Truman," Getts said, using Grumpy's given name. "If I have to listen to you try to stick another lie up my ass, that's just what will happen."

Grumpy shrugged again but licked his lips. "Orders."

"What does that mean?"

"I got orders to shoot the son of a bitch. Hey, they didn't want him kidnapped. He had to be taken out, Skipper. The order came from high up."

They all heard a sudden sound and turned their heads as one. A high-speed patrol boat, its powerful searchlight sweeping the water, was moving in their direction.

"Peach, how much time to the EP?" Getts said.

"Ten minutes," Peach responded.

If the patrol boat caught up with them while the Sea Knight was overhead, they would all have their asses in a tight wringer. The Sea Knight had no weapons to compete with a gunboat.

Cloud cover, as the Met people had predicted, was almost total. They left the black cliffs of Bosnia directly behind them and headed back out the Korculanski Kanal. The island of Otok Hvar and the peninsula of Poluotok Peljesac acted as a venturi for winds bearing down at them through the slot, increasing their velocity and pushing mansized whitecaps in their wake. In a few minutes they heard nothing but the sound of wind and the sea crashing into the IBS. As they rode to the top of a big swell, the stabbing PB light caught them and held on.

"Redbird Four, this is Redbird One," Doc said into his mike. "Redbird Four, Redbird One, come in." Doc was casting at 100 KHZ and, after contact, would go to 10 KHZ to talk. "Redbird One, this is Redbird Four, I read you five by five," a voice came over Doc's earphones. "It's scratchy but I got 'em," he said to Getts. Then he spoke into the mike set again. "Redbird Four, we're one point five west our hot LZ, speed approximately ten knots, running seas. We have a patrol boat in pursuit. Over."

"Roger that, One. Hold your course while we look. Standby." After several minutes the airborne radio operator came back to Doc. "Roger, One, we've got your transponder. Dial in four sixes and confirm." Doc keyed in the requested four sixes on the transponder and pushed the Ident key. The airborne voice came back. "Gotcha, One. You're in the Blue Sector. We're twenty-five off your port side. How about your hostile?"

"Still with us, gaining. If he gets too close, we'll give you a wave off," Doc said.

"Negative on the pass. We're coming down. Five coming aboard?" the heli crewman said.

"Four. That's one, two, three, four."

"Roger, you're four. Listen for us in about seven. Redbird Four out."

Peach looked away from Doc and saw Bobby looking at him. They had to deal with the patrol boat, which was now gaining fast. "Six hundred meters," Getts said. As if in answer to Getts's range estimate, the patrol boat began firing a deck gun, probably a 40mm from the sound of it, but the shells were landing beyond the IBS. "We'll give him three hundred meters, then we open up with twenties. Wait for the top of a swell, then aim at the deck line."

The four SEALs, including Grumpy, who locked in the outboard motor, checked their selective fire and stood by for Getts's command. They all watched the searchlight intently; several 40mm rounds fired from the Serbian, now getting closer. "Stand by," Getts said. As the words left his mouth, they could hear the Charlie Hotel overhead. Then the IBS was raised by the sea to the top of a swell. "Fire," he yelled over the sound of sea and helicopter engines.

The SEALs opened up simultaneously. Heavy firepower leaped out of their weapons in a steady, deadly stream of high explosive rounds. As the rubber boat began to run down the other side of the swell, the SEALs could see numerous hits on the boat. Peach gave Getts a thumbs-up. Doc punched Grumpy in the shoulder.

"Stand by," Getts yelled again. The IBS rose again on the next swell, and again the four SEALs poured fire into the patrol boat. This time there was no answering fire and the searchlight, miraculously immune from destruction, began to turn, unfocused, into other areas of the sea. The PB was no longer a threat, and all the wet and exhausted team wanted right now was to get the hell out of the area.

The Charlie Hotel, its rotors spinning overhead, was so loud that it felt like their brains were being concussed inside their skulls. The SEALs cracked two more chemical lights, fastened them to the gunwales of the IBS, and started to peer through the haze.

They finally spotted the Sea Knight descending slowly through the gloom, banking slightly as the pilot made eye contact with their chem lights. The huge, 120,000-pound giant bug, painted dead black, appeared like a goblin out of a junkie's nightmare. It descended toward the rubber boat, its ramp opening up like giant mandibles.

They saw the cave ladder lowered and, still making forward headway, the pilot slowed his speed to about five knots for the pickup. The SEALs dropped all of their equipment over the side of the boat, except their OICWs, then took turns grabbing the ladder overhead. The clamor of those giant rotors banging the heavy air around their heads sounded like the hammers of odin, streams of seawater sucked into the vortex then blown back out stinging their exposed skin. The last man up the ladder, Bobby Getts, let go a burst from his OICW into the IBS to sink it, then followed the others up the cave ladder to the interior of the copter.

Jesus. What a way to make a living.

United Nations

Hazeltine could feel a crimson flush that had started at his collar now light his head like the top of a Christmas tree as he sat in the secretary general's outer office, cooling his heels. He stood up and paced the opulent room, not looking at the African art that decorated the walls, and the carefully selected sculptures molded by the best artists from around the world.

Hazeltine had been summoned, *summoned,* to Luumba's office. Who the hell did he think he was? And who the hell did he think put him where he was? Hazeltine had tried to explain—brush off, really—Luumba's aide by saying that his schedule was hopelessly filled for the day and that a meeting with the secretary general would have to wait. But Kishua, the male aide, was resolute. The meeting would not take long and it *must* occur this afternoon by three o'clock. Unable to appeal directly to Luumba, Frederick Hazeltine had stormed from his office at 799 UN Plaza to the thirty-eighth floor of the UN building in a state of high rage. To be kept waiting like a supplicant was more than he could bear, both personally and as the ambassador of the most powerful nation in the world. By the time he was shown into the small African man's office, he was livid.

Luumba sat behind his grandiose desk, like an annoyed traffic judge in a small southern town who did not like what he saw on a policeman's citation. Rather than rise, he motioned Hazeltine to a chair across from his desk. The final indignity.

"Unan," Hazeltine began even before his pin-striped suit coat had touched the back of the chair, "I tried to tell that man who works for you that I had business in Washington, and that a meeting today was going to be a bitch. He doesn't speak English very well and he didn't seem to understand. We have to make this very, very short."

Luumba raised his eyes, the corners of his mouth pulled down as though he had bitten into a juicy lemon. He regarded Hazeltine for what seemed to the American ambassador a long, insolent, time. "So. Your president could not find the time to call me about Krabac."

"Good God, Unan, is that why you called me over here? Are you still hung up on that Balkan embarrassment? The President of the United States is without question the busiest man on the face of the Earth, and if you don't like the fact that he can't call you at your convenience then you have something to learn about the way the world works." Hazeltine almost rose from his seat. Almost.

"Yes, I have much to learn about the way the world works. I understand that he did not have time to call me about Vadim Krabac because he was too busy murdering him," Luumba said starkly.

Hazeltine sat up straight against the back of the chair, his eyes narrowing. "I don't know what the hell you're talking about, but on a personal level as well as professional one, I want you to know that I don't appreciate that kind of language. The President is not only a public figure but a close personal friend of mine."

"Too bad. Because I must then conclude that you were involved in the decision to assassinate Krabac as well. Your president does nothing in a vacuum. I know that he is incapable of making a decision by himself. You would have been the obvious choice to aid and abet," Luumba said.

The American ambassador's face turned a deeper shade of red, a vein pulsing at his temple as his fingers gripped the edge of the chair. When he spoke, it was only with supreme effort that he was able to control his rage. "You've gone too far, Luumba. You've just thrown away your career."

The African sighed. "We shall see whose career is to be lost. Sources from UN offices in Geneva have supplied me with some of the details of two days ago, March 11. Vadim Krabac was executed by masked terrorists in a government villa near Zga, in Bosnia-Herzegovina, during early morning hours. Gunfire was exchanged between the terrorists and security personnel of the government. Nine men were killed, six wounded, no terrorists were injured. Elements of the United States Atlantic Fleet were detected operating in Adriatic waters forty miles off shore from the atrocity. It is believed that the terrorists were picked up at sea by an American helicopter."

"You say it was an American fleet. An American helicopter. I assume you also mean to imply the terrorists were American. Do you have proof, or are you simply throwing around accusations?" Hazeltine said.

Luumba shrugged. "Just my intelligence sources and my personal beliefs. I can assure you that my associates are still evaluating data. I will receive more clearly defined reports."

Hazeltine rose to his feet. He rejected the urge to wipe a rivulet of sweat from the side of his nose. His knees felt a bit shaky. He made a mental note to have his secretary check his blood pressure when he returned to his office. "I have better things to do with my time than listen to mud being thrown at the American flag. Even by you." He turned toward the door.

"Yes, you must be very busy, Fred. Tell me, how is Roger Demerit? When will he be allowed to go home from the hospital?" Luumba said.

Hazeltine again felt weak in the knees. "It doesn't look good."

"Ah. Too bad. A courageous man. But I agree that he probably will not improve. He said as much to me this morning," Luumba said.

"This morning? You saw him this morning? In the hospital?"

"Yes. He was deeply troubled. I worried that our conversation might have tired him, but he insisted that I stay to hear it all," Luumba said, leaning back in his chair as he regarded the ambassador.

Hazeltine reached for his snowy white handkerchief.

Chapter Nine

Peach and Getts went back to their pre-Navy days when Getts was in college and Peach was learning martial arts in an Oakland dojo and applying what he learned in the streets of the city. Peach enlisted in the Navy three years before Getts graduated from Stanford. Each volunteered for SEAL training at BUD school, but were two full years apart. Still, they had been together ever since. While he knew Peach like a road map, Getts knew Truman Lynch not at all.

Mob 4 were handpicked men, and Grumpy was supposed to be as tough as they came, always determined to carry through a mission, and highly motivated. While this could be said of almost any SEAL, Truman had won a medal for valor in Desert Storm by rescuing a downed British pilot and concealing them both for forty-eight hours, until they could be reached by elements of the First Platoon, 4th SEAL Company. A first-class, capable guerrilla fighter, Truman's fear threshold had yet to be reached. But he was off center. Unbalanced. Truth to tell, maybe they all were, to one degree or another, but Getts thought Grumpy was farther off the scales than most.

Getts was sure this was so when Grumpy cold-bloodedly murdered a prisoner in their charge. Well, hell, their kind of hit-and-run operations behind enemy lines called for a "no prisoners" mind-set, even as a practical matter, but this time it was different. They were there to bring the man back *alive*. Getts gave the general his word, only to have Grumpy wig out.

When Getts got him alone, he tried to explain to him that they were in deep shit because of what he had done.

"I carried out orders, Bobby. Me, Doc, and Peach," Grumpy said.

"But not me," Getts said.

"No. Not you."

"Where did you get orders that I didn't know about?" Getts said.

"Same place you got yours, sir. John Barry," Grumpy said.

"Where did you see John Barry?" Getts said.

"At the Conch."

They were presently outside the BX on the sidewalk at the Creek, and people passing by were starting to get interested in their heated conversation. They could tell that what was between them wasn't exactly friendly. Getts and Grumpy moved farther down the sidewalk.

"He just happened to be there?" Getts asked sarcastically.

"How the fuck should I know how he got there? Everybody in south Florida knows we hang out there," Grumpy said, his temper heading north.

"He tells you he wants Krabac dead. And he wants *you* to make it happen. And you agreed. Is that your story?"

"Yes, sir," he snapped. "I followed orders from the same man you took 'em from. Anything wrong with that . . . sir?"

"So why didn't he find the time to give those orders to me?"

"He said you didn't need to know."

"Come on . . . ," Getts started to say.

"His exact words, Lieutenant," Grumpy said. "Hey, look, Lieutenant, don't sweat it. They're going to back us up. The orders came from the very top."

Little Creek was a U.S. Navy amphibian training base located in Chesapeake Bay among a big-time complex of Navy strategic bases that included CINCLANT (Commander in Chief Atlantic), NAS Oceana, JTASC/USACOM, NSWC Dahlgren, NATC Patuxent, Aegis Combat

Systems Center Wallop Island, Ft. Story, and Dam Neck near Virginia Beach. Little Creek is the Fleet Combat Training Center, Atlantic. While SEAL teams 2, 4, and 8 operated out of Little Creek, there were also SEAL groups training at Dam Neck. All SEAL units were under the command of SPECWARCOM (Special Warfare Command) and were only tenants on each base.

Getts had been ordered to wait in his room at the BOQ at Dam Neck for Captain James P. Rolland, one of the original BUDs (Basic Underwater Demolition) and a stand-up guy who, in any other command in the Navy, would have been a three-star admiral by now. Getts had met Captain Rolland several times, the first at his graduation from BUD in Coronado in 1990. When Getts was assigned to SEAL 6, Captain Rolland was a kind of mentor to him and they developed a personal relationship that included many hours of swapping bourbon-and-coke-fueled stories, with junior officer Getts doing most of the listening.

It was on Jim Rolland's recommendation that Getts took over command of Mob 4 at Pamino Beach. Getts had no illusions, though, that this meeting with him was going to be a joyous reunion. Getts wasn't under house arrest, but it was pretty clear that he wasn't encouraged to stray far from the officer's club or its BOQ until Rolland arrived.

It was late in the afternoon, the final rays of the sun casting a dull orange glow on the bottom of cumulus clouds that sat, thick and unmoving, on the water's horizon. It was probably a warm day. Getts didn't pay any attention. He had a tightness in his gut that he couldn't spit out. He realized that he was depressed, but he also knew that all the medication in the world wouldn't help the way he felt. Thanks to Grumpy and some bogus order, his life was going to change into a massive shitstorm.

He sucked on a bottle of beer, aware that alcohol, no matter how slight, would only make his depression worse. He looked up from his reflection on the ocean to see Jim Rolland step out onto the deck.

He was in a khaki uniform, a gold braid adorning his hat. It was a working uniform so he wore no ribbons, or his Navy Cross, three Bronze Stars, two purple hearts, four battle stars, and two unit citations, to name just a few. His badges alone would have weighed down a lesser man. They included master jump wings, the Budweiser, the SAS recognition, and many others. Captain James Rolland's tight frame was forged of battle-hewn sinew. What hair he had left on the sides of his head was white, his eyes as deep blue as the sea on which he had chosen to spend most of his life. His eyebrows were bushy and had turned to light gray, giving his face the image of a person pleasantly surprised. His lips were full and red, as though oxygen had just been pumped through his blood vessels; his skin, made leathery from excessive exposure to the sun, was mahogany. He smiled when he saw Getts, revealing straight, white teeth. In his left hand he carried a small, zippered note case which he dropped casually into a chair near the table by which Getts sat.

Getts came to his feet and, because of the circumstances of their meeting, put his heels together and came to attention. Because they were at the O-Club, Getts did not salute, but he felt that he should be somewhat formal. "Good afternoon, sir," he said.

"Hello, Bobby," Rolland said, extending his hand. "Sit down. Relax." Getts shook his hand. It was as strong as steel, warm and dry. He regarded Getts for a long moment in a way Getts thought was friendly. Rolland glanced around the patio deck to see that they were alone, except for a waiter who appeared at the table to take their order. "Beer for me. How about you, Bobby?"

"I'll finish this one, sir," Getts said. The waiter left for the inside of the club and Captain Rolland and Getts took chairs at a small, circular patio table.

"How's Buzzy, Bobby? Still in good health, I hope?"

Captain Rolland's memory was either extraordinary or he had gone to the trouble of studying Getts's personnel file. Either way Getts was impressed. He didn't know whether to be wary or comforted by Rolland's obvious effort to make himself familiar with his past as well as his present. "She's well, sir, and I'll tell her that you asked about her."

"Do that. You're a lucky guy to have a mother like that. I had a damn good one, myself. My father, too. I was an Army brat, you know."

"Yes, sir, I remember you saying that. Your father was stationed at Fort Sam Houston for some time. He was a doctor, I think, sir," Getts said.

"You've got a good memory. He took good care of everybody except himself. He died at the age of fifty from a heart attack. I think I dodged a bullet from that gene pool. My mother is eighty-five and still raising hell out in Long Beach. We keep in close touch." Getts waited for Captain Rolland to come to the real point of why he wanted to see him, but the man was not ready yet. "I thought about studying medicine like my father, but it's funny . . . at the time, when I was in my early twenties, I didn't care much about who lived or died. Matter of fact, I could usually come up with a rationale for putting a lot of folks out of their misery forever. Can you believe that attitude? I saw myself as a warrior. Not only did I regard myself as a man of action, I thought that the more people you killed, the better man you were." Rolland shook his head slowly. "Now I'm older and I don't think that way. These days I wonder what kind of doctor I might have been. Or, if I had been a lawyer, I wonder if I could have made people's lives a little easier. Even a schoolteacher. I know I could have made a difference if I had taught kids how to read and write."

Getts did not think that Captain Rolland expected a response from him and he made none. Rolland's drink arrived and he took a large swallow, then unzipped the leather attaché. He produced a document of several pages which Getts immediately recognized as his AAR, after action report. It was not a copy, it was the original. "Well," the captain said, "this is what I want to talk to you about. I wanted to give you some time to consider this."

"Yes, sir, I thought that might be what this was all about," Getts said.

He placed the document in front of Lieutenant Getts. "I'm Acting IG for all SEAL teams, Bobby. I'm supposed to look into this." He nodded at the report. Getts didn't need to look at it. He was very aware of what it said. "What you're saying in here, Bobby, is that your men obeyed an illegal order and carried out an assassination. Did you give them that order?"

"No, sir, I did not give them that order, but I do not avoid my responsibility for the fact that I was the team leader when that illegal order was carried out," Getts said.

"Noble. I expect a good officer to say something like that, and you're a hell of a good officer. This is off the record, not part of my duties of IG, but it really isn't true, is it, that you helped your men do anything illegal?" Before Getts could answer, Captain Rolland continued. "Tell me something, Bobby, if you didn't give an illegal order, who did?"

"Sir, it's in my report. It was a man who called himself John Barry. Chief Petty Officer Peach Crosley and I met three weeks ago with John Barry in Miami, Florida. He gave us our mission folder, a briefing, and I believe he later ordered Lynch to execute General Krabac."

"You believe, but you don't know. What does Lynch say?" Rolland said.

"Ask him yourself. He'll tell you about his private meeting with John Barry."

"Who's John Barry?" Rolland asked.

"I don't know, sir. I assumed he was White House. I confirmed his command authority through Colonel Arnold Talent, SpecOps," Getts said.

"Colonel Talent has no knowledge of any such conversation with you, Lieutenant Getts, and he has no knowledge of a man by the name of John Barry," Captain Rolland said.

Getts felt a chill run through his body. "Sir, Mr. Barry's identity seemed to me a cover name. I have that in my report," Getts said.

"The White House knows of no man there by the name

of Barry. They have a Barnard, but her first name is Nancy and she is an assistant in the PIO," Rolland said.

Getts's throat constricted and he found it difficult to form words. "With respect, Captain Rolland, sir, are you calling me a liar?"

"I wouldn't do that, Bobby. I'm talking to you now as a friend. Look, I have a different report for you to look at. It's all filled out and ready for your signature." He produced a second set of papers from his note case. It wasn't an AAR but a special warfare training report. Getts scanned the material. It said that on the days of 9, 10, 11, and 12 March, Getts and his men of SEAL 8, with elements of Second Platoon, were practicing an underwater beach survey in the Bay of Salerno and that on the nights of 9, 10, 11, and 12 of March they were in or near their billets at Atlantic Fleet Com, Naples, Italy. The report went on to say that upon satisfactory completion of their training exercises they returned, via military air, to their permanent assignment at the Naval amphibious base in Little Creek, Virginia.

"I can't sign this, Captain Rolland," Getts said.

"Why not?" he said.

"Because it isn't the truth, sir," Getts said. For a moment he believed that he saw a flash of pain race through the window of Captain Rolland's eye.

"Bobby," he said, "you've been on hundreds of training exercises just like this one. You can sign this report with a clear conscience. But suppose you don't. Suppose your AAR goes in as written. What you are telling the Navy Department, the Secretary of the Navy, and the entire United States government is that you were ordered by the President of the United States to assassinate an official of a foreign government. You're on the promotion list for full lieutenant in August. Your promotion will be held up until this is clear. There will almost certainly be a court-martial and your men will be accessories to an assassination. Do you understand that?"

"Yes, sir, I do. But I can't change what occurred. That's why I'm telling you and the U.S. Navy that my man was given illegal orders and that the responsible parties should be—"

"Hold it right there, son. Don't tell me who's responsible for what. If I told you to drop your trousers in a downtown shopping mall and flog your weenie, would you do it? No? Then who the hell are you to parcel out blame? You're responsible for what you do and so are your men." Captain Rolland's chin was firm and his eyes were steady. And he was absolutely right.

"With respect, sir, my report will have to stand as written. I don't see that I have any other choice," Getts said.

Captain Rolland leaned back in his chair and took a deep breath, his eyes holding Getts's for a long moment. It seemed that he was trying to think of something further to say that might change the situation. "Okay," he said, getting up, "that's the way it is, then."

Getts rose and saluted him. Captain Rolland did not return the salute, but turned his back and walked into the doorway of the O-Club.

Chapter Ten

Doc couldn't believe it when he heard that Bobby turned in an AAR. Most of the missions they did weren't reported at all, and he damn sure figured this one would be no exception. So Grumpy spazzed and shot the war criminal. Bottom line: mission accomplished. Nobody's business was nobody's business, especially in SEAL 6. But Bobby couldn't get over it. They had a conversation about it, but Getts did most of the talking. They were all "temporarily relieved of duties." They knew there was a formal investigation going on and there damn sure was going to be a court-martial. Someone's ass was going to get hung out to dry.

One day the three of them—Peach, Doc, and Grumpy—had just emerged from the base theater where they saw *Saving Private Ryan.* Bitching movie. They thought it was really, really good, and there's Getts waiting for them when they came out. He wanted to talk, he said. Well, no shit, so did they. They walked slow down Fifth Street, over to Eighth Street and up Helicopter Road, talking.

"Hey," Getts said, "I'm sorry that shit is starting to slide downhill. Didn't have to be that way."

"How come we're standing still for a court-martial?" Peach asked.

"Why?" he said. "Because we did an illegal mission. We murdered someone."

"You mean Grumpy, here, murdered someone, not you, Bobby. Certainly not we," Peach said. "Unless there's something you're not telling us."

"I absolutely do mean we. We're a unit," Getts said.

"Bullshit, sir. You didn't get the word. That's what you're going to tell them, that you'll take responsibility, but in the end it's his ass, not yours," Peach said.

"I don't see it that way," Getts said.

"No, Peach's right," Doc said. "What's all this Court of Inquiry crap, anyway, Skipper? Scuttlebutt says you can just write another report. They'll let you do that, way I heard it," Doc said.

"That right? Depends on who you're listening to, Doc. Bad enough we assassinated someone, I'm not going to compound the problem by falsifying an official government document," Getts said.

"So we go to Leavenworth? That's what you're saying, sir? Just so we can pretend we're the goddamn Musketeers," Grumpy said.

"I think we don't lose our heads. We've got friends on our side. Right, Grumpy?" Getts said.

"That's right, sir. I got an order. And the people who gave me that order are letting you fill out a different report. Only you won't do it. That fucks us good. Sir." Grumpy spat the last word out.

"You fucked yourself when you failed to come to me with that order," Getts said. "People you think are your friends aren't your friends, Grumpy. I'll give you a piece of news. I'm your true friend, understand? I'm also your commanding officer. I would never have given you an order to do anything that would put you behind bars. Even you should be able to figure that one out," Getts said.

"You're turning on the unit," Peach said.

"He's the one who's turning on the unit," Getts said, pointing to Grumpy. "He cut me out. He killed a prisoner to whom I had just given my word of safe conduct. He's ratting everybody out, not me."

"We don't see it that way. There are three of us. You're turning us into the brass because you don't have the balls to take the rope they're throwing us. Sir."

Getts's fists clenched. You can call a man a lot of things but nobody called Getts short on balls. The team thought they'd get it on right then and there, but Getts cooled himself off quick.

"How about it, Lieutenant? You going to stick to the truth or are you going to get our ass out of the fire?" Grumpy said.

"I told you I'm not going to make it worse with another lie. If no one serves the truth, this country is in the toilet. We're all in this together but—"

"You telling me you've never told an iddy biddy lie in your whole life, Lieutenant Bobby?" Grumpy said. "And you're not going to start now? Suppose they got you strung up by your thumbs in a bamboo hooch, sticking needles under your fingernails and a pair of pliers around your nuts. They're asking you where the rest of your unit is hiding. You going to tell them the truth or are you going to lie?"

"Not the same thing and you know it," Getts said. "This is a matter of principle. It's what the service is all about, doing the right thing."

"Sorry. For a minute I was getting confused the lies we should tell and the ones we shouldn't. You know what I think, Bobby? I think that anyone out to string up our asses is the enemy, and I don't give a fuck whose uniform they're wearing at the time. I'll lie to them and I'd advise you to lie, too," Grumpy said.

"You're borderline insubordinate, Grumpy. Watch yourself," Getts said.

"Come on, Skipper. Since when is it a sin to lie for your buddies?" Doc asked.

Bobby's neck stiffened. "I don't like this, either. Not a Goddamned bit. Whatever happens to you happens to me, too," he said.

"That's thanks to you, with all due respect, sir," Grumpy said. "I'd rather see you fall on a hand grenade and get blown up to save my ass. Why don't you do that, Bobby, you're so fucking excited about saving us?"

Bobby looked hard at Grumpy. Maybe he was trying to intimidate him. "Hey, Grumpy, I'm beginning not to like what you're saying or the way you're saying it. Would you feel better if we fell out on the beach and settled this thing? I'll be happy to take my bars off."

Before Grumpy could say or do anything, Peach stuck his oar in. "Bobby, you don't appreciate what we're saying to you. I know you don't. See, if you let your report stand, we're going to jail. Ever think of that? We'll get convicted right along with Grumpy, here. Maybe we can keep Doc out of it because he was covering from the perimeter and we can fix up a bullshit story for him, but me and Grumpy will go to Leavenworth Penitentiary for twenty-five to thirty for murder. Can you dig that, Bobby? Do you understand what we're saying to you?"

"I'm not going to let that happen," Bobby said.

"Yeah?" Peach said. "How? With you being the JAG prosecutor's chief witness against us, how are you supposed to save our ass?"

"It's not going to happen," Bobby repeated, as though trying to convince himself.

"Pardon me, sir, if I don't sleep real easy 'cause you said that." Grumpy had an evil grin on his face that sent a chill through Getts. "I'll make it even clearer. We're not going to jail. I'm thirty-one years old. Doc's twenty-seven and Peach here will be twenty-nine in a month or so. You think we're going to spend our young-ass lives in a jail cell because you got some kind of weird fucking George Washington hang-up? Ain't gonna happen, pardner. I gauran-fucking-tee you."

"That sounds like a threat, sailor." Getts's eyes narrowed.

"I don't make threats, sir. Ask anybody."

They all knew what Grumpy was talking about. It made Doc swallow hard, but Grumpy left them no choice. None. They would have to eliminate Getts or go to jail for life just because Grumpy followed orders.

At the Creek, NIS (the Naval Investigative Service) is located at area 2008, which was where they told Mob 4 personnel to show up, Grumpy first, at an annex near building 16. His foot was feeling a whole lot better but it was

still bandaged and he limped as he made his way across
the compound. The annex wasn't anything fancy, wood sid-
ing on a concrete slab, probably five rooms at most. A
female rating sat at a desk out front wearing a yeoman
third class rank on her fatigues. Grumpy told her who he
was and that he was to report to a Commander Fortier.
"Be right with you, Petty Officer," she said. "I'll tell him
you're here."

While she got up from behind the desk and went down
the hall, Grumpy took a seat without being asked. It was
getting to be a habit to sit whenever he could because of
his foot. The lady yeoman had a fat ass. Little pudgy
around the joints, too, and she wore glasses. Nothing wrong
with glasses. He kind of liked them on some girls, but
there's no excuse for fat, he figured. You can run it off. He
had no sympathy for people being fat. If he had to carry
one out of a jungle, down a mountain or up a river, he'd
just stick a flag in his or her asshole and wish him a lot of
luck when the Federales showed up.

He was sitting there thinking about her ass when it was
his own he should be worrying about. His and Doc's and
Peach's. What was Bobby Big Shot trying to prove? That
he had honor? What the fuck exactly is that? Grumpy had
honor. So did Doc and Peach. Honor is what made them
what they were. You had to have it to get through BUD
training. You had to have it to get through Hell Week
without quitting. You can't run fifteen miles soaking wet
with saltwater carrying a full field pack for two hours and
go for eighteen more without food unless you got something pretty goddamn close to honor helping you along the
way. Honor is knowing you're better than anybody else.
Except your swim buddies. And the team. Your honor is
to the team. And, by God, to yourself. So Bobby thinks
the team is fucked up and he's got some kind of special
insight about right and wrong. Well.

"Last door on your left down the hall," the yeoman said
when she returned.

He followed her directions, knocking once at an open
door. "Come in." Grumpy could see an officer sitting there.

He walked inside, came to a brace, and snapped a salute to the officer behind a desk. On one side of his desk was a floppy briefcase that couldn't stand up by itself, and in front of him he had pads and papers spread all over the place. Commander Fortier had thick black hair on his forearms, just like on his head, and on his ring finger was a class ring but it damn sure wasn't the Academy. He was wearing a pair of those little half-glasses on his nose while he looked down at his papers. Then he looked up and smiled like he was trying to be friendly. Grumpy knew better than that. This was the first motherfucker whose business it was to put him in jail. Him and his swim buddies.

Chapter Eleven

It seemed to Commander Fortier that SEALs have a special way of coming to attention. They don't quiver like the Marines or the Brits. They kind of slide into it. When they salute, their right hand raises up a little bit slower, so that when their movements are finished they seem just about perfect in the way they set their shoulders back and their chin in. Not like plebes, but like fighting men. Petty Officer Truman Lynch was clearly good at what he did. He was close shaved, his camo uniform starched and ironed to a knife's edge. Commander Fortier got tired just looking at him. After all, Commander Fortier didn't run five miles every morning or even every month. His idea of excitement was to lie on a couch with a good novel, a bowl of nuts, and a glass of wine within reach. Lynch's nose seemed to twitch just a bit at the smell of Commander Fortier's pipe tobacco. Another bad habit of his, the commander thought. Looking at Lynch he was reminded that his own khaki uniform had been worn a few too many times between trips to the cleaners. He nodded toward one of the four chairs in the room.

"At ease, Grumpy," he said. "Have a chair. I'm Commander Fortier."

There were three chairs and a table besides the one he was using, all of them metal, government issue. Grumpy sat in one farthest from Fortier's desk. Fortier continued making notes for a couple of minutes, until the yeoman secretary came into the room, sat down at the table, and arranged her court reporting machine in front of her.

"This is Yeoman Agland," he said, introducing his legal

assistant. "She'll record what will be said in this room. You'll be asked to read her transcription, make any corrections that may come to your mind, then sign it. I do some of the Judge Advocate's Office investigations preliminary to formal hearings or court-martial proceedings. I'm going to take a statement from you today under oath. You will be expected to answer my questions fully and honestly to the best of your knowledge, under penalty of perjury. Your testimony will become a part of case number JA-52-323, involving Lieutenant Junior Grade Robert Getts, Chief Gunner's Mate Glenn Crosley, Quartermaster First Class Truman Lynch, Petty Officer First Class Jake Gathers, and elements of the United States Navy. The events which occurred on or during the days and nights of March 9, 10, 11, and 12 of this year are the focus of our interest. The purpose of this investigation is to ascertain whether or not Navy regulations or laws of the United States or any regulations of the U.S. Code of Military justice were violated by any of those personnel mentioned herein. Questions so far?"

"No, sir," Grumpy replied curtly.

Every investigator develops his own techniques of questioning a witness. One of them is to carefully watch the body language and voice inflections of the witness for contradictions between what is being said aloud and what is conveyed otherwise. It seemed to Fortier that Lynch's throat was a little tight. That, of course, could be the product of Petty Officer Lynch trying to assess which side the "blue suiter" was on, his or the Navy's. He was, on the one hand, in danger of going to jail for essentially the rest of his life, or, conversely, being exonerated. Commander Fortier thought that might constrict *his* throat, too. The U. S. Navy wanted the best to happen for Petty Officer Lynch and his "swim buddies." But he couldn't know that, yet.

"Does the name Grumpy mean anything to you?"

"Yes, sir." Grumpy replied.

"And what is that?"

"Wasn't that one of the seven dwarves?"

"You have no other association with that name?"

"No, sir. Should I?"

"I'll ask the questions. Who is John Barry?" Fortier said.

"I don't know, sir," Grumpy said.

"Never heard the name?"

"I don't think so, sir."

"Petty Officer Lynch, when you are ordered to execute a mission, who gives you your orders?" Fortier said.

"Well, sir, naturally my platoon leader, Lieutenant Getts, issues orders that I obey. Sometimes I get written orders. Everyone gets those," he said.

"Have you ever undertaken a secret mission?"

"No, sir."

He's lying, Fortier thought, even though it was a technicality. The commander knew that Lynch's team had operated in both Desert Shield and Desert Storm. They were all decorated for valor. "Who would give you orders if your mission was secret?" he said.

"Sir? I guess I don't think much about that. If we're told to saddle up, the order has to come from National Command Authority. Or USSOC. U.S. But that's pretty well filtered before it gets to me, sir."

"To what unit are you assigned?" Fortier said.

"SEAL 8, 2nd Platoon, sir."

"Were you ever assigned to SEAL 6?" Fortier said.

"SEAL 6? No, sir."

"Ever hear of SEAL 6, Petty Officer Lynch?"

"No, sir."

"Mob 4?"

"No, sir."

"Come on, Lynch," Fortier said, "I asked you a reasonable question and you're giving me a smoke-and-mirrors answer. Mob 4 is a unit of SEAL 6." Fortier removed his reading glasses from his nose and looked up. "For your information, I'm cleared for top secret. Does that affect your answer to my question?"

"Meaning no disrespect, Commander, I might have heard of a SEAL team that specializes in antiterrorist and hostage rescue work, but that's all. I've just heard about them. Rumors."

"I have an abbreviated copy of your personnel file. It doesn't tell me your hometown. Where are you from, Lynch?"

"Los Angeles," he lied.

"What did your father do for a living?" Fortier asked.

"He was a cop, sir." Grumpy enjoyed that part of his legend. He had even told some tall tales about how his father shot it out with the mafia.

"What part of the city did you live in?"

"San Gabriel Valley. Sunland. We lived on Fenwick Street," Grumpy said, unblinking.

"Did you like it there?"

"Sir?"

"I mean, were you happy? Did you like school?"

"Oh, sure. It was pretty nice."

"How old were you when you joined the Navy?" Fortier said.

"Nineteen, sir." That was true.

"Right out of high school?"

"More or less, sir. I did a year at a junior college."

Commander Fortier did indeed have an abbreviated personnel file on Truman Lynch, and the questions he asked the SEAL were based on facts that he already had in front of him, though Lynch had no way of knowing that. Lynch had lied, consistently and right down the line. Except about junior college. He had done a year of junior college but it was nowhere near California. The SEAL they called Grumpy was born and raised in the midwest. His father was a railroad engineer. If he was ever in California it was for BUD training. SEAL Team Six members often had a "legend," a cover story they would tell in case they were captured. Fortier apparently represented to Lynch an enemy interrogator. The realization made the commander angry and frustrated. He did not, however, allow his emotions to show.

Fortier looked at Lynch for several moments. Then he referred once more to his notes. "Where were you during the days and nights of March nine, ten, eleven, and twelve?" he said.

"Well, sir, my squad was doing a training mission in Salerno Bay, Italy. We did a beach recon that included currents, sand composition, gradients, beach profiles, and stuff like that. Pretty much of a routine training mission, sir."

"Did you HALO in?"

"No, sir. We inserted from an IBS. That's an inflatable boat."

"Day or night?"

"Night."

"What was your BSU?"

Petty Officer Lynch seemed surprised that Commander Fortier knew about Basic Support Units. "We staged out of an LHD assault ship. Part of COMNAVSURFLANT," he said.

"How did you injure your foot?"

"I stepped on a piece of rusty steel in the Bay of Salerno, sir," he said.

"Where is the town of Zga?" I said.

The SEAL shrugged. "How would you spell that, sir?"

Petty Officer First Class Jake "Doc" Gathers, like his swim buddy Grumpy, was impeccably military in his bearing; and if he appeared slightly nervous, Fortier regarded it as natural, and not necessarily a conflict with honesty. "Are you familiar with Executive Order 12-333, Petty Officer Gathers?" he asked.

"Not really, sir. I mean, I heard Bobby say something about it lately when all this shit started, pardon the expression, sir. But I never read it, if that's what you mean," he said.

"Have you ever been given an order to kill a man?"

"In combat, yes, sir."

"And you are a member of SEAL 6, Mob 4. Is that correct?"

"SEAL 6? No, sir. SEAL 8, Second Platoon, sir. Should be right there in my file, Commander." Doc's hands had stopped fidgeting with his starched fatigue hat and rested easily in his lap.

"I don't have your file," Fortier said. "I have an extract of the SEAL 8 staffing roster. Your name is on it."

"Yes, sir. Damn sure should be, Commander," he said and sat a little deeper into his chair.

"You are the communications man in your squad, is that right?" Fortier asked.

"Yes, sir, that's one of my specialties," he said.

"Who is Redbird?"

"Redbird? I don't believe I know that one, sir."

"It's a coded unit identifier, isn't it, Gathers?"

"Well, it could be, Commander. I mean, we use all kinds of code words. Everybody does all the time. I just don't know that one. Bluebird?"

"Redbird."

"No, sir, I don't know that one."

"Do you regard yourself as an honest man?"

"Yes, sir."

"Would you lie to protect a friend? A swim buddy?"

"You mean to an enemy, Commander? Like if I was captured or something? Sure. But would I lie to an officer, like you, sir? No, sir, I wouldn't."

"Where are you from, Petty Officer Gathers?"

"Rimridge, Wyoming, sir."

"Did you go to high school there?"

"Went to grade school there, sir, and then we had to take a bus into town for high school because Rimridge was too small to have its own high school."

"Were you a good student?" Fortier asked.

"Yes, sir. I generally made the Honor Roll most terms."

"College?"

"No, sir. I did a term at Idaho State but I always wanted to be a SEAL, so I joined the Navy when I was twenty."

"Ever been assigned to the Adriatic?"

"No, sir. Trained with the French swimmers—that's what they call their SEAL guys. Swimmers. I trained with them at Teulon. And I've been to Britain a couple of times and we've been to Naples a couple times. Like when we were there last March, in the Bay of Salerno. But not the Adriatic."

"Never to Bosnia? Never to the north side of the Adriatic?"

"No, sir. United Nations personnel only in Bosnia. That's what I understand. Peacekeepers. That's not our kind of gig, sir."

"Do you know what an illegal order is?"

"Generally speaking, I guess I do. Yes, sir."

"Give me an example," Fortier said.

"Hitler gave his men illegal orders. Killing innocent civilians and shit like that. Pardon my language. If you're told to do something like that, Commander, you don't have to do it. You're not supposed to do it."

"Have you received an illegal order of any kind in the past twelve months, Petty Officer Gathers?" Fortier said.

"Me, sir? No, sir. Never. Nothing close to it."

"Newspapers and television stations all over Europe reported that General Vadim Krabac was murdered by American commandos. Did you know that?" Fortier said.

"No, sir."

"The same story was carried this morning by CNN. That would tend to confirm Lieutenant Getts's AAR."

"If you say so, sir. I never read it, myself," Doc said.

Chief Glenn Crosley looked to Fortier like a man he would want on his side in a street fight. He was big, over six feet, well muscled, light on his feet, and had eyes that didn't miss a thing. His face showed scars, probably from combat, but he remained handsome. Virile. "I understand you hold a black belt in karate," Fortier said to him.

"And aikido," he said.

"I don't suppose you were ever an unarmed combat instructor for SEAL Team Six?" Fortier asked.

"That would be SEAL Team Eight, sir."

"Never been assigned to Team Six?"

"The Phantoms? No, sir."

"Why do you call them phantoms?" Fortier said.

"Well, we hear all these magic kinds of bullshit about

some slick SEAL outfit, but I've never seen them. Never seen them on anybody's TOE, either."

"So you don't think they exist?"

Peach shrugged. "I don't give much thought to rumors."

The chief was borderline disrespectful, but Fortier's assignment was not to instill discipline, it was to learn facts and evaluate them. "You testified in your written account that during the nights and days of March 9 through 12 you were with your squad doing training dives in the Bay of Salerno. Is that right?"

"Yes, sir," he said.

"Are you a religious man, Crosley?" Fortier said.

"Can't say that I am, sir."

"Do you believe that morality comes from the Bible?"

"Get it wherever you can, sir. If that works for you . . ."

"Crosley, would you lie to save yourself from court-martial?"

"I'm not a liar, sir," he said.

"That wasn't my question," Fortier said evenly.

"That's my answer. Sir."

"Would you lie to save the life of a swim buddy?" Fortier said.

Peach started to respond then checked himself. Finally, he said, "There are times when I would lie. When you're captured, for example . . ."

"How about in peacetime?"

"How about oh-two-hundred hours when the bar is closing and I tell a lady she's the most beautiful woman I've ever seen in my life? Am I lying?"

Crosley seemed to have an adjustable moral system. But then, don't we all? Fortier thought. "Lieutenant Robert Getts said he led you and his unit on a mission to Bosnia, near the town of Zga, on the night of March 11. Is that true?"

Peach knit his eyebrow as though he were thinking about it for the first time. "Why, no, sir. I guess he made that up."

"What reason would he have for that, Crosley?" Fortier asked.

"Reason? I love Lieutenant Getts. But he's a sick man.

Depression. Hell, I've seen him so bad he was hallucinating."

"Can you prove that?" Fortier said.

"Hell, yes. Sir. He's taken all kinds of medications. Benzodiasepine is one of them. Trazodone was another. Desyrel, Prozac. Shit, there were days when this guy was staring at the wall while we did his work for him."

Peach looked at Fortier without blinking, straight in his chair, fully relaxed and confident. The commander's stomach knotted at the potential implications he had presented to him and to the U.S. Navy in trashing Getts. "I suppose you could supply me with the names of doctors who have treated Lieutenant Getts?"

"Certainly could, sir. Civilians, of course. Navy doctors would have closed him out. But you can ask Bobby about that. He's no liar, sir. Man of his fucking word. That's why I have to think he was delusional when he filled out that action report. None of us did what he thought we did."

"I've never heard anything so off the wall. Are you saying that you covered for a man whom you knew to be mentally incompetent, Peach? That he didn't know the difference between the coast of Bosnia and the Bay of Salerno?" Fortier said, his voice rising in anger.

Peach's tone remained maddingly modulated. "We all covered for him, yes, sir, but he wasn't incompetent. Fact is that he's a hell of a leader. So smart he's scary, and he doesn't know the first thing about fear. That's why we went where he said to go. Sir, I followed him before and I'd follow him again. It's just that sometimes he'd get these kind of attacks that would last for a week or two, then he'd be all right."

"You're a liar," Fortier said.

Peach's eyes narrowed, his lips pressed white, and the color left his face. "Commander, I'm going to let you get away with that just one time. I think you're emotionally upset. Because if I didn't think you had lost control, just for a minute there, I'd come right across that desk and tear your fucking throat out."

"Commander . . ." Yeoman Agland started to leave her chair, extreme nervousness in her voice.

"Don't record the chief's response to my remark, Yeoman Agland. I . . . uh . . . I used an improper form of question." Fortier considered what to say next for a long minute. Then he turned back to Peach. "What kind of attacks did he get?"

"Like I said, he'd hallucinate sometimes. You know, imagine things. Couple times he thought he was floating around in the room. And he harbored anger. Lots of it. He'd just walk around in a rage for days, sometimes weeks, then he was okay again."

"How long would he be okay?"

Peach shrugged. "A month. Month and a half, sir."

"Furnish my office with the names of those doctors who treated Lieutenant Getts by oh-eight-hundred hours tomorrow morning, Chief."

"Yes, sir."

"And you said you followed this man, took orders from him. Even when he had a gun in his hand," the JAG officer said.

"Hell, sir, we all had guns."

It was more than April showers in Little Creek. The skies had literally opened up and it was pouring. A system called El Niño had turned the weather upside down and it flooded everywhere. Commander Fortier saw Lieutenant Robert Getts walking erect along the cement walkway toward the building. He was dressed in camouflage uniform, shined jump boots that glistened even in the rain, and a three-quarter-length raincoat turned up at the collar. He was a handsome man, Fortier thought, appearing young for his age. Too young for what he knew supported his service record. He wasn't privy to all of it.

The part of Getts's record that he was able to get his hands on told Fortier something about the man's determination, his character, and what his commanding officers had written about him. "Courage beyond . . . Willpower consistent with the highest demands of SEAL . . . A born leader . . . An officer of tireless dedication . . . unswerving patriotism, an American flag for a heart." Unusual attributes for any officer, even in an unusual branch of the American military system. There was a story told by men of the SEAL teams that might have been more myth than fact. It was certainly unverified in Navy records. Glenn Crosley was in SEAL training before Bobby Getts was accepted into BUDs as a fresh ensign out of Stanford ROTC. Crosley, already a black belt in martial arts, had become an unarmed combat instructor at Little Creek when Getts began BUD training as one in a class of 175. Only forty-nine finished the school, confirming that the object of the rigorous training was to get rid of the weak and adopt only the tough, the determined, the cunning. Officers, by design, had it rougher than enlisted men because they were leaders, and if any man fails on a mission it better not be a leader who can cost lives beyond his own. Officers were singled out for harassment and encouraged to drop out. For some reason, an instructor by the name of Schlicker had decided that he was going to get Ensign Getts sent to anyplace other than the tough Navy SEALs.

Bobby Getts had no special physical attribute to separate him from the others. He was average size, without any fat on his body, because of his intensive running regimen prior to his arrival at the Creek. But he apparently had more than enough heart. The fact that an instructor by the name of Schlicker beat up Bobby Getts in martial arts classes was apparent for anyone to see. But the harder he was thrown, the more viciously he was punched and kicked, the more fuel there seemed to be to the fire in Getts's belly. He became a walking, running, crawling mass of tape and bandages. Peach prepared to step in and stop the one-sided conflict between his old friend and a cadre man, but Getts insisted on handling the battle himself.

The story went that one Sunday night, Schlicker was on a date with a woman from town. He was walking up the beach near the EM Club at Dam Neck when he was ambushed by a person or persons wielding a two-foot piece of driftwood. Schlicker took two blows to the head and numerous strikes to the body. He suffered four broken ribs, a broken nose, concussion, bruised kidneys, and class-three bruises to his legs and arms. Then a petty officer third class, Schlicker walked unassisted to the club, where an ambulance was called. He was in the hospital for three weeks. A search was conducted for Schlicker's assailant, but the victim claimed it was too dark to provide a description of his attacker. No suspect was found.

Four weeks later, Ensign Getts graduated first in his class of forty-nine officers and enlisted men. Two years after that, when Lieutenant Robert Getts was given a special assignment to the Middle East, he asked for Glenn Crosley as his second in command. Off duty as well as on, the two men had been inseparable since, though Crosley had never caught up with Getts in rank.

Getts had hung up his hat and raincoat before Yeoman Agland ushered him down the hallway to Commander Fortier's office. He took a chair at the gesture of Commander Fortier's hand. Yeoman Agland took her customary place at her stenographer's machine.

"Good morning, Lieutenant Getts," he said. "How do you feel?"

"Wonderful," he said.

"You don't feel wonderful at all, do you?"

"No, sir, I don't."

"I didn't mean to get into it so quickly, but since we're on the subject of how you feel, do you have a problem with depression?" Fortier said.

"Yes, sir. Don't we all?"

He was naturally defensive in his response but Fortier decided not to press him. He'd let him play it as he felt it. "You know what I mean. Do you take medications for depression?"

He took a deep breath and smiled. "Yes, sir. Not much. One hundred milligrams of Desyrel every day. I take it as a kind of prophylactic. I can live without it, of course."

"One hundred milligrams is not a small dose. Is that the only drug you take?"

"Yes, that's all," he said.

"How about Trazodone? Ever take that for depression?" Fortier said.

"Yes, sir. It's generic for drugs like Desyrel."

"They weren't prescribed for you by military doctors?" Fortier asked.

"No. I didn't want a military doctor to put it on my records. My depression is very mild. I have no serious effects either from the illness or the medication. I just thought it was my business, no one else's," he said.

"Have you ever hallucinated?" Fortier said.

Lieutenant Getts hesitated before answering. He knew exactly where Commander Fortier had received his information. "Yes, sir. I think every SEAL has hallucinated at least once, probably many times. We're deprived of sleep a lot, we get hypothermia at times from swimming in cold water, or hypoxia from going without air on a dive or on a HALO jump. So I know what it's all about. Yes, sir."

"I don't mean from that kind of cause. I mean have you ever hallucinated because of your depression?"

"No, sir. Never."

"Ever find yourself in a rage for no reason? I mean one that might be caused by your depression?" Fortier said.

"Never."

"I wish you had told me about this sooner, at our first session, for example," the commander said.

"I didn't think it was pertinent to your inquiry, sir. It certainly wasn't important to me," he said.

Commander Fortier had been thinking hard about who was telling the truth. Instinctively, as well as circumstantially, Lieutenant Getts seemed the bearer of facts in this case, and the other three enlisted men had strong motives for dissembling. Still, he couldn't recommend a court-martial based only on what he suspected. He had to know more about Lieutenant Getts, despite the fact that most of his records were closed.

"Lieutenant, I find it . . . well, hard to believe, that the Navy would send you on a mission to a place on the Adriatic to wipe out an official of a foreign government. Legality aside, that seems to me to be a job for a substantial strike force. Company size, not a squad. Certainly not four

men. And your background . . . I know that you're tough
and reliable. SEALs are tough, no question about it, but
this whole idea of four men going off, almost unsupported,
seems like a mission far beyond what you are experienced
enough to accomplish." Watching Lieutenant Getts's subtle
reactions, he knew he had struck a nerve.

"I have the experience," he said.

"It's not in your records," Fortier said.

"You don't have my records," Lieutenant Getts said.

"Then tell me."

"Off the record," he said.

Fortier considered for a moment. Then he said, "All
right. Nancy." Yeoman Agland withdrew her fingers from
the machine and sat back in her chair. Lieutenant Getts
glanced first at Agland, then back to Fortier. "Confidential.
Just you and me," he said. Fortier nodded to Agland, who
left the room.

Commander Howard Fortier believed Lieutenant Getts's
story. Getts might have regular bouts of depression, he con-
cluded, but he wasn't crazy. The method to his madness
was patriotism. He followed orders. He was loyal to his
troop—as long as they were loyal to him. His action report
was the work of a man troubled by a breach of military
protocol, and an order he clearly regarded as illegal or non-
existent. Telling the truth was the only way he knew how
to deal with it. Imagine that.

Even then there might have been a way for the Navy to
wiggle out of the whole mess, but the *New York Times* and
the *Washington Post* picked up the story that had begun in
the European media and was supposedly supported by a
source inside the Pentagon. Second page headlines announced
*AMERICAN MILITARY ASSASSINATES VADIM KRA-
BAC* and *NAVY OFFICER ADMITS KILLING.* Secretary
of Defense Arnold Blessing quickly announced through his
Public Information Office that charges had been made but
nothing proven. It was not the policy of the United States
government to use assassination against any foreign state
official the country was not at war with. Certainly Vadim
Krabac, however odious his participation had been during

the Bosnian wars, would have been no exception. An official investigation was under way, and the American public would soon have all of the facts.

The *San Francisco Chronicle* reported the closest thing to the truth, that a U.S. Navy SEAL officer had led a team to Bosnia-Herzegovina in order to kidnap a notorious general wanted for war crimes during that country's conflict. The officer, according to the article, admitted to his superiors that it was necessary to execute the prisoner before the team was able to bring him out of country.

White House Press Secretary Charles Goudy tried to minimize the affair by assuring the White House press corps that the President had just heard of the alleged incident and was looking into the charges to see if they had any foundation in fact. Naturally the President would be following the investigation with great interest.

Members of Congress, sensing the President's administration was vulnerable to scandal over the event, convened hearings into allegations of officially sanctioned assassination by military personnel.

Commander Fortier was called hastily from the officer's mess, where he was eating a late night meal, in order to take an urgent telephone call from United Nations Ambassador Frederick P. Hazeltine in Washington. Leaving his hot food to turn cold on his plate, Commander Fortier rushed back to his office and called the number he had been given.

After he had waited briefly for an aide to put him through, the honey-cultured voice of Ambassador Frederick Hazeltine came briskly through the earpiece without preamble. "I want your assurance, Commander, that no American military personnel were involved in whatever happened to General Vadim Krabac."

For a brief moment Commander Fortier wondered where a United Nations ambassador stood in his chain of command. No matter where he stood, Fortier realized, Hazeltine was a close friend and advisor to the President of the United States. This was no time to hesitate or equivocate. "Well, sir, the matter is still under investigation. It's too soon for me to give any kind of assessment," he said.

"Assessment? What the hell's to assess? Navy SEALs are the finest young men this nation can produce, aren't they? Then let's wrap this thing up so we can put out the official word. We're not looking so good around the world right now, Commander, so let's not give our enemies any more ammunition than they already have," Hazeltine said.

"I understand, sir, but the unit commander has made a written statement, an after action report. He says they were ordered to kidnap Krabac and that one of his men killed the prisoner on direct orders from the White House," Fortier said, the palms of his hands beginning to sweat.

"What's the officer's name?"

"Lieutenant Junior Grade Robert Getts, sir," Fortier said.

Chapter Twelve

Getts hadn't had a leave in almost two years and he decided that now was a good time to take one. He was now an official "prosecution witness" and the term damn near made him sick. He told everybody in JAG and his superiors that he had nothing prosecutorial to say, and that whatever they wanted from him they could get from his AAR. He was pissing into the wind, though, and he knew it. He was ordered not to have any communication with his former teammates, an order he summarily disregarded. If they didn't like it, he thought, they could convene another court-martial for him right behind the one they were starting. Matter of fact, he tried to contact Peach and Doc, but they were nowhere to be found. He tried the number in Pamino Bay, on the off-chance Grumpy would be there, but there was no answer. Getts didn't know if they were avoiding him, but he still thought they could work something out among the team and go after the people who'd given the orders in the first place. If Peach and the others didn't turn around fast, it would be too late. Their own predictions of life spent in jail would likely occur.

He didn't want to stay around Little Creek and have to explain himself to every SEAL he saw on the base. He even thought several times about talking to his mother, and when he finally did call her to chat, she was in the south of France with friends. Since the summer house was empty, Getts thought he might go out to the west coast and use the place. None of the team knew where his family summer home was located. It would be a good location to be alone, where he could think.

He also thought about calling Lydia. They talked regularly, but for the past several days he couldn't bring himself to tell her what was happening, and he had no appetite to lie to her. If you can't be honest with the people you care most about, what's the point of being alive? So he avoided her calls and made none of his own. He knew that couldn't go on forever, but he kept hoping for a positive turn of events, something that would make it all clear up. Waiting it out in Portland sounded better all the time.

His family summer home was on Lake Oswego in the southwest part of Portland. The lake, about three miles in circumference, had a connection with the Willamette River that flowed through the middle of the city of Portland. The Columbia River bordered the city on the north. The Columbia bore ships of seagoing size, while the Willamette was smaller, no less beautiful, and hosted tugboats pulling rafts of logs from inland logging sites to paper mills downriver. When Getts was in high school, during summer months he rafted logs for the Scooter Tug and Barge company. The pay was good and the adventure high. Logs moving on water are not as placid as they look, and the violence of their dynamic size and weight always fascinated him.

The house where they used to spend summers had to be about ninety years old by now. It was one of the first built on the lake, constructed by a retired sea captain who made the house's outer walls with lapstrake molded boards. There was a three-gabled roof and an outside staircase that led to the second floor of the house, where there were two bedrooms in addition to the two downstairs.

The front door key was original with the house. Six inches long, it weighed a quarter of a pound and was made of solid brass. When Buzzy went out, she locked the front door and put the key above the door ledge, where everybody on the lake, and probably in the village, knew it was. She had a philosophical attitude toward material things.

Getts sipped a dark Arabian coffee that Buzzy had on hand and it tasted great. It tasted even better after a few bites out of a croissant. He tried to call Lydia, but when he got her machine, he decided just to say, "Hi, it's me. I'll try you again." Still, he left his number on the lake and cautioned her not to reveal it to anyone, even the team. When he read the morning *Oregonian* newspaper, he came across a follow-up article on page two concerning Navy SEALs about whom conflicted reports failed to explain events that took place in Bosnia. Names of those involved were not disclosed by the Navy Department. The incident, if one had actually occurred, was still under investigation.

The telephone had rung several times during the first two days that Getts was at the Oswego house, but he had not answered, leaving the machine to pick up. When it rang that morning, however, for some reason he wanted badly to pick it up.

"Hello?" he said.

"Hi there, sailor. I'm selling sex and I know the fleet's in port," came the familiar, desirable voice.

"I don't know who this is but I'm a little short on cash. We haven't been paid yet. Can I have your body on credit?"

"Nope. I found this number on the wall of the bus station and thought I'd see if you were in the market. I guess I'll just keep dialing," Lydia said.

"If you do, I'll break your pudgy little fingers."

"Oooooo. Rough sex. Okay, I'll come there and give it away."

Getts hesitated. He wouldn't put Lydia at risk for any romantic meeting but he was also confident that no one knew where he was, especially Mob 4. "That's possible," he said.

"Is something wrong? The stuff in the newspapers—that was you, wasn't it?" Getts' nonresponse must have told her what she had already guessed. "Tell me where to find you."

Getts gave her the address of the lake house and cautioned her again about telling anybody where he was.

She would be there Saturday, she said, and would call and give him the flight number.

He took another drink of his now cold coffee while he studied the bottom of the cup for a long minute. His hand wasn't shaking but his guts were doing flips under his belt. The thought of a Navy SEAL trying to kill him was scary. The thought of three of them after him was more than he wanted to think about.

He didn't sleep at all that night. He called Lydia's number a couple of times, but she was either out or she wouldn't answer.

The next morning he had the *Oregonian* newspaper spread all over the kitchen table looking for anything more about Navy SEALs. There was a small, half-page column quoting a White House press secretary who denied that any American military personnel were involved in assassination, particularly not that of General Vadim Krabac. The *Oregonian* had always been too liberal for Getts, even to the extent of refusing to use team names like the Washington Redskins or the Atlanta Braves because they thought it contributed to racism. The Fighting Irish, in their estimation, should probably be the "Pleasant Celts." By the time he finished the paper, he was feeling depressed. He thought about increasing his dosage of Desyrel by fifty milligrams but decided that the loss of reaction time wasn't worth the benefit of simply feeling better. Happiness is overrated.

It was so simple. Grumpy wore a blue workman's coverall with a wide tool belt around his hips and a telephone dangling from a metal clip on the belt. He had on a white hardhat like those worn by employees of Southern Bell, and in his hand he carried a small blue tool box. He parked a panel truck across the street from 1131 Shell Street, Pampino Beach, and whistled as he walked up the outside stairs to the second floor and knocked on the door of apartment D. "Southern Bell," he said in a full but normal voice. He waited. No one answered, as he'd expected.

From his pants pocket he withdrew a set of lock picks. The lock was at least thirty years old, as old as the building itself, and in less than ten seconds the door was open and Grumpy was inside. He didn't waste time looking around the apartment. He went immediately to the wall telephone near the dining area, unscrewed the mouthpiece, and dropped in a small transmitter. He replaced the mouthpiece and repeated the process in Lydia's bedroom, the only other telephone in the apartment, then let himself out. The door locked itself after he left. Total time, three minutes and fifteen seconds.

Still whistling his happy work song, Grumpy started the engine on the panel truck and drove it halfway around the block, parking on Flores Way. He switched on a passive receiver, adjusted his seat back to a comfortable position, and waited.

Three hours later, at 1300 hours EST, his receiver emitted the sound of a dial tone, then the varying tones of a touch telephone. Grumpy had nothing to do. His electronic equipment was on auto-record. There was the sound of a telephone ringing, then a male voice.

"Hello?"

"It's me. Got a pencil?" a woman's voice said.

"Always prepared. Fire."

"Northwestern Flight 612 to Portland, arrives Saturday at seven-fifty."

"I can't wait."

"Only four days. I love you, Bobby."

"Lydia . . ."

"Yes?"

"Be careful. Make sure you're not followed."

"Don't worry, I will."

The connection was broken.

The members of SEAL 6 always carry guns. Always. In his room, Getts removed his 9mm HK from the suitcase that he had checked through from Virginia and considered whether or not he should take it to the airport when he picked up Lydia. If the piece was spotted by security people, there would inevitably be a messy event.

Out of nervous habit, he examined the semiautomatic. He punched out the magazine and worked the slide a couple of times, then looked inside. It wasn't obvious at first because he wasn't looking for anything in particular, but he quickly broke down the gun, removing the barrel and firing chamber to get a better look. He held the action up to the window to benefit from the extra light. Then he saw it. The firing pin had been filed.

The job was well done, carefully accomplished, so that the pin wasn't flat against the bolt, but filed just enough so that the pin would fail to reach the primer on the shell case. He would pull the trigger, then *nada*.

They had to have gotten to the gun before he left, and now Getts was wondering how they would do it. Telescopic rifle was a good one. Sniping was something they all did very well. The drawback of sniping was staying in one place for a long time until the target walked into your frame. That meant considerable study of his or her habits and avoiding discovery by a third person while you were setting up for the hit. Still, if the target was even a little predictable in his movements, it was an effective way to go. For the first time since he got back from Bosnia, Getts was grateful that their armorers had taken away their OICWs when they were reassigned. If the others still had them, there would be virtually no escape, outside of maybe running away to Manchuria and raising yaks.

Getts made a mental note not to use the front door again and to check the field of fire in a complete radius around the house. He was glad Buzzy was gone, and started worrying all over again about Lydia. On the other hand, they weren't after her. And there was no way they could find this place, even if they traced him to Portland.

So did he think they'd make it a personal hit? Like sticking a knife into him or facing him with a gun at close range? He already had the answer. They didn't file his firing pin in order to play fair. They wanted him to stop breathing and they'd do it any way they could. Getts found a set of keys to Buzzy's Jaguar convertible.

He went out the kitchen door and stepped behind a tall fir tree, then took two more steps to the garage door. He removed a lock-blade knife from a pocket and opened the blade. He thought he was alone but it always paid to be ready.

He turned the knob, then pushed the door quickly open. The garage seemed empty except for the cars. He stepped inside and pressed the wall button that opened the electric garage door. He got behind the wheel of the luxury car and fired up the 250 HP engine, dropped it into gear, and, keeping low in the seat, drove fast out of the driveway and onto Lake Lane, then turned south on Stratford Road. He entered the 205 freeway on ramp west, and noticed a light-color Mustang a block away. He mashed the accelerator and kicked the Jag up to eighty miles an hour. He could see the Mustang accelerate with him. He worked back into the right lane, weaving in and out of modest traffic, and took the transition to I-5 that went through the heart of west Portland.

He stayed left on 99W where I-5 crossed over the Willamette River. At Madison he swerved to make a left turn through three lanes of traffic and a red light. Getts ran the Jag up on the median strip, cut inside the waiting cars and, horns blaring and cars sliding out of the way, made it across the one-way traffic. Just as he got through the traffic, the light turned green and the Mustang slid through. Some people have all the luck. He turned onto Third Street, accelerated, and terrorized other drivers as he raced through red, green, and yellow lights until he got to Jefferson, where he pulled another hard right. The Mustang was hanging in there. Damn. Getts knew it was harder to follow than to lead in a rat race, and whoever was at the wheel of the Stang had nerve. Why was he not surprised? He made a fast right turn, then another out of sight of the Mustang into a large parking structure at Portland State University campus. He barreled up the ramp and careened around one corner. It was 1500 hours and afternoon parking slots were starting to open up. He found one and ducked in. Getts wondered how much trouble he was in, thinking of their battle bags. Each of them in Mob 4 carried what looked like a duffel bag, specially built to carry the goodies they used on ops: explosives of various kinds, automatic weapons, com gear, grenade launchers, even diving gear and shoulder-held rockets, depending on what the team thought it might need for a given assignment. Getts didn't have his, but the others damn sure would have brought theirs.

The Mustang first rolled slowly by the entrance to the parking structure, then stopped and backed up. The driver then began to drive slowly up the ramp and toward Getts's position. Getts flicked the electric control on the Jag's outside mirror so that he could lie low in the front seat, unseen, and still track the progress of the Mustang. Luckily the driver was moving fairly slow, searching. As he rounded the next corner, Getts dropped the transmission into reverse, used the parking brake to hold it in position, then, when his rear end was lined up on the Mustang's front bumper, stomped on the gas pedal and popped the parking brake. Getts laid serious rubber for ten feet. The Jag's rear bumper smashed into the Mustang's front wheel housing. Getts hoped it would cause enough damage so that the other driver couldn't steer. Getts kept his foot on the accelerator until the front of the Mustang was turned 180 degrees and he had an open path to the exit ramp. Getts had to raise his head slightly to see where he was going, and the hair on the back of his neck stood on end while he waited for a bullet to tear away his skull.

None was fired. Getts slid around the exit ramp, tearing off the wooden guard arm as he sped past the cashier's island and exited back on Broadway. On the way past the Mustang, Getts could see it was Grumpy driving, and he seemed to be alone in the car. As Getts burned out of the parking structure, he could see his teammate in the rearview mirror. Still coming.

Getts turned west on Clay, his right foot on the accelerator pedal, his left on the brake. He only slowed to avoid certain collisions, cutting people off, narrowly missing pedestrians, and running red lights. At Knights Park he whipped around onto Twentieth, sped several blocks to Burnside Boulevard, and hung a hard right. The Jag wanted to spin out, but Getts romped down on the gas pedal, turned the wheel into the slide, and she straightened right out. Burnside was downhill and he punched it, flying through intersections, all colors of lights, hoping that a traffic cop would show up and stop the chase. Getts would rather deal with an angry cop than a vengeful SEAL anytime.

The Mustang roared up behind him, glued to his tail. As he blasted through Fifth Street, a car slid behind Getts sideways, braking to get out of his way. The Mustang hit the car in the rear quarter panel and turned ninety degrees in the street. Several more cars clogged the intersection, giving Getts a two-block lead before the Mustang maneuvered out of the jam and was back on his track. He had to wait precious seconds at a line of cars turning west from Front Street, which ran along Portland's waterfront. A movement across the river caught his eye. An ocean-bound grain ship was moving slowly downstream from its berth near the Burnside Bridge. It would have to pass under the Steel Bridge—and that bridge would have to be raised to let it under.

Getts made the Jag groan as he held his foot down on the accelerator and wove in and out of traffic on Front Street, one eye on the rearview mirror, another eye scanning the waterfront as he watched the ship moving toward the Steel Bridge. Less than a quarter mile from the entrance to the bridge he could see that the crossing barriers were being lowered. Getts kept the Jag screaming for the bridge. The Mustang was four cars behind but closing. In front of him cars were stopping for the barrier. Figuring he had a good chance of dying either way, Getts wheeled left into one of the oncoming lanes. He hit the barrier at high speed and broke it to splinters. Cars coming in the opposite direction swerved crazily out of his way, one ricocheting off a bridge wheel guard and bouncing it back into the left-hand lane. Getts could see that Grumpy had tried to follow his maneuver but the oncoming car was headed directly at him. Both drivers stood on their brakes, burned rubber, slid sideways, and stopped.

On the opposite side of the river Getts could drive easily around the barrier and onto an exit ramp, now devoid of cars. Red lights were blinking, a siren sounding. He was sure that the bridge master was already on the telephone calling for a police patrol unit, but Getts had gained the precious minutes he needed. He swung north on I-5 to Stafford, then picked up 30 East. He was home free and, best of all, Grumpy had no idea where he was going.

Getts didn't want to look at the damage he'd done to the rear end of Buzzy's Jaguar, but he knew at least it could be fixed. Pulling a bullet out of his head would have been a more demanding job. He got on Highway 25 and headed east toward Harold Jannings's gun shop to do something about his filed H&K.

Getts had known Harold since he was a kid. Harold was the one who got Getts interested not only in firearms, but in the Navy. He was a retired chief gunner's mate, having enlisted the USN during WW2 at the age of fourteen. In 1963 Jannings was captain of the U.S. Navy's competition shooting team and had won the world's military rifle competition firing an M-1, using only iron sights, from distances of six hundred yards and one thousand yards. In ten days of firing he had been outside the bull's-eye only three times, a record that still stands today.

He parked in the familiar gravel-covered lot in front of Harold's gun shop and went inside. Harold had two daughters and a son, Ronald, who was working behind the counter and didn't recognize Getts when he walked through the door. It was just as well. Getts didn't have time to spend catching up on years past.

"Can I help you?" Ronald said.

"Harold in?" Getts asked.

"He's in the back. I'll get him." Ronald started to walk around the long counter but Getts stopped him.

"I'll go back there myself, thanks." The whole shop was probably a thousand square feet or so, catering to sport hunters and packers. Harold was never an exceptionally neat person where his stock was concerned, his interest more in how well his guns worked. Getts remembered some of the deer and elk racks still on the wall, along with a moose head by which he'd been awed as a pre-teenager. Rifles were displayed behind the long glass counter, handguns locked behind plate-glass display cases. The back room was more typically Harold—messy. There were metal supply cabinets for ammunition, specially built to withstand fire, machinery for repairing firearms closely jammed together, and parts and pieces of weapons occupying odd boxes and shelves.

"Hi, Harold," he said. The aging gunsmith looked up from his bench vise. His glasses seemed a little thicker, his hair thinner, and his shoulders might have been bent forward a bit more, but the corners of his mouth twitched upward in the understated way Texans admit they are pleased.

"Hi, there, Bobby," he said. The two shook hands without hurry. Harold's grip was still firm, his hand and broad fingers warm. "You look fine."

"So do you, Harold. Just great. I saw Ronnie on the way in."

"He's all growed up."

"Your girls, too, I guess. I didn't see them," Getts said.

"Caroline is twenty. Off to college. She isn't dumb like her father. Betty's married now. Lives in Gresham."

"They were cute little girls. They stay that way when they got big?" Getts said.

"I guess so. I had so many boys hangin' around this place I had to shoo 'em out like flies. Glad those girls are gone," he said with a twinkle in his eyes. "How's the Navy treatin' you, Bobby?"

"Not so good. I'm in a little trouble, Harold."

His face clouded, then he nodded his head. "That you the newspapers is talking about?"

"Yep."

"You worried?"

"Not so much worried as mad. My team could get hurt. I wouldn't like that." Getts didn't elaborate, especially about the fact that his team had now turned on him; so he simply produced his 9mm from behind his back and handed it to him. "Needs a new firing pin."

Harold accepted the semiautomatic and looked over each part of the mechanism. "Somebody wanted you out of commission," he noted, not expecting a reply. "I'll tend to this firing pin right now."

It didn't take him long. Before they walked out the front door, Getts said, "I need something else, Harold. Twelve-gauge pump shotgun with a pistol grip, if you have one. Thirty-six inches, no longer. Six- or eight-shot magazine and a couple boxes of double-ought shells."

"So you brought your trouble home with you," Harold said.

"Made a mistake. I guess I didn't know it was that bad," Getts replied.

"Go to the police. Right now."

Getts shook his head. "It won't settle out that way. Somebody's just making a wrong move, and I owe it to them to correct it before they do something they'll never live down. Or through."

Harold opened a large bin drawer, moved a heavy cloth to one side, and extracted a pump shotgun. "Mossberg," he said. "Modified it myself. Never gonna jam. I'll loan it to you."

"I better pay for it, Harold," Getts said, realizing that he was not a good candidate for future returns.

"Your father paid for this gun years ago when he lent me the money to start business here. And I lost forty thousand dollars to him playing poker on hunting trips. Never paid him."

Getts knew it was the other way around. Getts's father told him that Harold Jannings was the best poker player he'd ever faced and it was lucky that they were only playing for matches or he would have lost everything he owned to the Texan with the third grade education. "Thanks. I'll try to bring it back," Getts said.

Outside in the parking lot Getts got his first good look at the damage he'd done to his mother's Jaguar. The bumper was bent, as was a good bit of the body above the bumper, but the trunk lid was intact and it still opened and closed. He locked the Mossberg in the trunk after loading it with eight shells and dropping seven more into his jacket pocket. He retraced his route, got onto Eighty-second, followed it to Portland International Airport.

As he drove, Getts thought about how Grumpy—and surely the others—knew about the summer house by now. Could Lydia have been followed to Portland? To do that they would have had to be on the airplane with her. If they were careless enough not to use disguises, she'd spot them in a minute.

He parked in short-term parking, feeding quarters into the meter. Inside the terminal building he took an escalator to the concourse for Northwestern Airlines but stopped short of the security machines. Though the Mossberg was in the trunk of the car, he still carried the H&K under his belt and he wasn't about to give it up, even in the relative safety of the airport. He looked around at the inbound monitors and saw that Lydia's flight was twenty minutes delayed. There were plenty of places to kill time, like food shops, bars, souvenir stands, and the like, but Getts didn't want to have his nose buried in a taco if one of his swim buddies happened to figure out where he was and decided to finish him off. So he found a wall, put his back to it, and kept his eyes open.

Chapter Thirteen

Lydia always pulled Doc's heart strings. She was his kind of woman—one to whom they never had to explain where they were going or when they'd get back or what they were going to do when they got there. Whenever they partied, they included her. They introduced all of their women to her, even the ones they were embarrassed about. Maybe they just wanted to impress the girls with the high-class act that was Lydia. No doubt about it, she was special. He almost felt bad when they tapped her phone to set up the ambush. Jesus. Well, Getts had to know they were there now, and when he almost took Grumpy out on the bridge, the team knew Getts wouldn't give up until either he, or they, were dead.

There were two Northwestern planes coming into PDX from Miami, both within an hour of each other. Doc took one, Grumpy took the other. They wanted to meet them both just in case Lydia and Getts were running a decoy game on them. Doc wore a pair of wire-rimmed glasses, a phony mustache, and a hat. He wasn't sure he could fool Lydia, but if he kept a discreet distance he should be able to blend invisibly into the crowd. He carried a backpack and a tube that looked like a standard fishing pole carry-on. Going through the concourse security system—what a joke—they looked at the electronics in his pack and believed him when he said they were stereo parts.

The 737 from Miami pulled up to gate 55 at 16:40 hours, right on time, and Doc watched the whole two hundred plus passengers drag their sorry asses out of the chute. But Lydia wasn't one of them. "Anybody left on board?" Doc asked one of the stews. "I'm not sure which flight my sister caught out of Miami."

"Nope. That's everyone," she said and smiled. She was just a hair on the heavy side, but she had a dimple that Doc liked, and the way her eyes lit up was intriguing. He wished he had time to use some hustle. He went down to the baggage carousels, where, sooner or later, everyone on the flight would show up. But this wasn't the flight she was scheduled for, so he merely glanced over the crowd when it arrived.

Doc watched for Getts. He wanted to find the skipper before Getts found him. He walked among a group of tourists, favoring one leg like he had a slight limp, his hat brim pulled down. He looked at the ETA monitors and saw that the other Northwestern flight, the one Grumpy was watching, was ten minutes out, the baggage scheduled to dump into carousel 3. The lost and found office was next to carousel 1, so Doc walked inside and, ignored by the clerks, watched out of one of the windows. He could see all three carousels from there. Carousel 2 was filling up. There were four people, young, wearing hiking shorts, packs, carrying down jackets. College kids, maybe, starting or ending their Easter vacation. When the hell was that, anyway? A businessman wearing a gray suit and a gray face, looking impatiently at his watch, waited for a black leather hang-up bag that was next to last coming down the slide. Two more men wearing sharp pin-striped suits. Lawyers—what else?

A nervous man in his late forties, with a blond surgically enhanced broad clinging onto his arm like her newfound life might suddenly slip away, struggled with at least six Gucci bags. A cop stood waiting with a prisoner. Doc picked them out easily—he could see the bulge at his hip where the lawman carried his piece, and the bracelets on the other guy's wrist peeping underneath a raincoat. Unusual lash-up. The perp must be nonviolent, or they would have shipped him con-air.

Two women held hands by a carousel. One was a knockout, the other looked like an offensive tackle. Families swarmed everywhere, one including grandma and grandpa

and three little kids. Another family was Oriental, some
others Cuban. A quadriplegic in a wheelchair was steered
by a man about thirty.

Doc then spotted a man and a woman, walking briskly
together, but not talking. When their bags came down the
conveyor, they pulled off each piece, then she walked out
of the baggage area ahead of him, leaving him dragging his
ass to keep up.

An old man walked by who looked like Doc's grandfather, Jacob. Large nose, mustache, not real tall, dignified
in a humble way. Doc was named after the man, and he
was sitting alone with him on his bed when he died. The
old man off the plane even wore a hat like Jacob. Nobody
wears fedoras anymore. He wondered what his grandfather
would think of his grandson if he knew Doc was going to
kill his best friend.

Doc had to look away from the old man, and when he
did, he saw Lydia. She was standing near the entrance of
the baggage area, waiting. Doc felt another twinge, big
time. She'd put herself into the field of fire and there wasn't
anything he could do about it. Damn, she was sexy. The
baggage area was a big place, but he spotted Grumpy
standing near carousel 4 reading a newspaper. Doc looked
back to the carousel and, sure enough, there was Getts.
Looking at him, Doc experienced a couple of feelings. In
a flash, he thought about all the shit they had done together
and he wanted to put his arms around Getts and kiss the
son of a bitch. But he reminded himself that his skipper
was a traitor. He had turned on the team. He didn't give
a damn if the rest of them went to the gas chamber or did
life in prison. Doc tried to hate him for that. He remembered once when he was so pissed off at an officer on another team, Doc had to be restrained from hauling off and
kicking the officer's ass. Bobby stopped him by telling him
that frustration was the only thing that caused anger. Well,
Doc wanted freedom and Bobby was the guy trying to take
it away, so Doc had big-time frustration. And anger. He
watched while Getts took Lydia's luggage off the carousel,

then the two of them walked a little way to a car rental counter.

She looked great, Getts thought. She was wearing white cotton shorts that came almost to her knees, a yellow cotton blouse under a navy blue double-breasted blazer, and tan flats. He told her she looked delicious.

"Thanks," she said. "All the sailors tell me that."

They talked easily, like two good friends finally back together, until her Skyway bag arrived on the carousel. When they had cleared baggage claim, Getts pulled her to a corner of the room. "Truman and Jake are here. They . . . they're trying to kill me. You have to go back."

"Because of the Bosnia thing?"

Getts nodded his head.

"Well," she said, "they're not after me, are they?"

"No, but that's not the point," Getts said.

"I think that is the point. And I'm not going to just turn around and get on another airplane. I need a shower," she said.

"May I help you, sir?" A clerk was talking to Doc.

"No, thanks. I'm just getting out of the cold."

The clerk looked at Doc like he was a little nuts, as it was just a couple of degrees under seventy. Bobby was filling out forms for the rental car. Lydia had her arm around Bobby's waist. Doc couldn't see Grumpy anymore, but guessed he'd probably gone outside.

Doc waited until Getts was through the outer glass doors before he followed them. Sure enough, Doc could see Grumpy already watching the rental area from the cover of an overhead walkway. Doc went to where they had parked their rental car less than two hundred yards away. He started the engine, pulled out of the spot, then picked up Grumpy as they followed Getts's Mercury four-door.

The two SEALs waited until they had five or six cars between them before keeping pace. They drove west, back toward downtown Portland. They stayed almost a mile back on the Banfield Freeway, driving a few miles per hour over the speed limit. At the Willamette River they crossed a bridge that split three ways on the west side. Bobby got on the center lane that indicated Highway 26, to the coast. With several cars between them, Doc and Grumpy followed.

The highway passed through a tunnel, up a hill near a place called Sylvan, then evened out into a more or less straight road through North Plains. A sign said *Seaside 74*. It made sense to Doc, now. Seaside was a place Bobby went to as a kid. It was Portland's beach town. He remembered Getts mentioning it before—it was on the coast eighteen miles below the town of Astoria. Doc referred to a map. One car between them stopped at Staley's, a roadside restaurant; another car stopped for gas. There were now only two cars between Bobby's car and theirs, and they knew he'd be looking, so Doc turned off at the Vernonia junction. They sat there for about two minutes, until Bobby's Mercury had rounded a couple of curves at the top of the hill, then they took to the road again. Doc sped up a bit now because it was important to have him in sight when they got to Seaside, if that was indeed where Getts ended up. A little over twenty-five miles out from Seaside was Oney's, another restaurant, and Grumpy slid down into the seat in case Getts had pulled off the road to check his six o'clock. Doc looked out of the corner of his eye and, by God, there he was, watching the road from the parking lot. The two SEALs roared by at seventy, Grumpy slumped out of sight and Doc turned the other way.

Five or six more miles down the highway Doc slowed, pulled off the road onto a rock-clay logging road, and waited. Sure enough, eight minutes later, Getts came cruising by, never seeing the two SEALs. They let a couple more cars go by then pulled onto the highway again.

In Seaside, Getts made a left turn over the Avenue U Bridge, drove by a golf course on the left, and proceeded almost all the way to the ocean. He turned into a motel called the Tides, an aging but classy place, while Doc and Grumpy drove on by. They now knew where Getts would be when they wanted to drop the axe.

Chapter Fourteen

Getts had always liked the Tides. His family had stayed there when he was a kid. It was elegant for Seaside and their unit had a full kitchen, a fireplace, and cozy woodwork in the living room and bedroom. Each unit had a view of the Pacific, which was only fifty yards away. This was the end of Seaside's beach, dominated by Tillamook Head, which rounded into a cove, the sands dotted with huge boulders. Getts had seen a lot of beaches in the Navy, but the rocky, wind-beaten coast of Oregon was unmatched for raw natural beauty. Mountains cascaded right down to the sand, while sharp rocks jutted upward through waters of high tide, creating treacherous undertows during neap tides. Huge trees—fir, cedar, and hemlock, among others— grew fifty to one hundred feet tall in misty clouds, the underbrush below them dense and all but impassable. The Promenade, or Prom, as the locals called it, began at the cove, the cement walkway, built in the 1930s, running along in front of opulent beachfront homes.

Getts's sense of urgent danger and certain violence lessened as he carried their bags up the narrow stairs to their room on the second floor. Lydia would leave on the first flight out tomorrow, but tonight was theirs.

There was already firewood near the hearth, along with kindling and newspaper. The sky was broken by cumulus clouds and there was a definite nip in the air, giving them a perfect excuse to light a fire. "There's a store down the street," Lydia said, referring to the Avenue U Market, "I'll get us a bottle of wine and a bite."

"Why don't I go to the market and you light the fire?"

Getts wanted to look around alone before she walked any
streets without him. He figured he had succeeded in evad-
ing Grumpy and Doc, but he also figured that's exactly
what they'd want him to believe.

"We'll go together," she said.

Getts picked up a canvas bag, into which he had placed
the cut-down Mossberg. He had used a razor blade to make
a slit in one end of the bag near the seam so that he could
slip his hand into it without unzipping the top. He slung it
over his shoulder as they began walking the two short
blocks to the store.

They walked by the Seaside Golf Course, where Getts
had been many times in the past.

"My folks used to drink cocktails up there," Getts said
to Lydia, pointing to the Par-Tee Room above the pro shop
of the golf course.

"What were you doing while they were drinking cocktails?" Lydia said.

"Playing with starfish that I caught on the rocks at the
cove," he said. "I'd put them in a bathtub and at night I'd
shine a light on them to make them move."

At the Avenue U Market they bought a bottle of Chardonnay along with a South African Merlot and a couple of
bottles of French Rothschild burgundies. They picked out
a loaf of French bread, sharp Tillamook cheddar cheese,
crackers, smoked oysters and salmon, and, for bourgeois
Getts, potato salad. On the way back to their rooms he
explained to Lydia that tonight they would eat razor clams,
a shellfish so delicious that God, despite His clumsy work
almost everywhere else, had seen fit to plant them in only
three locations on the face of the Earth, one of which was
Seaside, Oregon. So delicious were they that the once plen-
tiful mollusk had been dug up to near extinction, mostly
by tourists who flailed at them with everything from suction
cups to fire axes, only succeeding in killing more of the
creatures than they bagged for dinner. Nowadays, he was
told, the clam police would apprehend and execute viola-
tors. He explained to Lydia that Buzzy was the best razor
clam cook in the world and that she taught him everything

that she knew. It was simple—dip the shelled critters into whipped raw egg, then into crushed soda crackers, then drop them into a hot skillet for the count of ten on each side. Eat with ketchup. Damn, them're good.

Lydia looked cautiously at his athletic bag as Getts lowered it to the floor with a clunk in the small living room at the Tides.

"Shotgun," he said.

"We going duck hunting?" she said.

"Lydia, Doc and Grumpy are dangerous. I thought I could talk them out of it before you got here but . . . there wasn't time. I don't think they know where we are, but it's possible. I shouldn't even let you stay tonight—"

She put her finger on his lips, then replaced it with her mouth.

When she broke it off, he was breathless.

"They aren't after me. Stop worrying."

"Sometimes worrying's the natural thing to do."

"How does it help?"

"For one thing, it can help you keep from making a horse's ass of yourself a second time."

"I want to be with you, no matter what. Everything's cool."

He knew it wasn't cool, but she was right, they weren't after her. And she didn't blink as he removed the H&K from his belt and then the combat knife strapped to his ankle. He couldn't say that hardware created a romantic mood, but after their second glass of burgundy he thought it was forgotten.

"So?" he said. "What do you think so far?"

"It's all so beautiful. I've never seen trees that big in my life," Lydia said, referring to the seemingly unending forest on their drive down the Sunset Highway from Portland.

"Douglas firs," he said.

"It must rain a lot around here."

"All the time," he said.

"And you were here in the summer?" she asked.

"Yep. We'd come down a lot of weekends. Even in the winter. My folks had friends here and they had parties that were knockouts. When I went away to high school and college, I'd come down with my buddies and we'd spend spring break here. Beach parties and beer."

"Wild ones?"

They had their arms around each other now, pressing close. "Real wild. I hate to admit this but we knocked over the lifeguard tower one year and carried it down Broadway. About thirty of us got arrested. Little bastards that we were, we deserved it."

"You were amateurs," Lydia said. "Ever hear of Daytona?"

"Parties? Riots?" Getts said.

"Um huh." Lydia drank wine the way he liked to drink it, in large measure but still savoring the taste of the stuff.

"You were a riotess? One of those topless babes we saw on the news?" he said.

"Well, I don't know if you saw me on television," she said. They sat facing each other on a sofa, the ocean at their elbows, food and wine on a coffee table nearby.

"I'm really, really glad you came," Getts said, "though it makes me feel selfish." They spent several moments looking into each other's eyes. He felt like he was back in school, on a first date, tingling. It always seemed to be that way when he was with her. He was finding it very hard to imagine life without her.

They went for a walk on the beach. Before they got very far, day turned to night. They carried their shoes and even the dry sand was cool to the touch. As they held hands and strolled down the beach toward town, they passed by people who had built fires among the logs and driftwood that lay scattered along the sands. Lydia and Getts shared a quart of English Ale as they walked, talking about nothing; music, movies, things they liked and some they didn't. They turned up the beach at about Avenue A, headed toward the prom and Broadway, which was just a block away. They had just stepped onto the concrete walkway when Getts got a tingling sensation in his throat and ears. He looked around carefully at all the people. Nothing seemed out of the ordinary. It was school vacation and the place was over-run with high school and college kids. He scanned them all.

Nothing.

He peered into shadows. There was a last house on the prom, then an apartment building, then an old building that once housed the American Legion Club and the public swimming pool.

Getts spotted movement.

"Lydia, I'd like some caramel corn. Get us a bag, would you?" he said, nodding toward a popcorn stand not far away. Lydia didn't trust his reason for sending her away, but she went. He moved up against the wall of the old building, then looked around the corner. A pathway par-tially covered in ivy led to an alleyway behind. He stepped into the darkness, pulled his 9mm from his belt, and moved deeper into the black. He scanned off-center with his eyes. To detect an object in the dark, it was necessary to locate it with your peripheral vision—looking directly at something might actually make you miss it. He kept his eyes moving constantly, high, then to each side, giving quick glances downward before shifting high again. Getts was in a crouch when he saw a movement at the opposite end of the path. A man? A dog? It didn't seem possible for the team to have picked up his trail so quickly, if at all. But the unlikely was what he should expect in order to stay alive.

He was satisfied that they were alone. Replacing the H&K, he returned to the prom. At the end of Broadway Street was a turnaround where car traffic and strolling pe-destrians made a large circle, got a nice view of the ocean, then started down the other way on the street. Lydia was standing on the turnaround with a bag of caramel corn in her hand. It was untouched. "Everything okay?" she said, her brows knit.

"Sure. I thought I saw somebody I knew," he replied.

"Shit, you had me scared for a minute," she said.

"Sorry. I didn't want to do that," he said. "I told you this isn't where you're supposed to be right now."

"Where you are is where I'm supposed to be." The bold way in which she took his arm left him speechless.

They walked down Broadway, literally bumping into people as they strolled through Seaside's carnival atmosphere. Leonard's Salt Water Taffy shop had been there for as long as Getts could remember, along with the souvenir shop across the street from the bumper cars. There was a Ferris wheel and other rides nearby, as well as a hamburger shop and the local theater. Across the street and farther down on Broadway was a penny arcade, which hadn't had a penny machine in it for fifty years, and a tavern called the Grill, a hangout for locals that served dynamite fried razor clams.

The intoxicating smell of hot, heavy cooking oil greeted their senses as they went inside. The Grill had an ambiance of its own—bright lights, clattering dishes, and worn-out waitresses who knew all the answers to tourists' smart-ass remarks. A sexy Greek woman owned the place, and staffed it with her family members. Its counter had a dozen stools, and three rows of booths filled the rest of the premises. Getts and Lydia didn't glance at the menu. They knew what they had come for, and when the waitress arrived at the table, he ordered a bottle of beer and a carafe of wine for Lydia, confident that he would eventually help her drink it. "Razor clams," he added. "Two orders."

The waitress looked up from her pad and studied Getts's face. "Aren't you Robert Rawling?" she said. She had blond hair worn as though she had just stepped out of a shower and forgotten to comb it. She was unusually tall but well proportioned, with freckles that made her face seem especially pleasant. With her upturned nose she might have made a poster girl for an Irish cruise line. "I'm Molly Miller," she said. "Sue Weller was a good friend of mine."

"Sure, I remember you, Molly. And I remember Sue," Getts said. It had been a long time since he had heard his real name.

"God, wasn't it awful? So sudden. I mean, she wasn't sick at all, then she was dead. It happened in Mississippi. Her husband was playing down there with his jazz band, you know."

"Yeah, I heard that. This is Lydia Brooks, Molly."

"Hi."

"Hello."

"So," he said, "you stayed right here in Seaside, huh?"

"No, I got married and moved to Sacramento. My husband was in the Air Force. Then we got divorced. I've got a girl, she's six. Sharon and I went to Portland and I took up glass blowing."

"Interesting," Lydia said. "Could you make a living at it?"

"Yeah, kind of. I got pretty good but the company I worked for ran out of contracts and so I'm sort of killing time until they get another one. Hey, what are you doing, Robert? Last I saw of you, you were going to college somewhere."

"Stanford."

"Oh, wow. Brains. How are your folks?"

"My dad died a few years ago. My mother's fine, though." Through the large plate glass windows of the Grill, he could see crowds of people moving up and down Broadway. On the opposite side of the street he saw a man who looked like Grumpy. Without speaking, he got out of the booth, pushed past Molly, and walked out of the restaurant, looking up the street. The tall man he thought was Grumpy turned out to be somebody else. When Getts returned to the Grill, Molly was back in the kitchen and Lydia was sitting alone.

"Somebody else you thought you knew?" she said.

"Yeah. Sorry."

"Not a problem. I like Molly," she said.

"She's nice. She had a brother, too. Forgot to ask about him," Getts said, still thinking about Grumpy and Doc. And Peach. Where the hell was Peach?

"So your real name isn't Bobby Getts. It's Bobby Rawling."

"I didn't think people would still recognize me. I haven't been here for a long, long time."

"Why did you change your name?" Lydia said.

"We all did in our unit."

"How dangerous is this business?" she said.

"The Navy SEALs?"

"I mean whatever is going on now. In the *Miami Herald* this morning it printed the names of the four Navy men who carried out the assassination. Lieutenant Getts was one of them," she said, her voice soft as she sipped her wine.

"Yeah, well, I guess that it had to go public sooner or later."

"So?"

"I think they're here. In Seaside," he said.

"After you?"

He nodded. He could only hope they wouldn't hurt Lydia. He talked himself into thinking he wasn't hiding behind her. It wasn't his style and they knew it. But who knew how—or when—they planned to jump him.

"What shall we do tomorrow?"

"Tomorrow we're going to the airport."

"Know what I'd like to do? Snorkel. Or SCUBA. Whatever you want to teach me," she said, ignoring Getts.

"Lydia—"

"You don't seem to understand, smart as you appear to be otherwise." She took his hand in hers. "I'm here. I'm not leaving without spending time with you. It's why I came all the way across the continent. Get it? You can't unload me that easily."

"You aren't safe with me," he said.

"I am safe. You're just being careful. Come on."

"Okay, we could rent some gear in Astoria. We'll do it in the morning. You can take an evening flight."

She made no comment. They ate the clams. Lydia ate like a lady, while Getts devoured his like an unemployed logger. He was tempted to order another plate but changed his mind when Lydia said "Let's go."

"Down Broadway?"

"No, to the motel." She took his hand, kissing him carelessly on his fingers.

As they walked down the prom back to the Tides, Getts had the feeling that they were being watched. He didn't bother to look behind him because he knew he wouldn't see them anyway.

Chapter Fifteen

Damn, Grumpy breathed out, Getts almost caught him in the alley but for some reason he didn't press it. Grumpy didn't know why. The waitress he talked to was an old friend, Grumpy guessed. She was kind of cute. He felt like warning her, "Hey, lady, watch out for this fucking rat. He'll stab you in the back." Grumpy wondered what she'd say to that. Anyway they'd get it done sometime tomorrow.

The next day started out overcast, with cumulus clouds hovering around the mouth of the Columbia River, seeming to concentrate around Point Ellice on the Washington side before marching south. But rain wasn't in the forecast for that day as Getts and Lydia drove along Highway 26 toward Astoria. Over one hundred years ago Astoria, named after John Jacob Astor, had been as rough and tough as it got, making port cities like San Francisco and Oakland seem tame by comparison. They passed by Camp Rileah, named after a one-time National Guard general, following a winding road through Twin Spruce and Warrenton, and around Smith's Point into the old cannery factory areas. The river was about nine miles across at this point, and the mouth of the river, where a sandbar separated the Pacific Ocean from the mighty Columbia, was a treacherous rush of tidal action that had sunk a thousand ships and boats over the years.

They drove past Portway to a place on Basin Street that Getts had located on a Chamber of Commerce map. Along the refurbished dock area they found a dive shop on the south side of the pier, and a yacht broker on the north side. It didn't take long for Getts to make a deal with Gordon Cross, a master diver himself. Cross's nose looked like a Little Leaguer had used it for batting practice. His hair cut short, he had blue eyes and broad shoulders that stood him well for swimming and, Getts was about to confirm, football.

"Are you the same Cross who played football for Oregon?" Getts asked.

"Well, I wore number eighty-four and got free meals at the training table, but was definitely not All-American caliber," he said. "We can fix you up with what you need. I'll give you two days for the price of one. How's that?"

"Sounds good. This is Lydia. We're not going out far, maybe to Lower Sands Light," Getts said. Lower Sands Light seemed to have fish most times of the year. If the weather suddenly got bad, they could get back easily. The visibility was never wonderful there, but then it wasn't that good anywhere along the coast until you got to Puget Sound.

Cross fitted Lydia into a Theremelle wet suit. Getts took a slightly more humble Rynell suit. They used off-the-shelf Imprex masks and fins, but Getts was more particular about getting Liberator tanks and BCDs. He picked out a couple of Omega regulators with a two-stage valve system. They didn't need gloves and boots because the water wasn't that cold, and Getts had no desire to keep Lydia in the water long enough to make any difference. He picked out a couple of Halogen lights, 7.5 watts each, and they were ready to go. Getts signed a receipt and paid Cross, asking, "What's Niemi Marine like? We want to rent a boat for a couple of days."

"Niemi's a good man. He'll give you good equipment. Kind of pricey, though." Price, Getts didn't mind. Quality was paramount when things started to go into the toilet, which is always what you should expect around water. "I'll bring your gear over there," Cross said.

Jack Niemi was about sixty, with a full head of gray hair. He sucked on a pipe and seemed not to suffer fools easily. Getts told him he needed a power boat to do some diving, about thirty feet with a galley and a diesel engine. He gave him a short-form sketch of his experience with boats. Niemi's eyebrows shot up with the mention of Navy SEALs. "You still with them fellas?" he asked.

"Yes, sir. I'm on leave for a few weeks," Getts said.

"Stationed down in San Diego?"

"No. Back east, place called Little Creek. It's in—"

"Hell, I know where it is. Amphib base," he said.

"You a Navy man?" Getts said.

"Two years aboard the USS *LaSalle*."

"AGF-3," Getts said. "Atlantic Fleet."

Niemi's chest seemed to expand and just a flicker of a smile lighted at the corners of his stern Finnish jaw. "Yeah, well, I was goddamn glad to get off her. Rolled around the North Sea till I was sick of the water. Never wanted to see it again."

"Retire?"

"Nope," he said. "Just got the hell out. Went into the logging business and got myself broke and bone tired. Figured as long as I was going to be tired and broke, I might as well do it having fun."

Niemi looked neither tired nor broke. "I got a Gunnerson, strake hull. Let you have it for a hundred dollars a day," he said.

A Gunnerson was a custom-made boat, beautiful craftsmanship, seaworthy in all weather, and much too good to be diving out of. One hundred dollars a day was a gift. "That's mighty generous of you, Mr. Niemi," Getts said.

He waved a hand in the air. "My personal boat. Tired of looking at it tied up here. Needs to have the engine run, anyway. Give me a driver's license so's I know you won't steal it."

Getts filled out a minimum of paperwork and they walked out to slip number 9. "You look like a nice girl," Niemi said to Lydia. "What the hell are you doing hanging around someone like this?"

"I'm trying to change him into a nice man. Do you think that's possible, Mr. Niemi?" she replied.

"I think I'd change if you asked me to," he said. "Here,

now, I got all clean bedding on board. You use 'em and don't worry a bit about washing them later. Hear?"

"Do you supply sheets and blankets with all your boat rentals?" Lydia asked.

"You bet I do," the old man lied. "Don't let a boat go out without what it should have on board."

Lydia looked at Getts, and gave him a smile he would not soon forget. "But you're leaving tomorrow," he reminded her.

They put their diving gear aboard and went into town, stopping at a store on Commercial Street for enough food to get them through the next twenty-four hours. Wine, cheese, bread—the basics. He thought they might even get lucky and catch a salmon while they were swimming around Lower Sands Light or Skipanon Waterway. The Gunnerson had an efficient galley for cooking treasures of the sea.

Getting lucky, he thought in his selfish heart of hearts, was something Getts was looking forward to.

By 1300 hours, the scud had burned off and they had the Gunnerson set at 50 percent power heading west, Lydia at the wheel. Her concentration was acute as they made for Skipanon Waterway Light, the wind tousling her hair and spray alighting on them both. Occasionally she would look aside to catch him watching her and she would break into a huge smile before returning to her responsibilities at the wheel. For the first time in months Getts felt really good, and reasonably relaxed. He had debated with himself about bringing weapons on board, finally compromising with himself by leaving the Mossberg in the trunk of their rented car but bringing the 9mm along on the boat. He still had his assault knife fixed to his ankle, a piece of equipment that would not look out of place on a diving expedition. Despite his preparedness, Getts thought what he really needed was to be on the offensive, hunting, instead of cowering in the marsh like a game bird.

Jack Niemi had left two fishing poles aboard and had added a container of clam necks for bait in case they wanted to throw a line over the side after they anchored.

Naturally, his rods and reels were top of the line, and Getts knew that he wouldn't be able to resist trying to snag a sturgeon, which were known to feed around the Youngs Bay Entrance and Tansy Point Turn.

They passed north of the Skipanon Light and Lydia throttled back to a slow crawl as he peered into the depth sounder for a place to dive. In a few minutes he got a forty-foot bottom readout and motioned to Lydia to cut the engine. On the leeside of a rock formation jutting out of the water at high tide, where the Gunnerson was invisible to land, he dropped a stern anchor over the side, then played out the line, letting the current take them slowly downstream.

He secured the anchor line to a gunwale cleat and then dropped the forward anchor off the bow. He could feel Lydia's presence as she poked her head over his shoulder while he tied off this anchor. He was still on one knee as she sank onto the deck, her legs between his, arms around his neck. She felt perfect. They kissed, her breath sweet, the wind in her hair tickling the sides of his cheeks. As they parted, she was wearing that I-know-something-that-you-don't-know smile on her face, and he found himself looking forward to the coming of night. Lydia was an interesting human being, one Getts knew he could spend a lot of time with. And he knew exactly why: she could make him take leave of his senses. "Hungry?" he said.

"Yeah, but first things first. Let's go below and check out the bedding," she said.

It was after 1600 hours when they finally emerged from the cabin to the main deck and began shrugging into diving gear. He had assumed that he would literally have to dress Lydia for the dive, a job he was frankly looking forward to, but she had already pulled the wet suit around her otherwise naked body before he could lend a hand. "Are you sure the only lessons you got were the two I gave you back in Pamino?" he asked.

"That's right. Doesn't mean I've never done it before."

"How much experience do you have?" Getts said as he

helped her into her harness system and buoyancy compensator.

"I can probably avoid drowning in forty feet of water," she said.

He began to get a sneaky feeling that his leg had been pulled, but it felt just fine to Getts. She could pull anything he had. He was able to rig himself out easily, including a depth and pressure gauge, knife, compass, body weights, and snorkel. He then helped her into her gear, which gave him a chance to recheck her automatic inflation hose, BC mouthpiece, tanks, and regulator. He made sure her face mask was a good fit, taking the opportunity to kiss her lingeringly before he was finished. She tickled his ear with her tongue until he wanted to make a another dive into the bedding, not the water. He cautioned her to stay close to him at all times under water. Visibility was never good in the Columbia, but even if they were in one hundred plus feet of visibility, he would still want her nearby.

He secured a boarding ladder onto the side of the boat and, after he had checked Lydia's equipment one more time, and delivered yet another lecture about staying close to him, they rolled backward into the water. Visibility was limited to about eight to ten feet—acceptable, he thought— and they began a descent to twelve feet, then twenty, then thirty. The ocean tide was high, so the Columbia's current was slowed to less than 3 mph at their location. Lydia was comfortable at her present depth and she gave him a thumbs-up. The bottom of the bay was less than ten feet below now, giving them plenty of room to roll and play, if that's what she wanted to do. Getts had brought along a Hawaiian sling, the simplest form of fishing device ever invented, consisting of a hollow cylinder, with rubber tubing attached to the outside to propel a fishing arrow.

There were many fish in the waters outside Youngs Bay, certainly enough flounder to make a tasty meal, but Getts kept his eyes open for salmon and, if the gods of the seas were amenable enough to smile upon his humble butt, a sturgeon. The big, ancient fish liked to snuggle into sand holes in this comparatively slow water and eat whatever it could find on the bottom, growing to a very large size by maturity. Some of the world's tastiest sturgeon were as much as seventy-five or more years old and, unlike Michael Jordan or movie starlets, they got better with age. Making sure that Lydia was close behind him, he swam toward the Skipanon Light.

The light appeared, sure enough, about twenty yards away, straining against a two-inch mooring cable around which grew a healthy amount of kelp. Where there was seaweed, Getts knew from experience, there would be fish. You have to be careful SCUBA diving around the stuff, but if you don't do anything stupid and keep your cool, it's safe enough and a great visual experience. He thought he had made no more than a couple circuits inside the kelp when he turned to check behind him.

Lydia was gone.

Getts made a right turn and headed toward the outer perimeter of the kelp bed in order to increase his range of vision. She was nowhere in sight.

Getts never panicked in water, and he had solid knowledge of what to do in emergencies, but his heart hammered in his throat as he kicked hard to go around the green forest of kelp.

He found her following a sockeye salmon, about six meters downstream. He didn't know if she planned to strangle the salmon, as she didn't have a spear, or just get a closer look, but Getts's anger with her for getting out of his sight dissipated quickly enough to put his arms around her when he reached her. She turned and smiled at him through her face mask. He patted her on the shoulder and motioned upward.

There was no need to decompress for the depth and time, just over thirty minutes, that they were under the water, so he climbed the ladder on the side of the boat, then turned to help Lydia aboard. He easily removed his gear and began to unfasten hers. "Were you worried about me?" she said.

"Nope."

"You looked like it."

"I'm a SEAL. SEALs don't worry."

"Want to make out?"

"I suppose I could do that before I take my nap," he said. He realized, as he helped her lithe, slippery naked body out of the wet suit, that he wasn't sleepy at all.

Getts had caught two big Dungeness crabs simply by picking them off the bottom of the bay. Next to razor clams, Dungeness crab was the best shellfish in the world. Better even than Maine lobster. They couldn't find a galley pot on board large enough to hold the two four-pound crabs, so Getts cleaned out a bait bucket, filled it full of water, and put it on the gimbled galley stove. While they waited for the water to come to a boil, they sipped wine, nibbled on cheese, celery, and French bread, and talked. Looking back, he did not recall what they said to each other, but at the time he was totally impressed with everything she had to say. He never tired of looking at her bottomless brown eyes, her rich chestnut hair and fascinating mouth. Was that love? If not, then, like his mother used to sing, "it'll do until the real thing comes along."

When the water came to a boil, Getts dropped in the crabs. One of them had previously got a pincher around the web of his thumb and forefinger so he took special delight in making him the first cookee of the evening. They were in the briny water for about a half hour before he removed them and cooled them in cold water. He tore the backs off the still warm shellfish, scooped out the lungs and what the Japanese call "brain butter," and snapped the bodies in half. In the meantime, Lydia had made garlic bread and a lettuce salad with pieces of fresh onion adorned with thousand island dressing. They cracked the shells of crab legs open with their teeth, shook out the meat, and built a couple of crab Louies that would have cost a day's pay in any gourmet restaurant in the country. As they feasted, they washed down each delicious mouthful with Chardonnay.

Boat traffic on the river and bay was not heavy. But trollers and sport fishers arrived over the bar heading for port before the neap tide turned to flood. It was almost

2000 hours and all the boats had their running lights lit. Getts switched on their anchor light for the night and snuggled back down with Lydia in the lazaret, a wool blanket spread over the two of them. "Let's spotlight some fish," she said.

"You mean to catch?"

"No. Let's just snorkel around the Skipanon Light and use our flashlights to look around. It'll be great," she said.

Getts knew it was kind of fun to surprise a fish in the eyeballs with an electric torch and see how it reacted. Some of them even wanted to follow you home. "Okay," he said, "let's do it."

They pulled on their dripping wet suits, attached flippers, put on masks and snorkels, and, with flashlights in hand, rolled over the side. They swam at a comfortable pace, using the bent-knee kick that UDT personnel learned the hard way was the best performance technique for speed and endurance, and using their lights to chase after an assortment of fish and crustaceans. Getts's heart skipped a beat when, below him, he saw the distinctive form of a sturgeon about five feet long cruising slowly on the bottom. He had not brought along a spear so the animal was perfectly safe from Getts's open-ended appetite. It was a good thing, he guessed, because the magnificent fish was as awesome to watch as he was to eat. He felt a tap on his back. Lydia pointed over her shoulder, indicating that she was returning to the boat. She seemed to be in no distress but, to be safe, he turned to accompany her. She placed both hands on his shoulders to stop him, shook her head in the negative, waggled her finger to tell him there was no need. She turned and swam off. Within seconds she was gone from his view.

Getts turned back toward the direction of the sturgeon and swam twenty meters more or so to see if he could pick up its trail again. But it was gone. He then swam in a northern direction for several minutes before coming up.

He blew air out through his snorkel, surfaced, and looked around. It was fully dark now, and he could see the phosphorous wake kicked up by Lydia's fins as she swam smoothly back toward the boat. They had wandered more than one hundred meters from the Gunnerson, farther than he had planned. Lydia was within fifty meters of the boat when he noticed something unusual.

A sport fishing boat, her outriggers stowed, was heading directly toward the Gunnerson, on an approximate course of sixty degrees, which would take it north of Youngs Bay Entrance Light, toward Smith Point. It showed no lights. Had the fisherman come from Tansy Point or Warrenton without Getts noticing? If the boat had been out to sea and returned over the bar, then why had it veered so far off course and moved close to the Gunnerson? The logical possibility occurred to Getts that the boat had originated from the Smith Point direction, near Astoria's docks, shielded from their view by the Gunnerson while they swam, and was now returning along the same route.

But he hadn't seen it while they were aboard, and they had been snorkeling only thirty minutes or so. The troller might have gotten as near as a quarter mile without coming to their attention.

Plenty close enough for a SEAL.

"Lydia," Getts shouted.

But she couldn't hear. She was under water moving toward the Gunnerson at a leisurely pace. Getts was approximately seventy meters northeast of the Gunnerson, and about equidistant from the sport fisher.

The sport fisher had slowed, then stopped dead in the water. There could be any number of reasons why the sport boat hove near the Gunnerson. Boaters are notoriously gregarious. For all Getts knew, the sport boat people might want to talk or offer a beer. Or there could be an engine problem. Happens to the best of boats. Getts could hope for any of those things. But running without navigation lights or anchor lights was a dangerous thing to do in those waters.

Unless whoever was on board did not want to be seen.

Getts cursed himself for his carelessness and passionately wished he had strapped his 9mm to his side before going into the water.

Quickly he pulled off his tank harness and let the tanks sink. Now freed of the heavy weight but retaining his mask and snorkel, he kicked out for a point between the sport boat and the Gunnerson, hoping to intercept anyone attempting to come or go from one boat to the other. He couldn't use his light lest he give himself away, but he left it hooked to his belt anyway. A bright flash directly in an attacker's eyes was good for a moment's hesitation, at least. It might make the difference between life and death. Ten meters from the sport boat, on its north side, Getts slowed his pace through the water to survey the scene. He could see no one on the deck of the sport boat. Still in the water, sixty meters to the south, Getts could see Lydia's underwater light. She could not see or hear anything on the surface. Getts quickly hyperventilated, then dove for a run underwater.

It was very dark, with visibility of only a few feet, yet he swam rapidly, about six feet under the surface. He sensed, rather than felt, a form near his ten o'clock. Strange, but Getts thought it was swimming away before it swung toward him. In less than two seconds, Getts came face to face with an underwater swimmer. Even in the dark, he recognized Doc's form. Doc went immediately for his knife. Getts had anticipated the move and, using one hand to grasp the hilt of Doc's knife while at the same time ripping at his antagonist's face mask, he coiled around the other SEAL, the two of them spinning underwater like two deadly sea snakes seeking to kill. Getts could feel the wire of a UTEL, an underwater communication system for talking to another swimmer or to a surface craft. When he pulled Doc's mask, he also yanked out the UTEL transceiver, and the entire unit came away from Doc's head. Getts knew that Doc's underwater vision was severely degraded, but a SEAL is never blinded in the water, his true element.

Doc now had in hand his ten-inch serrated combat dive knife. Getts quickly clamped his hand onto the knife, gripping a piece of the hilt and some of Doc's fingers. Getts dug his nails into Doc's hand with all of his strength. He knew that it must hurt. But Getts had exhausted his lung capacity and was badly in need of air. He kicked his legs as hard as he could and began to bring both of them to the surface. Just as they would come near the top of the water and precious air, Getts knew Doc would try to pull them both down again, depriving Getts of badly needed breath. After all, it was a tactic taught to them both, to instill panic and fear in an opponent underwater.

Getts was forced to let go of Doc's right hand, and with his left, he made another desperate grab for the mouthpiece of Doc's Aqua Master two-stage regulator. He succeeded in tearing it from Doc's mouth, and pulled once more at the circulating hose and succeeded in ripping it from the system. They would be on even terms now, but by now Getts was literally dying for air only four feet away. He let go of his hold on Doc's hand, kicked hard for the surface, and broke through. At the same instant he sucked hard on the snorkel and was rewarded with the most delicious tasting helping of oxygen he had ever felt in all of his years of swimming and diving. Knowing that Doc had a free hand with a very sharp knife in it, Getts lunged to change locations. His maneuver almost worked, but Doc's combat knife caught him in the side of the calf muscle of his left leg.

The pain tested Getts's blackout threshold, the blade slicing deep and hitting bone. When Doc yanked it out for another thrust, Getts's line of vision was not clear. Ignoring the stinging of his wound, he turned back under his antagonist. As Doc ducked down, Getts jammed the flashlight in his face. The bright halogen light, aimed directly at Doc's pupils, blinded him completely. Getts seized the initiative, and had his own knife out of its scabbard in a flash, thrusting forward with all his might. He felt the big blade slice Doc's wet suit, stab through the hardened rubber tank harness, then penetrate flesh. Blood immediately clouded the darkened water.

Getts pulled the knife out and was preparing to thrust forward again when the bowels of hell ripped the water apart.

The AMS-26 Limpet mine, packed with ten pounds of tetrytol, can blow a hole in the side of an armored battle cruiser six feet wide. Attached to the hull of a boat like the Gunnerson, it will vaporize every atom of wood, metal, and fuel on board. The underwater concussion was enormous. For the instant that Getts was cognizant after the explosion, he felt like he had been kicked in the torso by a team of Clydesdale horses. Then everything went black.

When his senses returned, he was aware that he was on his back, kept afloat by the buoyancy of his rubber wet suit. He was aware of incredible stabbing pain in one leg, which competed with the shock the rest of his body felt. For what seemed an eternity, he could not move, then he willed his hand to move, then an arm. He rolled in the water, trying to move his head about.

The awareness of where he was gradually returned. The Gunnerson was nowhere to be seen. The sport fishing boat was also gone. In the pitch of night, he could only make out small splinters of wood, pieces of cushions from the Gunnerson's lazaret, dead fish, and other jagged flotsam.

The explosive blast was too great to even allow a fire.

Lydia.

Struggling to overcome the internal trauma that made his organs feel like mush, Getts covered the distance to where he had last seen Lydia. He found her, floating facedown, her arms out from her body, her shredded wet suit waving around her peacefully, as though she were still languidly examining the water below her.

Except that her mask and snorkel had been blown from her head.

As he reached her, he could see that blood was flowing freely from her ears. He rolled her over, cradling her in his arms. Blood not only oozed from her nose and mouth, but from her once flashingly beautiful eyes, now weeping grotesquely from tiny exploded blood vessels, rolled back and lifeless. Though he felt her carotid artery, he knew she was already dead.

*　　*　　*

As Grumpy steered their stolen sport fisher, Doc refused
to look over his shoulder at the roiling spot in Youngs Bay
where Bobby and, heaven help them, Lydia existed minutes
ago. It was more than the deep stab wound in his chest
that hurt Doc. Something else inside him died right then,
and, amazingly, he wanted to cry. He couldn't remember
the last time he'd cried. It was probably back when he was
three years old, when his old man was beating up on his
mother. But he felt the same way now, like something valuable was lost forever. Big-time gone. They had talked themselves into it, he thought, and it was the only way. They
had to do it. It was the first rule of war—him or me. But
now, having done it—having killed a swimbuddy—he
wished he had never been born.

In the distance they heard sirens. Grumpy looked
through the binocs again. He could see flashing lights coming from the direction of the Coast Guard station at Warrenton, and police activity on Highway 26 along Astoria's
waterfront, wailing sirens there piercing the night.

They were more than halfway back to pier 12 in the
Basin when the heli took up station at the Skipanon Light,
and swept the water with spotlights on its way to the blast
site. Grumpy couldn't make out what kind it was, but he
didn't give a shit, either. "He's gone, Grumpy," Doc
groaned.

"Let's wait until we read it in the papers," he said.

Oh, God, I'm so sorry I did it, Bobby, Doc grieved.

Near midnight Grumpy tied the boat up at the pier and
looked at Doc's wound. "It isn't good, Doc," he said. "I'm
taking you to a hospital. Hang in there."

Grumpy hoisted their war bag onto his shoulder and prepared to step off the boat. The car was a block away. He
would stow the bag, then come back for Doc. But as he
glanced over his shoulder, he saw that Doc had not moved.
Grumpy dropped the bag and knelt beside his fallen companion. "Doc," he said. He felt for a pulse, but couldn't
find one. "Doc, goddamn it! Jake!"

Doc was dead.

It didn't seem possible. They were bulletproof. Especially Doc. He was too good to die. The best of the team. Grumpy sat in the dark for a long, long time, thinking. Maybe Getts was dead. Then again, maybe not. He was a SEAL after all, and they couldn't stick around to confirm the kill. But the price had been Doc. Grumpy could feel his throat constrict, his senses shutting down, his hearing quieted by the pain in his head, his fingers numb as he touched his head. Considering the options, and they were very few, Grumpy began rummaging around the sport fisher. He found a sleeping bag stowed in a forward locker. With some difficulty he managed to place Doc's body inside, then wrapped it with coils of anchor chain from the bow, and finally with the anchor itself. Grumpy was not a religious man, nor did he have the time to say prayers over Doc's remains. He just slipped the corpse over the side. Then he used an oil-stained rag to wipe down the boat, eliminating fingerprints. He retrieved their war bag, climbed onto the boat dock, and walked off into the night.

There was no reason to think that that particular boat would be searched or that anybody would look for them, but you never knew. It would be written off as a fuel explosion on the boat, Grumpy was sure. It happened all the time. Fuel vapors get trapped in the engine compartment, then, without the fumes having been vented, the key is turned, the ignition switch is actuated and . . . boom. Happens everywhere.

An hour later, as Grumpy was driving back to Seaside from Astoria, KAST radio reported that a woman had been found, the victim of an explosion aboard a boat in Youngs Bay.

Grumpy knew it had to be Lydia. They had eavesdropped on Bobby making a reservation for her to fly out, then spent the day picking up his trail from when they thought he was dropping her off at the airport. Even before the radio later updated news of the explosion, he realized that Getts and Lydia had changed their plans at the last minute. She must have been aboard the Gunnerson, or

close to it in the water, when the limpet vaporized the
boat. Okay, so there was collateral damage. Can't always
be avoided, no matter how well you plan. Grumpy felt a
shiver run through his body.

Did we get him or not? he wondered.

Chapter Sixteen

Captain James Rolland more than liked Bobby Getts. In his opinion, Getts carried inside him the best things that the Navy, and the country, were all about. He was steady, he was a leader, and he was honest. There was no question in his mind that Getts was telling the truth, just as there was equally no doubt that a court-martial would find against Getts's men in Mob 4. Peach, Doc, and Grumpy were lying about their role in the Balkan raid, he believed; but he also believed that they were lying for a very good reason.

Rolland paced the office that he shared with the base personnel officer, gnawing on his mechanical pencil as he glanced at his telephone. He had made a number of calls this morning and some of them, uncharacteristically and suspiciously, had not been returned.

"I've made some fresh coffee, Captain," his secretary called out. Ostensibly, Kendel Gross was still a "pool" administrative assistant, but she had quickly insinuated herself into a role that had somehow made her indispensable to the operation of the base. She seemed to have an answer to every question under the sun, and even when no spoken questions were given, she had answers before being asked. She often irritated James Rolland, but he told himself that (a) she was often right, and (b) her sheer dedication to running other people's lives was a greater force than he could control. So he gave in.

"No, thank you," he said.

"Have you taken your Advil, today?"

"Yes. No. I'm, I'm going to do that," he said, suddenly

aware of the arthritis in his fingers of his right hand and left hip.

"Luckily," Kendel said in a motherly tone, "I brought you a rice cake and a power bar to go with your coffee. If you don't have food when you take anti-inflammatories, you're going to ruin your liver."

"I hate rice," he said. Why didn't Bill Stewart at JSOC return his call? Maybe he should call him again.

"Nonsense. I saw you eat it when we had Chinese food brought in two weeks ago," Kendel said.

"And those power bars taste like shit."

"You've never had one," she replied patiently, placing a fresh cup of coffee, a rice cake, and a mountaineering ration bar on the captain's desk. "Anything else?"

"Any phone calls come in for me this morning?" he said for the third time today.

"I'd tell you if they had, Captain," she said admonishingly.

"Yeah. Well . . . thanks. Close the door when you leave, would you?" When Kendel had left the room, Rolland snatched up his telephone and dialed.

"JSOC Analysis, Sergeant Voigt," a male voice said on the other end.

"This is Captain Rolland, IG, Little Creek. Is Bill Stewart back yet?"

"Oh, hello, Captain Rolland, sir." There was a long pause while the sergeant on the other end considered.

"Look, Sergeant," Rolland said forcefully, "this is urgent. I need to talk to Commander Stewart right now. If he isn't in the office, I want you to go out and find him. Is that clear?"

"Ah, hold on, sir. He must be in the building here, somewhere." There was a click as Rolland was put on hold. Well, fine. He'd hold. Captain Rolland sat impatiently at his desk for several minutes before the telephone clicked again and the unmistakable growl of Commander Bill Stewart came on the line. "Stewart, here."

"It's Rolland, Bill. Where the hell have you been? I've

been trying to get hold of you for almost a week. Have you been hiding from me?"

"Hiding? What the hell have I got to hide about?" Stewart's voice first reflected anger, then softened in tone as though he was worried about being overheard. Which he was. "I'm trying to do you a favor but you want it done yesterday."

Rolland's voice lowered sympathetically. "Sorry, Bill, but I need to know where Arnie Talent is or there's going to be big trouble. Want to know what's going to happen?"

"No," Stewart grunted. "I've got my own problems. Besides, I think I know the kind of trouble you're talking about. I might have some information for you."

"What is it?"

"He's in Germany. And he's been moved up on the list," Commander Stewart said.

"Really? Where in Europe?"

"Germany. Headquarters, Seventh Army. Talent is the new deputy chief of staff."

Rolland whistled to himself. Nice move up, buddy. "Got a phone number for him, Bill?"

Commander Stewart passed it on to Captain Rolland.

Rolland reached HQUSAREUR/7A but was directed to another number in Stuttgart where Colonel Talent was TDY (Temporary Duty). As Rolland was waiting for his call to be placed through various extensions, he suddenly had the idea to change his rank and branch of service. He didn't want to be dodged, if that was the name of JSOC's game. "This is General Scott," he said to a civilian office worker, and waited. After a moment a familiar voice answered. "Colonel Talent."

"Arnie, this is Jim Rolland. Little Creek."

"Jesus."

"Hey, I'm glad to hear from you, too."

"How did you find out where I was?" Talent said.

"Why? Is that a secret?"

Talent gave no response.

"Arnold, some good men are going down if we don't back them up. I need you to talk to me," Rolland said.

"Sorry, I don't know what you mean."

"You know *exactly* what I mean. Four Navy SEALs went on a mission to Bosnia. They knocked off a war criminal on orders that came through JSOC. You were one of the authorizing officers. I need you to say that in court."

"I don't know what you're talking about. Do you mean those crazy Navy types I've been reading about in the papers? That's wild stuff. Are you working on that, Jim?"

"Listen to me, goddamn it! You think I don't know what the fuck is going on? I don't know where the order originated, but I sure as hell can guess. You'll be moved up on the promotion list for general if you keep your mouth shut. Well, Arnie, good men are going to die or go to jail for the rest of their young lives just so that you can wear those stars. You're too good a soldier to let that happen." Rolland paused, and took a deep breath. "Colonel Talent, who is John Barry?"

Talent clammed right up. Rolland let the silence grow until it was all but unbearable on both ends.

"We're not on a secure line," Colonel Talent finally said.

"I'll come over there."

Talent exhaled resignedly. "All right."

"I'll get a SAM flight out of Langley. Be there tomorrow morning."

Getts was in a deep, spiralling, black hole and he couldn't see any way out. He thought he was under control, but he knew that if he thought too hard about it, he would lose it at any moment.

Humans have something against the dark that other animals don't have: fear. Shit happens when the sun goes down. Placid beings become hunters. Strong men and women can become weak and vulnerable when it is dark. That's why SEALs trained for so many hours over all kinds of terrain, always in the dark. So that they would lose their fear. So they could dominate in it, could operate effortlessly while their prey became paralyzed.

Getts didn't want to be paralyzed.

He had trained, operated, and faced death with Doc for

almost a year. He wanted to talk with him, plead with him, apologize to him. Getts felt the strength oozing out of his system. The longer he sat still, the blanket pulled up to his chin, the more he seemed to slip away. Despite the pain in his leg, he became more comfortable, resigned, as if he were drowning, surrendering to death, looking forward to the big sleep, the one that lasts forever.

The street lamps of Astoria's waterfront buildings, the running lights on passing boats, and the billion little mirror images of moonlight rippling on the water, all seemed to dim as Getts's eyes became fixed in a catatonic stare. Forcing himself out of his stupor, he continued to search the slips, dragging his leg, looking into one boat, then another, trying to locate the sport fisher.

His leg was tightly wrapped in a bloody rag, which had once been a clean towel taken from the transom of an unattended boat. He limped like a fairy tale ogre as he shuffled along in the dark, the Mossberg gripped under one arm.

The blackness of his soul was beginning to invade his weakened brain, a white searing anger spreading through his chest. Getts seethed while he reeled from dock to dock, looking for yet another friend to reveal himself so that he could murder him in hot blood.

He had no sense of time when he finally passed out from loss of blood.

Getts hurt in every fiber of his body when he awoke in the emergency room. He had received two pints of blood and fifty-two stitches in his calf. His body had been hammered by the underwater explosion, and the ER doctors believed he might have badly bruised vital internal organs. He wouldn't be walking anytime soon, they said.

One doctor informed Getts that he was the only survivor found in the boat explosion, and that the police wanted to talk to him more about the woman who'd been aboard. Getts stared back at him, his eyes as vacant as his heart.

A while later he was in a recovery room full of painkillers when two Astoria policemen came into the room. They

wanted to know who he was, of course. He gave the name
Lieutenant Robert Getts, USN, and explained that he had
rented a Gunnerson boat from Jack Niemi, the same vessel
that got blown up near the Skipanon Light.

"And the woman with you? What was her name?"

"Lydia Brooks."

"What was her address, Lieutenant?" Getts was asked.
He told them her street and apartment number in Pampino
Beach, Florida.

"What was she to you?" one of the policeman asked,
scribbling notes in a small notebook.

"Friends," he said. "We . . ."

" 'We' what, Lieutenant?" one of the cops said.

"Nothing."

"Where'd you go after your boat blew up?" one of the
plainclothes cops asked.

"Got picked up by another boat. Fisherman. He took me
back to our pier," Getts said.

"What was his name?"

"Who?"

"The fisherman who picked you up."

"I don't remember. Jerry something."

"Whose boat were you looking for at the Portway pier?"
a uniformed cop by the name of Gustafson wanted to
know.

"I don't know," Getts said.

"You were pretty badly hurt. Lost a lot of blood. Why
didn't you call for medical help? Or the police?"

"Well," Getts said, fighting to keep his mind coherent.
Deniability. Must maintain that. "You know, I was pretty
much out of it. Confused."

"You were found with a shotgun in a canvas bag. What
were you going to do with that, Lieutenant?" Gustafson
asked almost mockingly.

"Keeping it dry," Getts said, his words slurred.

"Hmmm. Well, what caused the explosion on board?
Any idea?"

Getts slowly moved his head left to right. "Fumes,
maybe."

"You mean gas vapor? Wasn't your boat a diesel?"

Getts did not respond.

"Well," the cop said, "we'll find out later. What were you doing on the boat?"

Again, Getts didn't answer.

"Maybe you were looking for somebody on the pier? That possible?" the detective said.

Getts allowed his eyes to remain still, unblinking. His head pounded like the bottom of an empty oil drum.

"What's your address here in town?" the detective said.

"I'm passing out," Getts said, closing his eyes.

"Like hell you are. . . ."

"Leave it alone, Howard. We'll get it tomorrow. He's not going anywhere," Gustafson said.

Getts heard them walk out.

By the time they were serving breakfast the next day in Astoria Mercy Hospital, Getts was long gone. He had a cabdriver take him to the bottom of the hill, and from Commerce Street, Getts directed him to Cross' Dive Shop, where he had parked his rental car. He paid the cabby, then searched underneath the car's frame where he had hidden a magnetic box that held a key. In the process of looking for the box, his hands roamed across an ELT. No wonder they knew exactly where he was. They might have tagged him at the airport, or more likely, in Seaside. When he moved, they moved. Getts continued examining the underpart of the car, including the niche above the frame on the opposite side. Sure enough, there was the second transmitter. Nicely thought out. You allow the subject to find the device and he puts it on another vehicle headed out of town, like on a motorcycle or bus, figuring he's gotten rid of his tail. Getts would have used two transmitters himself. He put both ELTs back where he had found them, climbed into the Mercury, started the engine, and drove back to Seaside, numb inside and out.

His leg was killing him when he got to the Tides. Once inside the room he double-locked the door, swallowed a handful of aspirin, lay down on his stomach and fell asleep.

He awoke when it was getting dark, chewed on some cheese and day-old bread, had a swallow of wine, then took a shower and discarded every trace of his indulgence with Lydia, apologizing to her as he did so. "Why did you have to be so stubborn? Why couldn't you have just gotten on that plane?" He tore of strips from clean washcloths, taped them over his stitches, finished off the bottle of aspirin, and fell down on the bed again. He slept for twenty-four hours.

The next afternoon, he felt a little better. His body was still a constantly throbbing, and his calf was still sending strong messages to his brain about the true meaning of pain. Well, his brain could handle it. Pain was good for Getts—it reminded him that he was still alive, that he had a mission to accomplish still. It wouldn't allow him to get careless again.

Getts needed a weapon. The H&K had gone down with the Gunnerson, and the Mossberg was in police custody. There were two gun stores in the area, but a flea market open seven days a week at the Gearhart junction would serve his purposes better.

He left the room through a window over the sink in the kitchen. His car was parked on the street out front and that, he was sure, was what Grumpy would be watching. Getts walked through a couple of neighbors' backyards, crossed Downing, and, sure enough, found Grumpy parked around the corner, leaning back against the driver's door. He had a perfect view of Getts's front door and the Mercury. Getts returned to the Tides whence he came.

Inside the room, he looked up a telephone number and dialed. The phone rang twice before it was picked up. A voice said, "Seaside Police Department, Officer Gue."

"Officer Gue, my name is Oscar Albright, 3114 South Downing," Getts said.

"Yes, sir."

"Here's the situation, Officer Gue, I'm a reasonable man and I expect to meet nutballs once in a while in a resort town like Seaside, but there's a man who's been following my wife around for two days. See, we're both in our fifties and, frankly, she's not very attractive. In fact some of our friends in Portland thinks she's downright ugly. But she is my wife, you understand."

"Yes, sir."

"So, when a man chases Gladys around town, then parks in front of our house watching for her, I think the man's got to be a real sicko. You agree?"

"Yes, sir. Uh, have you ever seen him before, Mr. Albright?"

"Never."

"You say he's parked in front of your house?

"That's right. We're renting the place for the summer."

"He's there right now?" the policeman said.

"I can see him right through the window. Nasty looking man, I might add."

"Just stay inside your house, Mr. Albright. I'll send a car right now. An officer will be there in less than five minutes."

"Good. Oh, by the way, Officer. The man may have a gun. I could be wrong, but I thought I saw him get one from the trunk of his car."

"A gun? Are you sure?"

"No, I'm not," Getts said. "But if I were you, just to be safe, I'd look in the trunk of that man's car."

"All right, sir. We'll want to talk with you after we check him out."

"I'll be right here, Officer."

Not one, but two cars arrived. One car parked behind Grumpy, another behind and to the side. The cops opened their car doors and used their radios to talk him out of his car.

Getts took his time limping out of his motel door, walking to his car, then driving slowly by the flurry of police activity. Grumpy looked right into Getts's swollen eye as he cruised past. Getts knew he'd talk his way out of the jam. After all, he hadn't done anything wrong. He just wanted Grumpy to know he'd been made, and that the score would be settled on Getts's own terms. Ten minutes later, Getts was at the north end of town on his way to the Gearhart junction.

*   *   *

The backbone of the flea market was an old corrugated warehouse that once stored root beer and assorted other sodas for an area dealer. White pines stood tall behind it, and a few hundred yards beyond lay the confluence of the Necanicum and Wahanna rivers. Tables, tents, and umbrellas protected assortments of jewelry displays, pottery, leather hats, live squirrels, food bars, auto and motorcycle parts, used clothing, vegetable slicers, sandwich machines, popcorn makers, and, of course, guns. There were new automatics, old revolvers, ammunition, reload outfits, scopes, knives, and hunting gear of all description. Getts found a man wearing a genuine leather frontier hat with a pheasant feather sticking out of the crown and a leather vest over bare skin, his arms decorated with attractive tattoos depicting a variety of LSD-induced hallucinations. He had a cigarette hanging comfortably under a graying mustache, which was turning yellow from carefully selected Kentucky tobaccos. At his waist he carried a six-inch Buck knife in a sheath.

God had sent Getts to this man. "Nice pieces," Getts said, nodding toward the guns on his table. The man had a length of stainless steel wire, about three-eighths of an inch thick, running through the trigger guards of the pistols, and the end fastened to a welded loop and locked with a padlock. Getts could have made them all disappear before the trader could get his Buck knife off his belt. But today, he had important business on his mind.

"Looking for something special?" the man said.

He had a Bersa .380 semiauto that looked decent, but suffered from a deficient 6-round magazine. He also had a Mitchell 9mm, a Frontier Colt .44, and a few .22 target pistols.

"I need a stopper," Getts said, not seeing what he was looking for.

"How about a Glock? Got a seventeen right here. Ten-round mag, damn good shape. Used to belong to my sister. Scared the hell out of her so she gave it to me to sell."

"That's bullshit," Getts said, not bothering to look up.

He laughed. "You see this Bersa? Three-eighty will stop anybody," he said.

Getts began to stroll away. "Hey," he said. Getts turned. "I got a compact forty-five Star. My own gun, man," he whispered, glancing around nervously, as though he were selling Getts a stolen gun, a possibility that pleased the SEAL. Getts nodded his head. The man walked a few steps to a twenty-year-old pickup truck, reached underneath the dashboard, and came up with a piece wrapped in a rag. He removed the rag, popped the magazine out of the grip, ejected the chambered round, and lay the gun on the table between him and Getts. Getts knew the weapon very well. It was just over seven inches long, had a short grip frame, a throated barrel, and a flared ejection port. It was a dependable gun. And it had a 10-round magazine. Getts operated the slide, looked inside and down the barrel. It was well cared for, not over oiled. With a proper diet of ammunition, it would earn its keep.

"How much?" he said.

"Six hundred."

"That's the factory price. Tell you what, you quit trying to fuck me on this one and I'll buy one of your shotguns back there." Getts nodded toward three shotguns the trader had leaning against a wooden crate.

The man nodded his head. "Kind you want?"

He had a double-barrel Savage, a Winchester Black Shadow turkey gun, and a Winchester 1300 Defender— pump action, 12-gauge, chambered for magnum shells. The 00 ammo Getts already had in the trunk of his car would fit the Winchester just right. It had a short barrel, built for close-in work. He could saw six inches off the stock and it would be perfect. "What do you want for the thirteen hundred? Couple thousand?" Getts said.

He laughed. "Man, you're funny. Tell you what. The Winchester is worth over two hundred fifty . . ."

"You're fifty high. I'll give you seven hundred for both, and a box of shells for the forty-five. No paperwork."

"Cash?"

Getts reached into his wallet and came up with four hundred and fifty. He handed these to him. "There's a bank in Gearhart. You and I can drive over to the ATM for the rest."

They took Getts's car and finished the deal in ten minutes. The gun trader offered to buy Getts a beer. It sounded good in principle but Getts had other things to do. "Hey, man," the man said as he stepped out of Getts's car, "good hunting." Hunting, indeed.

Getts drove back to Seaside, parked on Broadway, and went into the Rexall Drug to buy more bandages, tape, and aspirin. His calf muscle was still screaming at him. But he was long over feeling sorry for himself. And he had a gun now.

Chapter Seventeen

Peach sat at the bar in the CPO Club knocking back straight shooters of tequila, a cactus nectar he had loved for as long as he could remember. There was nothing especially tasty about the liquor today, however. He was just in the mood to drink. He had been informed, along with others of his unit, that there would be Senate hearings into the political assassination of Krabac, but that he and the others in Mob 4 would not be questioned or required to testify until the U.S. Navy had finished its own proceedings against them. He knew he was at a crossroads, and didn't like how it felt. They were leaving tomorrow, and he honestly didn't know if he could bring himself to go with them.

"Hey, Peach," another SEAL named Sy Burgher said to him in passing. "Leave some for the cleanup crew."

Peach glared in Sy's direction but turned back to his booze and threw down another shot. "Come on, man," Sy said, worried about the man he had seen only occasionally in the past several months. "Lighten up."

"Fuck you."

"Are you serious about marriage or are you just flirting?" Sy said.

Peach slowly climbed off his stool, approached the SEAL chief in front of him, and screwed his lips into a smile. "I don't think I know you well enough to marry you," he said. "Maybe we should just date for a while."

"That's sensible," Sy said. "You may call for me tomorrow night."

"Do you fuck on the first date?" Peach said, staggering slightly.

"Not usually, Peach, but in your case I'll round up some guys from the barracks and we'll oblige you."

Peach giggled. He pulled his fatigue cap from his pocket, put it onto his head as best he could, and headed for the parking lot, where he had left his car. Whether someone had placed a call to the base provost marshal, or the two Marine guards just happened to be passing as Peach destroyed the side of two parked cars attempting to maneuver out of the lot he never knew. It became a moot point when they placed their vehicle in front of his and stepped out.

"Hey." The gunny sergeant didn't like drunks, and was extremely pissed at all the paperwork he would certainly have after he arrested this asshole. "Where the fuck you think you're going?"

Peach did not reply. Instead, he breathed deeply, exhaled, and belched.

"Get out of the car, Chief," the Marine said. The Marine wore a white cartridge belt upon which he carried a side arm and a baton. One hand was on each weapon.

"Oh, no, no. That is not what you want, jarhead. That is definitely not what you want," Peach slurred.

"What did you say?"

Marines were often called jarheads by the Navy, and other services, but seldom to their faces. Gunnery Sergeant Richard F. Miller, five feet eleven inches, two hundred and fifty-five bench-pressing pounds, had tangled with SEALs before. They were tough, all right, but so was Sergeant Miller. It was a major disappointment to Sergeant Miller that there was not currently a war going on in which he could take full advantage of his body, a piece of prime weaponry, honed straight and true by America's quintessential fighting force. But lacking national targets sanctioned by the President, secretary of defense, and General Walter R. Laughlin, commandant, this sorry piece of SEAL shit would do nicely. While his autonomic nervous system began to hold blood in strategic places in his body, causing his face to go white, Sergeant Miller's voice took on the satisfied, almost melodious level of command. "Chief Dickface," he said calmly, "you are under military arrest. You must remove your sorry ass from that vehicle peacefully and surrender to me and Corporal Charles Seine, here, or we will be obliged to use force and beat the sad fuck out of your young ass. Anything about my lawful directive that is confusing to your one-celled SEAL-ass brain?"

"Why do they call you people leatherdicks? Is it because you sit around the barracks flogging your weenies until they wither up? Or is it because . . ."

Corporal Seine jerked open the door to Peach's 4×4 and reached inside. Peach couldn't believe his good fortune. He laid his left hand over the corporal's right, gripped his thumb, and turned quickly downward. The man's digit immediately dislocated from the ball of his hand and the Marine screamed in pain. Peach stepped almost leisurely out of the car and placed his left foot inside Corporal Seine's left instep, thus opening up his right side to attack. He dropped an elbow sharply into the Marine's ribs, breaking three of them. His aikido moves were fluid, automatic, and very effective.

Gunnery Sergeant Miller was surprised that a drunk could move so well. Seine was pretty tough, but he lacked certain street fighting techniques that Sergeant Miller learned the hard way in the bars of north Pittsburgh and the Kellerman Mines. Still, Miller would use his baton. He advanced toward Peach in an athletically balanced stance and, when he was the right distance from Peach, threw a vicious karate kick. The kick, as far as it went, was pretty fair. But Peach had seen thousands of them before, from martial arts experts to drunken frat boys. He moved his body only a few inches, but more than enough for the Marine's size eleven brogan to hit nothing but air.

Peach wanted to grab Miller's balls and stuff them down his throat, but it would probably be better to use the man's own baton as a rough kind of enema that would remind him of this meeting for days, even weeks, to come. In the art of war one should always use an enemy's perceived advantage against him. So when Miller used both hands in a well-timed lunge with his blunt-force weapon, Peach did not retreat but moved forward instead, deflecting the man's

leading thrust hand with his own, just inches inside the
intended point of attack.

Peach used Miller's own weight, and surprise, against him
to pull the Marine off balance. There was a snapping sound
as Peach wrenched the baton over up and down, the Marine's wrist breaking as the baton fell easily into Peach's
palms. The Marine knew he was whipped right then, but
Peach, his mind red with blind rage, was just getting started.

Lieutenant Commander Avery Bledsoe listened with increasing interest to Lieutenant (JG) Keith Grissom, as the
junior officer made his report. Lieutenant Commander
Bledsoe had a reputation for diffusing sensitive situations
that arose at Little Creek before they reached critical mass.
The base commander's daughter was a perfect example. At
the tender age of sixteen, the girl decided that what the
squadron softball team needed to win their league was an
infusion of oral sex. She proceeded to supply that service
under the grandstands at a non-league game while the men
and women of Amphib Division 5 divided their attention
between the action on the field and the action under the
bleachers. Commander Bledsoe and one of his minions arrived on the scene and, after placing Amy Connors in the
backseat of the security car, immediately took the names
of the game's spectators. That night and the following day,
Bledsoe visited each and every eyeballer to the Great
Event and threatened those persons with article 15 if they
so much as breathed a word of what they had seen to anyone on or off the base. He was bluffing, of course, but no
one wanted to test his resolve. Amy was hustled off to an
"exceptionally well-attended" school in Chicago and the
base softball team went on to finish last in the league.

"Where is Sergeant Miller now?" he barked at Grissom.

"Base infirmary, sir. Figures to be there awhile. He's got
broken ribs, a dislocated knee, and, Jesus, you should see
his face. . . ."

"How about the others?"

"Well, it ended up with nine of my people having to get
involved before they got him wrapped up," Grissom said.

"Any of them hurt?"

"All of them. Not as bad as Miller, but this Chief Crosley is some kind of marshal arts instructor. And a SEAL."

"What the hell started it?"

"Crosley was drunk and Miller tried to arrest him," Grissom said.

"That's it? He was drunk and wanted to fight?"

"I guess so. Except he was crying."

"Who? Crosley?"

"Yes, sir. He was crying when we locked him up," Grissom said.

Lieutenant Commander Bledsoe thought about it for a minute. "Yeah. Well, maybe it's that other shit he's going through. The court-martial."

"Could be, sir. I asked him if he wanted to see his defense counsel but he said no, he wanted to see Lieutenant Getts."

"Where's Getts now?"

"On leave somewhere. We don't really know."

"Look here, General," the President said, "I care about one thing. I care about protecting the honor of the armed forces, in this case the United States Navy, and I don't care about protecting anyone or anything else. Frankly, I don't see what we have to gain by court-martialing these young men. Hell, I love SEALs. Always have." The President had moved from behind his desk and began to pace the floor for dramatic effect. He rubbed the back of his neck with one hand just as he'd seen LBJ do in the newsreels. He was working in shirtsleeves for comfort, but thought that it gave him a forceful air when getting down to business.

Army General Connie "Peanuts" Chilquist, chairman of the Joint Chiefs of Staff, was as much politician as he was a squad leader, a battalion commander, a division commander, and a war planner. He understood that the court-marshal looming over the heads of the three Navy SEALs couldn't do anybody any good, no matter how it came out. He would gladly have erased the damn charges from JAG dockets if he could. "I think that's what we all want, sir. Exactly what we want."

"Okay, then. Fine," the President said.

The newly appointed Secretary of State Frederick Hazeltine spoke up. "Is there a 'but' in your statement of agreement, General?"

"Not as far as what we all want, Mr. Secretary. Not a damn bit. But I guess I'm not clear on exactly what we can do about it. I mean, the trial is scheduled, and every news organization in the world knows about it by now. I can't just order the charges dismissed."

"Why the hell not?" the President said. "Somebody drew them up, somebody can dismiss them. You're the top general, Peanuts. Give the damn order."

Chilquist looked imploringly at Hazeltine but found no sympathy there. "I can do that, sir, but only if I have your express authorization," he said.

"Is that supposed to be a joke? What do I have to do with any of this? I'm trying to help you, General, and the other armed services. If it looked like I influenced military affairs it would . . . uh . . . uh . . . ." The President fumbled.

"It could be construed as a political rather than a military crisis," Hazeltine finished smoothly.

"That's right," President Spalding said, returning to his executive chair behind the desk. "Peanuts," he began in a conciliatory tone, "before my National Security Council advisor Roger Demerit suddenly passed away, he was frustrated with this damn war criminal. He wanted him kidnapped. If he had said something to me about it, I might have agreed with him. Know what I mean? Hell, we all hate bastards like that Krabac. So Demerit's kidnapping scheme went sour. Why hang these gutsy Navy kids for it? They did the best they could."

"Sir," Chilquist said, the heaviness in his chest returning, "the CO of Mob 4 is prepared to swear that his men were given orders to kill General Krabac, not to kidnap him. He's going to say that a man called John Barry gave the order, and that John Barry was on your staff."

"Barry? Who the hell is that? I don't know any Barry. Do you, Fred?" the President said.

"No, I don't, Mr. President."

Chilquist knew exactly who Barry was. He was a White House lawyer, several layers down the line. "Yes, sir. Of course, if it was Roger Demerit who gave the order, and we could prove it. . . ."

There was a momentary silence in the room.

"Ah, he might have put that order in writing. I mean, I could go through his papers," Hazeltine suggested.

The President broke into a huge smile. "Well, hell, *now* we're getting somewhere. Sure, Rog would have written it down. His signature would be on the damn paper, wouldn't it? Those SEAL fellas were following a direct order from the national security advisor," the President enthused.

Chilquist had to squirm. "Yes, sir, I can see how it all happened, now. But if Lieutenant Getts doesn't change his story, it means that somebody gave an illegal order to murder a foreign state official. That's what the trial would be about. That's what the media would pick up on." He absentmindedly plucked a mote of linen from his uniform trousers.

"Has anybody explained the facts of life to this Lieutenant Getts?" Hazeltine said.

"It's my understanding that they have, Mr. Secretary," Chilquist said.

"Well, let's give it another shot. I'll talk to him, myself."

Grumpy had completely lost Getts hours ago when the Seaside cops had surrounded his car. He should have figured Getts for that. He should have stayed away from the car, out of sight, but he got lazy. Well, he couldn't afford to get lazy again.

Getts had either split for Portland, or for Little Creek, or for Butt-fuck Eurasia, for all he knew. But first things first. He would make sure he wasn't still around. Grumpy used a local AAA map to divide the town of Seaside into concentric squares, from the cove to Broadway, with Beach Drive as the southern and western boundaries, and from

Highway 101 to Bear Valley Road as the outermost eastern boundary. In the north he would use 101 as far as Gearhart. If he received no signal from the ELT on Getts's car, he would make one run to Astoria—as a very long shot—then to Lake Oswego for a final check before catching a flight back to Little Creek. He would then confer with Peach.

It took less than one hour for Grumpy to get a hit on his RDF (Radio Direction Finder). He had driven about two miles past Broadway on the coast road to a part of town called Venice Park. Grumpy found three access streets leading west in the general direction of the signal— Queen Street, Pine, and a third unmarked street, its sign long torn from the steel pole. None of the streets were paved.

Grumpy removed his Glock from his belt holster and laid it near him on the seat where he could get at it instantly, then turned down Pine Street. He adjusted the "bug" on his RDF as he drove. The high-pitched signal got increasingly louder as he proceeded, the ocean now visible. The road deteriorated to loose sand, and as he turned a corner, he could see Getts's rental car parked less than twenty meters away. It was necessary for Grumpy to stop, and to quickly put his own car in reverse. Just as he shifted gears, there was an incredible crash on the driver's side door that completely caved the window in, causing intense pain in Grumpy's shoulder. The blow was like a ten-pound sledgehammer, which was exactly what Getts used.

Grumpy had no time to move before the muzzle of a shotgun was pressed against his neck. "Now, Grumpy, pick up your piece with two fingers. Carefully drop it out this window. Do it now." The SEAL did as he was told. "Now get out of the car," Getts ordered, giving Grumpy room to move.

"How you doing, Bobby?" Grumpy said pleasantly.

"Real good. How about you?"

Grumpy shrugged. "If you want the truth, the day hasn't been much good so far."

"Hey, don't worry about it. We're going to take care of that right now," Getts said. "Pop the trunk."

Grumpy carefully leaned back to the open door of his rental car, then actuated the trunk latch. Getts moved to examine the contents of the trunk. Except for a fabric overnight bag, the trunk was empty. "So the cops got your war bag, huh?" Getts said.

Grumpy nodded. "They had probable cause. Can't blame the dumb motherfuckers for being nervous. I mean, if they had any brains at all they'd be SEALs. Right?"

"I don't know. How smart is it to deposit fifty thousand dollars in a Miami bank account when you're pulling E-6 Navy pay?"

"They get that already? That was just a place to put it until I could get it into an offshore account. Silly me," Grumpy said.

The nearest house was at least two hundred meters away. In front of the SEALs was an unkempt area where years of flotsam from the two rivers had emptied into the Pacific Ocean, bringing with it logs and roots of giant trees. "Walk in front of me," Getts said. "That way." He motioned with his shotgun.

Grumpy had a diving knife strapped to the inside of his pant leg and a .25-cal Beretta in an ankle holster. He was waiting for one single moment when Getts's attention would be distracted. Getts didn't give him the opportunity.

"Why don't you go for the gun first?" Getts said as they walked. "That way you don't have to get so close. I'm three steps behind. You know, save you a half second."

"Gee, I never thought about that," Grumpy said.

They reached an area near two very large pieces of driftwood where picnickers had built many fires, the logs blackened but whole.

"Is this where I get it, Bobby? Hell, I don't blame you, man. You know why? Because of Lydia. This may not mean a hell of a lot to you now, but we all loved that lady. Me and Doc didn't know she was with you on the boat. We never asked that old man if you were alone. That's the truth."

"Truth? What do you know about truth, Truman? You sold out your team, and your country, for money."

"No. I didn't do that, Bobby. I got an order. And the man who gave me that order attached cash to it. He said it was an authorized expense. Anybody would have accepted it. Maybe not you, because you're a rich cocksucker, but us little people, we'd take it in a heartbeat."

"It was an illegal order," Getts said.

"Say what? Illegal? When was the last time you disobeyed an order? Me, I don't think I ever have. And I've had a lot of shitty orders in my career. They told me to pop this Serb general, and I did it. End of story."

"So why wasn't I let in on the secret?" Getts asked.

"Think about it, Bobby."

When Getts didn't reply, Grumpy went on. "We figured once we popped the target you'd get used to the idea. We didn't know you'd go iron-ass over a fucking Serb killer and turn us all in. You were wrong, Lieutenant. We were your unit and your loyalty was to us."

"Doc was in on it?"

Grumpy nodded. "Sure. I may be a prick, but I do share." Grumpy took a deep breath. "Okay. I'm tired of talking about it. Do it already."

Getts did not pull the trigger. He stood for a long moment considering the man in front of him. His one-time comrade.

"I'm going to testify against you when it goes to trial, Grumpy. After all your other fuckups, you figured to fix them by killing your commanding officer, and in process, you killed a civilian. And the woman I loved." Something in Getts softened. Revenge was one thing—killing a swim buddy in cold blood was another. After all his pent-up rage, his grief, his feelings of utter betrayal, Getts found he just couldn't pull the trigger. "If I were you, I'd run. Change your name and beat it. Somewhere the Navy won't find you. Don't ever come near me again or I'll kill you."

Grumpy breathed out audibly. "You don't have to worry about that, Skipper. You let me go and I'm out of here."

Neither man offered his hand as Getts backed away, limping painfully to his car, leaving Truman Lynch standing by himself beneath cloudy skies on a remote beach. From a distance Grumpy watched Getts stoop, reach beneath his car, and withdraw one of the ELTs. Getts turned and saw Grumpy watching him as he pointedly dropped it on the cold sand. Then he stepped into his car, started the engine, and drove off.

Getts called the police station from a public telephone and identified himself as Mr. Oscar Albright. "I called in a complaint about a man who was stalking my wife. I told you that I thought he had a gun."

"Yes, sir, Mr. Albright, we'd like to have you come in and talk to us. . . ."

"I'll be happy to. Did you search the car? Did you find any weapons?"

"Well, we couldn't search his car, sir. We need to have probable cause to detain the man. That's why we need to have you. . . ."

Getts hung up the telephone. Grumpy had lied—he still had his war bag, and most likely the intent to use it. Getts drove north about seven miles to Surf Pine and pulled into a parking lot at Hertig's Meat Packing. Inside, he asked to buy four of the extra heavy plastic bags that the butcher used for packing cuts of beef and pork. He also insisted on paying for a quarter roll of plastic tape especially made for sealing processed meats for freezing and shipment.

When he returned to Seaside, he stopped at a Safeway supermarket on First Avenue and Holiday Street. Inside he bought a gallon container of Dial hand soap, a roll of adhesive tape, and a small box of birthday candles.

Across the street was an outdoor store that catered to hunters and fishermen, offering athletic equipment of all descriptions, such as running shoes, sleeping bags, guns, ammunition, tents, fishing equipment, and outdoor clothing. Getts bought a set of tiger-striped camos and a pair of Nike hiking shoes. He also purchased nylon rope, a large backpack, a camping shovel, a box of wooden matches, and a two-gallon gasoline can. He paid in cash.

At a local hardware store he bought a one-sixteenth-inch carbon drill bit and a plastic screwdriver that would accommodate the bit, a pair of vise-grip pliers, and a pair of channel locks. He also found a roll of five-millimeter wire, which he bought as well.

His last stop was the Shell gas station across from the post office, where he filled his two gallon gas can. He had noted that he was not being followed at all of his stops about town. Better that he wasn't, but it wouldn't really matter in the end. Satisfied with his progress, Getts drove back to the Tides.

Inside, with his packages and bags arrayed in two rooms, Getts chose to work first in the bathroom. His first order of business was to remove his leg dressing and examine the injury. It was red and blue, seeping fluid from the strain of hard activity, but he could tell that the wound was not infected. He applied disinfectant powder, then fresh dressing, and taped his entire lower leg as tightly as he could without impeding blood flow. He did the same to the wound on his thigh.

Getts next used his diving knife to cut the top off the Dial liquid soap container, and poured its contents into an open plastic meat packing bag. Then he carefully poured the entire two gallons of gasoline into the soap. He used a handheld mixer from the kitchenette utility drawer to stir the mess into a thick, homogeneous gelatin. He closed the top of the bag and used sealing tape to secure it.

Now, being careful not to cut too deeply, Getts used his diving knife to score the bag with small holes. He noticed to his satisfaction that the gelatin pushed out through the holes in little droplets. Now Getts laid a second meat packing bag atop the kitchen table and scored this bag across its middle. He filled the bag up with water and examined it. Water passed through it in streams. Clearly, he had cut too deep. He patched the bag with the strong plastic tape and scored it again. He repeated the process of filling the bag with water. He held it up to the light. He could see no liquid leaking through the bag despite the fact that it had been intentionally weakened. He placed the first bag, with the gelatin, inside the second and sealed it with plastic tape.

It was 1610 now, two hours until dark. Plenty of time.

Working again at the kitchen table, Getts removed the magazine from his .45 Star and levered the round out of its chamber. He then inserted the one-sixteenth bit into the plastic screwdriver. Gingerly applying the vise grips to the head of a lead hollow-point bullet, and securing the channel locks around the brass casing, he turned gently, removing the bullet from the casing. He then applied the drill bit directly into the hollow part of the bullet and began to twist. Within a few turns, the bit had completely penetrated the soft lead bullet, leaving a small hole through and through.

Getts cut the heads from three camping matches and gently stuffed the sulfur tips into the hole in the lead bullet. He removed a birthday candle from its box, lit it, and held the candle over the bullet, allowing hot wax to drop onto the bored hole. This done, he replaced the bullet back into its brass casing and crimped it tight using the channel lock pliers.

Getts repeated this process for the next three rounds in the magazine. As he did so, he reminded himself that tomorrow's actions would have to take place during the daylight simply because Grumpy possessed night vision glasses and he did not.

It was now fully dark and the pain in Getts's calf was becoming unbearable. But he dared not use painkiller, nor did he have time to rest, exhausted though he was. He had a long night ahead of him.

It was dark when he changed into the tiger camo. Getts took his shotgun, diving knife, and trenching tool, and eased out of his apartment door. He walked quietly to the end of the long corridor and, confident that the remaining ELT was still sending a strong signal from his parked car on the north side of the building, Getts made sure there was no one watching this exit, and stepped into the night.

He walked, carrying his equipment in his backpack, down Ocean Vista Way past the huge rocky cove that guarded the end of the city's limits in the south. The road began to slope upward, eventually becoming an entirely wooded way where the last of the town's houses had been built. A mile farther up, the road abruptly stopped at the foot of a dense forest. The Cannon Beach Trail started there.

The trail traversed Tillamook Head, an edifice several hundred feet high that jutted out into the Pacific Ocean, creating a sheer rock cliff at its westernmost side. Thick virgin forest and heavy green brush under tall fir and spruce trees surrounded the trail on all points of the compass. Getts moved along the narrow path for a distance of half a mile, then moved east, making no effort to hide his way through the undergrowth. About one hundred meters from the trail he halted, withdrew his trenching tool, and began digging. He dug steadily for an hour, willing the pain away enduring the physical agony wracking his entire body.

Once done, he cut green branches from trees and whittled both ends sharp, then placed them into the bottom of the pit he had just dug. He covered the pit with a mesh woven from fresh branches and leaves. He drank deeply from a bottle of water and rested for ten minutes. Because the northwest fog was beginning to settle its icy fingers upon the forest, Getts put himself back to work before the elements made the job harder. He moved two meters to his left, two meters straight ahead, then began the whole process over again, digging, cutting, sharpening, weaving foliage. And, by 0500 hours, he had completed the third tiger trap, and a single shallow spider hole.

Moving now only with great effort, he placed himself close to the earth and began to "clean" the ground surface of his tracks. He dispersed soil, fluffed leaves and pine needles, and brushed clumps of grass where the stems had been noticeably bent. Then, on the far side of the three tiger traps, Getts walked heavily, making no effort to disguise his footprints. He continued to leave this trail until he was able to "disappear" behind an outcropping of moss-covered rocks.

Lastly, walking backward, he retraced his steps. It took him an additional hour and thirty minutes to match his footprints precisely to those he had made going in. By the time he was back on Sunset Road it was 0735 hours. He made good time returning the two miles to his apartment at the Tides, entering the same way as he had left.

He fell heavily onto the floor of the main room and used a couch pillow to support his head. He would sleep for only twenty minutes. Then the action would begin.

Getts's car had not moved during the night. Grumpy had nothing but respect for Getts's fighting talents, but he thought Getts had lost his nerve when he backed away from killing him when he had the chance. There was no reason why the lieutenant wouldn't hike his ass back to Little Creek and run his fucking mouth to JAG just like he said. By himself, Grumpy could only watch the car and two of the three exits from Getts's Tides' apartment at one time, but he made sure to wake himself every thirty minutes to check the car and all the doors. There was no reason to think Getts was not getting a full night's sleep. Well, that was good. A man ought to have all the rest he wants before being put to sleep for good.

At 0916, Grumpy watched from inside his car while Getts exited the front door of the Tides and walked to his car. He was wearing a navy blue sweatshirt and khaki shorts. Grumpy could clearly see the two white bandages on his leg. Getts started the engine and drove out onto the street, turning onto Ocean Vista Way. He turned again, south this time, toward Tillamook Head, the ELT continuing to put out a weak but audible signal. Grumpy waited for Getts to get a good lead, then followed.

There was virtually no traffic going in their direction. Grumpy referred to the city map and could see that Ocean Vista Way became Sunset Road, eventually dead-ending about a half mile above the cove. Where the fuck was Getts going? he thought.

Within a few minutes, Grumpy's RDF indicated that the other car had stopped. Grumpy stopped as well, and waited for several minutes, not sure what lay ahead. He slowly approached the end of the paved road and spied Getts's rental car, apparently deserted. This place, the SEAL thought, was just as good as most. Perfect, in fact. He

popped the trunk of his car, opened his war bag, and retrieved an AR-14—the hunting weapon of choice for Navy
SEALs. He also had a choice between using the M26 fragmentation grenade or the M3A2 offensive grenade. He considered for a moment, then took one of each.

It was a cold, cloudy morning. A sad dreary day for killing but, Grumpy thought, it had to be done. Getts should
have used the shotgun. If Grumpy was in his place, he
certainly would have done it. Getts was an enemy, maybe
more now than ever. And Getts should have remembered
his basic SEAL training: never give the enemy a second
chance.

Grumpy pulled on his jungle pants and hat. As he pulled
a brown campaign sweater over his head, something niggled
at the back of his mind. What the hell was Getts doing up
this road in the first place? Well, whatever the fuck it was,
it was going to be his last act. He would be careful, Grumpy
would. As careful as a mouse in a snake den.

Grumpy strapped on a cartridge belt and made sure he
had plenty of spare magazines, although he didn't anticipate much of a firefight. He knew Getts had no rifle except
the shotgun. He considered taking water but decided he
would be able to move easier without the extra weight—
and, besides, he should be back to his car in a very short
time. Grumpy snapped his fire selector on full automatic
and started walking.

Within a few paces he was at the threshold of the Cannon Beach Trail. He looked down at the damp soil and
easily noted the shape of Getts's shoes. He began moving
along the trail, sweeping his gaze left, then right, then up.
He took tenuous steps, looking for trip wires, booby traps
of any kind. Four hundred meters up the trail, in a shadowy
place, Getts's shoe prints disappeared from the trail. He
had gone either left or right. Grumpy dropped to a prone
position, scanning the area and the trees above. Getts was
simply not there. Grumpy rolled slightly sideways and
watched the foliage behind him.

Crawling slowly now, he examined the grass and leaves
to the right of the trail. They appeared undisturbed. Check-

ing his six o'clock again before he moved, Grumpy rolled over the trail. He had good cover behind a fallen log and considered spraying his fire zone with lead to see if Getts would react. But Grumpy knew Getts was cool under fire, and he decided against betraying his own position. He stayed on his belly and peered more closely at the foliage around him. Got ya. Grumpy spotted bent blades of grass and a scuff mark here and there where toes or knees had disturbed the ground. Smiling to himself, he moved ahead slowly, silently, pulling himself forward like an anaconda through jungle grass.

Then he saw it.

About twenty degrees to his left was the glint of a wire. It was partially covered with leaves but still visible to the SEAL-trained eye. One end of the wire would be fastened to an explosive. Grumpy didn't know where the hell Getts would have come across a big-bang device but, hell, they all knew how to make one. The other end of the wire would either be fastened to a tree or a bush and would detonate when it was tripped. But this wire was positioned very low to the ground—touching it, in fact. Grumpy pretended not to see the wire. He moved his head slowly about him, as though still looking for Getts's position. By now, Grumpy was sure that Getts's camouflage was something like a hand-made gilly suit. Most snipers liked to make their own and Getts knew that end of the business better than most. Still, Getts's plan was blown, and he was about to step into a very nasty pail of shit.

Grumpy inched ahead. When he arrived at the wire, stopping so that it was just under his chest, he simply placed his entire stock and barrel down the wire in a perfect sight setup. There wasn't any need to eyeball Bobby because Grumpy knew he would be there, holding the wire's end. Grumpy depressed the trigger of the M-14 and held it down, ripping off a 20-round burst. Then, just in case he had not achieved a direct hit on the target, Grumpy rolled to his right.

Just like he was trained.

Suddenly the ground gave way beneath his body and

Grumpy felt himself starting to fall. Grasping as far out as his arm would allow, he managed to catch himself before striking the hideous punji stakes below. There were four rows of them, needle-sharp, placed ten inches apart and reaching two feet up from the pit they were buried in. As Grumpy struggled back to safety, there was a thunderous explosion behind him and to his left. Getts's shotgun. Grumpy made a split-second decision. Getts was trying to push him in a certain direction. To his right, toward the trail, away from the shotgun. Grumpy leaped to his left.

It was the wrong decision. But it wouldn't have mattered. Left or right, the result would have been the same.

This time Grumpy could not catch himself before plunging into the tiger's pit. He screamed in agony as the stakes drove through his feet and legs. But that was only the beginning. A soft plastic bag fell on him, hitting him between the neck and shoulder. When it struck him, the bag collapsed, disgorging its contents all over his body, clinging to him like—well, like liquid soap. And gasoline. Instantly Grumpy recognized the ingredients of homemade napalm.

"Getts. Getts! Jesus, Bobby, don't do it!"

Getts rose slowly from his spider hole ten meters away, his Star .45 in hand. He cautiously approached the edge of the tiger trap.

"I don't want to burn, Bobby. You can't do this," Grumpy pleaded.

Getts raised the .45. He fired one shot through Grumpy's right eye. He was dead before the incendiary bullet ignited the napalm into a giant ball of flame.

Chapter Eighteen

There was a message on his answering machine in Lake Oswego. There were very few people who knew that number; the IG, Commander Fortier, and Getts's division commander. The message said that he was to immediately get in touch with the State Department, and speak with Secretary Frederick Hazeltine.

Getts made the required telephone call, then drove to the Portland airport, doing a lot of thinking on the way. Before Bosnia, he never had to actually think about stuff like the meaning of life and even what was right or wrong. By the time he got to the airport rental parking lot, he remembered something that his father once told him about figuring out what's right. "Just get rid of the stuff that doesn't matter," he said.

As Getts passed through the short ticket line at American Airlines, picking up a first-class ticket, some of the stuff that didn't matter began to appear obvious to him. What was left, of course, was the things that did.

He thought about the past forty-eight hours. Two of his closest friends on planet Earth were dead. And he had killed them both. An enormous sadness overwhelmed him. There were things left undone, words unsaid. Truman Lynch. A dangerous man. Complex. For a while he was the perfect Mob 4 man, the best kind of SEAL. Then something went wrong. Maybe, Getts thought, he would look up Barbara, Truman's girl. Maybe he could explain to her what he couldn't understand himself. Tragically, Doc had just been thrown into the mix. At the wrong place at the wrong time. And how about Peach? Well, Getts swore to himself, he was not going to lose his last remaining friend.

His plane landed at Washington National at about 1330 hours, and from there he took a cab to the downtown Hilton. He called the number he had been given and was answered by a cultivated male voice. He had reached, the voice said, the office of the Secretary of State.

"Ah, yes, Lieutenant Getts," the voice said. "Secretary Hazeltine wants to see you immediately. Where are you now?"

"I'm, uh, at the Hilton Hotel downtown." Getts gave him the room number and the location of the hotel.

"Yes, we know where it is, Lieutenant. We'll send a car for you right away."

"Thank you," he said.

"Lieutenant . . ."

"Yes?"

"Are you wearing a uniform?"

"No."

"Good. Just come as you are. We're very relaxed, here."

Getts never took a uniform when he was on leave, but the bit about being relaxed at the State Department didn't sound right to him. He had seen Frederick Hazeltine give news interviews, and Getts thought he might have heard a speech or two that he gave to the UN, and Hazeltine always reminded him of a tense man who tried to look like he wasn't on edge.

Getts wore civilian khaki pants, loafers, a dress shirt, and a summer-weight blue blazer. After debating with himself for a few moments, he went to the lobby, where there were a number of shops, one of them a men's clothing store. He picked out a conservative blue-and-gold-stripe tie, paid the salesman a monstrous $90 for the thing, and put it on. Well, it was silk.

By the time he had arrived back on the sixth floor, there were two men standing in front of his door. One was a handsome African-American, the other a nondescript white guy. They were in their mid thirties, larger than average size, and wore summer-weight suits that were cut to hide the bulges around their waistlines and underneath their arms. Secret Service. Getts would have been surprised if they didn't have commo radio earpieces in their pockets. Their faces told him that they didn't like knocking on doors of empty rooms.

"I'm Robert Getts," he said.

"We know that, Lieutenant," the white guy replied. "Come with us, please." Getts immediately didn't like their condescending attitudes, unspoken or otherwise. They placed him between them as they walked down the hall and into the elevator, so that he felt as though he were being arrested rather than escorted. Well, maybe he was, he thought.

The ride downtown was not a long one. The white guy drove the car while the African-American sat on the passenger side and looked out of the window as though he had more important things to do than haul a sorry swabbie around town. They drove to the rear of the building, down into an underground parking area, and through a gate that said *RESTRICTED ACCESS*.

The car was parked in a place designated *Security*. They took an elevator from the basement up to what Getts thought must be the top floor of the building. Still flanked on both sides by the Secret Service men, Getts was walked briskly down a thickly carpeted hallway and turned into an outer office with another heavy carpet, this time with the State Department seal woven into it. The Secret Service men nodded to a woman sitting at a reception desk as they cruised by, then stopped in yet another office, where there were a couple of flags, a bigger desk, and a man sitting patiently behind it. There were two open office doors flanking him, revealing rooms belonging to the State Department secretariat. One of the Secret Service men spoke quietly to the man at the desk, who picked up a telephone at once, spoke into it, then replaced it immediately.

"Welcome, Lieutenant Getts. The secretary is waiting for you." As the Secret Service men took seats in the reception area, the desk man, who wore glasses, a well-cut conserva-

tive suit, and a pale gray tie, led the way into the office of
the Secretary of State.

Getts was not sure what he expected to see. He supposed
that one could say the secretary's office was lavish. Hazeltine, it seemed to him, didn't go out of his way to squan-
der more taxpayers' dollars than were necessary to make
his stay there comfortable. Windows were bordered in
heavy royal blue and gold tapestries. The walls were hung
with patriotic paintings and photographs, past presidents
like Washington and Lincoln, a Civil War oil, and a series
of charming watercolors that appeared to be contemporary
New England. There was a bust of John Foster Dulles
topped off by a shark-tooth wool hat, a gesture Getts
thought the secretary had fun with.

Hazeltine stood up from behind his desk as Getts entered
the room, his hand extended, his male secretary making
the introduction before standing off to one side for further
directions. "Something to drink, Lieutenant? Coffee? How
about something more interesting? I'm sure the sun is down
behind a yardarm somewhere in the American Navy, eh?"
The secretary turned to his man. "We'll get by here,
Charles. Hold my calls." Charles left and closed the door.

"I know you turned me down once. . . . What do they
call you? Bobby? Bob? Do you mind if I call you that?"

"No, sir. Not at all."

"I notice you're limping. Hurt your leg?" the secretary
said.

"Twisted my ankle, sir," Getts said.

"Isn't that ironic? One of America's warriors comes back
from a dangerous mission and gets crippled playing
pickup basketball."

"Hiking. In the woods, sir."

"Whatever. I know you turned down a drink but I'm still
going to have one. Please reconsider. I've got a pretty
decent single malt Scotch," he said.

"All right, sir. I'll have scotch and coke," Getts said.

"Well, good. Good. Sit right there," he said, indicating
an overstuffed sofa in the middle of the room. "Put your
foot up on the coffee table." Two massive chairs stood

sentry on either side of the sofa, both looking comfortable enough to sleep in. To Getts Secretary Hazeltine looked like a man who had to work at being relaxed. He turned away from a hidden bar with a drink in each hand and handed one to Getts. "Here's to the men of the Navy, God bless 'em." They raised their glasses and drank.

"Bob," he said, sitting on the other end of the sofa, an arm draped over its back, placing his drink carefully onto the coffee table, "tell me something about yourself. Where are you from?"

"Portland, Oregon, sir," I said.

"You were raised there? Went to school there?"

"Yes, sir."

"Ever know a couple by the name of Glen and Gloria Holden? They lived in Lake Oswego," the secretary said.

"Yes, sir. I can't say that I knew them very well but my father knew Mr. Holden." It was obvious to Getts that the secretary knew very well where he was from, and that his family knew the Holdens, and that he wanted Getts to understand that he knew everything else about him, too.

"Glen and Gloria are good friends. They support the party in a very big way. Let's see. You went to Stanford, as I recall."

"Yes, sir. Psychology was my major."

"I went to Yale. Class of '76. Plus Harvard Economics," he chuckled, as though he were holding four aces while everybody else at the table had a pair. Well, Getts never understood economics and he doubted if Hazeltine did, either. "Bob, I gotta tell you that the country has enough psychologists. But it doesn't have enough admirals." He raised his glass to his lips. Getts didn't raise his. "Did you know that the President holds the SEALs in the highest possible esteem?"

"No, sir, I didn't know that."

"Well, he does. Probably because he couldn't make the water polo team in college," the secretary laughed. "No, hell, I mean it. It probably gave him an insight as to what it took to be one of you guys, someone that can swim all day and climb out of the water and still kick ass. I'm not

choosing sides in an argument, but I want you to know that
there's one hell of a lot of admiration on Capitol Hill for
what you guys are doing out in the field."

"Thank you, Mr. Secretary."

"Let me freshen that drink." Ice cubes clinked, whiskey
was poured. "How do you like this stuff? I'm not big on
hard liquor, myself, but I have to admit the Scots got it
right. The British prime minister sent over six cases. Thirty
years old, they tell me."

"It's very good, Mr. Secretary."

The secretary loosened his tie and put his head back as
though he were giving something a lot of thought. "Bobby,
I don't want you to worry about this pending court-martial.
President Spalding knows that you and your team were
doing your best, carrying out orders as you understood
them. Nobody, but *nobody,* is holding you at fault. There
doesn't have to be a court-martial at all."

"You're dismissing the charges, sir?" Getts said.

"Well, we've kept you out of these damned Senate hearings that are happening now. So far, anyway. In the interest
of impartial justice. That's what we're after, Bob. Justice."

"How about the charges against my men, sir? Will you
get rid of those?"

The Secretary nodded emphatically. "We can do it like
that." He snapped his fingers in the air. "We just have to
all get on board."

"On board, sir?"

"Yes. On the same page. Bobby," he said, his voice low-
ering conspiratorially. "One of our people gave the order
to kill Krabac. It came out of the National Security Council.
We're not avoiding our responsibility in this business. Hell,
I'll even tell you who it was. An advisor, Roger Demerit.
We found the order and his signature on it. But what good
would it do his family and this government if that became
public? You agree?"

Funny. Ten minutes ago Getts would have agreed, despite the deaths of Lydia and Doc and Grumpy. It had
gone far enough, hadn't it? Getts would have thrown his
arms around Hazeltine and kissed his big fat cheeks. But

instead, he heard himself say, "I'd be a hyena's ass if I believed for one minute that a lowly advisor set this chain of events in motion, and that he conveniently died to spare somebody else the embarrassment. It was an unlawful order, sir, coming from high up in the White House. Assassination isn't part of the Constitution of the United States; it's not the business we're supposed to be in." Getts found that despite all the shit that had happened, he hadn't loosened up at all. He was still hard ass to the core.

The secretary inhaled deeply, leaning back a few inches as he regarded Getts. His words, this time, were slowly spoken, chosen with great care. "It was a mistake. A mistaken order. Ever make a mistake, Bobby?"

"Yes, sir."

"Damn right you have. If you take up space on this goddamn planet, you've made mistakes. Point is not to repeat them. We're trying to get you and your men out of the fryer, Bobby, and to do that we've got to be together. You know all about teamwork. I don't have to tell you about being on the right side, hanging in there together. Now, it's real easy. You go back to square one and fill out a training report, describing the mission you and your men did back in March. I guarantee that your corrected statement will be accepted by the secretary of the Navy without question and that your original statement, the AAR, will be lost. It never existed."

"Is that all there is to it, sir?" Getts said.

The secretary waved his hand in the air, dismissing all problems, healing all ills. "Gone. Just like that. Okay? We got a deal, sailor?" The secretary leaned forward and slapped him collegially on the shoulder.

"I was thinking all of yesterday and this morning, Mr. Secretary, that the stupidest thing I ever did in my life was fill out the AAR the way I did."

"Well, don't be too hard on yourself."

Because it cost the life of two of my closest buddies. And a woman I loved. Beautiful, innocent. All I had to do was lie and Doc and Grumpy and Lydia Brooks would be drinking beer right now in Florida. Not only did I fuck up and fail to lie, but I had a lot of chances to see the wisdom in lying, and I blew it every time. So now they're gone. Forever. And Peach is going to take the rap.

That's what Getts was thinking.

What he said was: "Some good men died or are in danger of doing jail time because you fat, diseased bunch of cocksuckers don't know who to back in a one-horse race."

"What? What did you say?" The secretary's jaw sagged.

"Did that pussy in the White House think this one up or did you? Do you really believe you can unzip your fly, pull your dick out, and piss on the United States Navy?"

"You insubordinate son of a bitch!" the secretary screamed. "Get out of here! Get out! I'll have you . . ."

"You'll have me what? Court-martialed?"

As Getts was walking toward the door, it opened. Charles appeared, almost on the run, and right behind him were Getts's two escorts from the hotel. Getts turned back around to the secretary. "Don't ask these guys to step in unless you want them to go to the fucking graveyard."

Then he left.

Getts wasn't going to sit on his ass and wait for a court-martial to happen. He had an idea about how to avoid it altogether, but he desperately needed Peach to help. Getts went back to the Hilton to retrieve his .45 and the shotgun out of his luggage, and checked out. He half expected to run into Hazeltine's bodyguards but, to his pleasant surprise, they were nowhere to be seen. He caught a taxi out front and had the driver take him to the train station. A commuter was the quickest way back to the Creek.

The first thing he did when he got back on the base was to call the CPO bachelor quarters and ask for Peach. He was told that Peach was locked up in the base brig on a number of charges, all stemming from a brawl with base security personnel. Getts couldn't think of any strings he could pull, or he would have pulled them a long time ago. But he found out that Lieutenant Commander Avery Bledsoe ran security. Getts went to see him.

When Getts was shown into his office, Bledsoe remained

seated behind his desk, letting the SEAL know that he regarded this visit with suspicion. "I'm Peach's commanding officer," Getts said, after introducing himself.

"Have a chair," Bledsoe said, nodding toward a gray metal chair in front and slightly to one side of his desk. "So, what do you want?" he said.

"I'd like to have Peach released to my custody, sir," Getts said.

"Sorry."

"It's important," Getts said.

"I'll bet it is."

"It's very important, sir, or I wouldn't bother you."

Bledsoe leaned back in his chair and crossed his arms— not a good sign. "I'm not even sure I should be talking to you. I understand there's a Senate hearing in progress about political assassination. I assume you've been subpoenaed."

"No, sir. I have not."

"Well, I can't let you have him, but just out of curiosity, aren't you the officer who is going to testify against him and two other men at his court martial?"

"I won't testify if I can help it. That's why I want to get him out. Peach may be able to help me obtain evidence that will exonerate him of all charges," Getts said.

"What kind of evidence?" Bledsoe said. He uncrossed his arms, leaning forward.

"With great respect, Commander Bledsoe, I can't reveal the nature of that evidence yet." Actually, Getts would have revealed it in a heartbeat if he had known what the hell it was. "I will give you my word, as a Navy officer, that Peach will return to this base within seventy-two hours to face whatever disciplinary charges are filed against him."

Bledsoe regarded Getts for a long moment, then said, "Lieutenant, how much of a chance do you really think you have of coming up with the evidence you're talking about?"

"Some people would look you straight in the eye, Commander, and tell you any line of bullshit that would move their interest forward."

"Are you one of those people, Lieutenant Getts?"

"Yes, sir, I am."

"Desperate men sometimes fall back on the truth, huh?" Bledsoe said.

"That's what I'm reduced to, yes sir."

"Well, this might be your lucky day. Regulations allow me to release a prisoner into the custody of an officer. It's kind of a stretch in your case since I understand you're not being prosecuted only because of a technicality, but I'm prepared to overlook that. Secondly, this case you're about to get burned for is big. Important. National TV and newspapers. If you were to come up with evidence that could spring you guys, I would appreciate some kind of a statement from you to the effect that I encouraged you to go look for it. Maybe even that it was my idea. Something that I could put into my 201 file that would make me look good. Understand?"

"Yes, sir. Exactly, sir," Getts said.

"Okay. Now, the charges to be filed against Chief Crosley . . . Is that his real name?"

"No, sir."

"Hmm. The charges could be pretty serious. He whipped up some hard ass a couple days ago, and I have a gyrene gunny sergeant still lying in the hospital who can't remember the name of his mama, thanks to your boy. Personally, it was about time somebody kicked his honkey ass because he was King Kong on this base for too long. But that's neither here nor there. What's important is I'm the man who files or don't file the charges against your man. Peach, they call him?"

"Yes, sir."

"Yeah. Well, it's gonna take two, three days to fully investigate the scope of these charges and, uh, I'm a pretty complete guy about paperwork. May seem like red-ass-tape to you combat types, but I represent law and order here and I'm not about to have a man railroaded. So Peach, there, is completely useless to me for a few days. Let's say seventy-two hours. That give you enough time?"

"I believe it will, sir," Getts said.

"All right, you can have him."

Getts stood up and saluted Commander Bledsoe. "Thank you, sir. It's a privilege to know you."

"You call me up if you run into trouble. I'll give you more time." He flashed a huge grin as Getts left his office.

Chapter Nineteen

Peach was told that Lieutenant Robert Getts was coming to see him. They could meet in a private room, the one where lawyers can get together with the clients they're representing. Peach had a couple of sharp emotions when he heard it. Not because they were meeting in a private room but because Getts was still alive. Funny, Peach could have kept in touch with Grumpy and Doc while they were out on the coast but he refused to. He had no idea what happened. It was a sunny, honest to God spring afternoon in Virginia, but Peach was shivering anyway. He wasn't in "population" with most of the other guys in the brig because he hadn't been charged with a crime—yet. Time behind bars was stretched out, made even more claustrophobic when he thought about doing a long slide. God, ten years. Twenty. Thirty. His mind couldn't come to grips with it and he had only been there four days. He could almost understand why Grumpy and Doc had to go after Getts.

Peach was ten minutes early for their 1730 appointment. He didn't know why. Maybe his curiosity was killing him. Did he want to see Bobby? Yeah. He had some things he needed to say. He realized that he must have subconsciously picked the fight with the jarhead because, somewhere, he knew it would put him where he wanted to be: in the penalty box, out of the action. Now it felt like there was battery acid sloshing inside his gut. He paced around the green room, maybe 150 square feet, with a table bolted to the middle of the floor and three metal government issue chairs around it. No windows, one door. Nothing else. He heard booted footsteps in the hall that abruptly stopped by the door.

The knob turned, and when the door opened, there was Bobby, in his summer khaki uniform, decorations over one pocket, along with his jump wings, SAS pin, Budweiser, and collar bars. Man, he was still one squared-away son of a bitch. Peach got a kind of glitch in his throat and for just a second, he wanted to put his arms around Getts. But he didn't. He didn't offer his hand, either. Neither did Getts, who just turned toward the guard and nodded his head. The guard backed out of the doorway and closed the door. It looked to Peach like Bobby was favoring one leg a bit.

"Peach," Getts said in way of a greeting.

"Bobby."

"I hear you fell in love with a jarhead and he didn't love you back," he said.

"He never gave me a chance to show him what I can do in bed," Peach replied.

"They don't know you like I do," Getts said.

"Speaking of you, you're moving a little gingerly, looks like."

Getts shrugged and tossed his head, but his eyes never left Peach's. "Caught a knife blade in the calf. Could have been a lot worse."

Peach didn't ask him who'd wielded that knife. "How's Buzzy?"

"She's okay. She's in Europe." Bobby's eyes fell to his hands, then back toward Peach. They both knew they were stalling the inevitable with idle chitchat. "She's about as good as she could be with a son that makes life hell for her."

It looked to Peach like Bobby had aged. Maybe Peach just saw lines in his face he had never seen before. His eyes didn't smile like they used to. Well, he didn't suppose his did, either, as far as that goes. He was going to lose his Navy career over his ego, not even over principle. He had always taken it for granted, being able to hold his head up, walk tall. Some people could live without that kind of self-worth, but damned if Peach could think about doing it himself.

Bobby's career was over, too, and he knew it. There was all that bullshit about doing the right thing, bringing honor to the officer corps and that kind of jazz, but Getts kept insisting he'd been co-responsible for an unauthorized killing. His promotions, if he was able to remain in the Navy, would be very few and very far between. He didn't deserve it, by God. He was more than just a good man, he was too goddamn good for the Navy—in Peach's view, anyway.

"She asked about you," Getts said. "She was afraid to, really, but she read about us in the papers."

"Appreciate that. She still own that Alfa Romeo?" Peach said.

Getts nodded his head. "She drives a Jaguar now, but she still has the Alfa. I don't think she'll ever sell it."

"Rained while you were there?"

"Nope. Sunshine every day."

They couldn't look at each other for a couple minutes. Then finally Getts said, "You want anything? Coffee? Something to eat? They'll bring it if I ask them to."

Peach shook his head.

"Well, Peach," Getts said. Peach did not want to hear what was coming, but he was unable to block it out. "I saw Grumpy and Doc."

Peach cleared his throat.

"Doc's dead," Getts continued, almost whispering. "So is Grumpy."

So there it was.

Oh, God. Little Doc. Peach tried to say something, but his throat closed up on him and he had trouble breathing. He stood up and walked away from the table. Seeing as there was nowhere to go, he just leaned up against the wall. Doc's mother and his father would never see him again. The team would never hear his giggle, the one that always got them laughing. He wouldn't take care of them again, he wouldn't see to it that Peach sobered up with coffee, that they always drank plenty of water. . . . Bad as Peach was feeling, he knew it would get worse later. He guessed that he had been expecting something like this in one part of his brain, but in his heart he couldn't believe it would actually happen. "Grumpy?" he asked.

"Grumpy had his chance. I let him go but he kept after me," Getts said.

"Well. He was . . . off-center, I guess. Never figured him out."

"He was going to jail," Getts said. "A least that's what I told him. Did you know he collected money for the job?" Getts said.

Peach nodded. "Yeah. He was going to split it with us."

Getts looked up sharply. "That right? I thought he lied about that, too."

"No, it wasn't a lie. He said it was authorized so we bought into that, too. Oh, well. . . ." Peach didn't bother to ask him how Doc and Grumpy died. He didn't want to know.

All Peach knew was that he was glad Bobby was standing here alive. Peach knew that if Bobby had been killed by Doc and Truman, it would have killed his soul. Because Peach was the only one who could have stopped it. He had to admit that he had hated Getts for turning on them. Peach allowed that hate to infect the other two, and he let them go through with their plans. Peach thought now that it was he who should have died, not Doc or Grumpy, for being stupid and headstrong.

". . . just wish I could do it all over," Bobby was saying.

"What?"

"I think I knew it from the beginning but I was all messed up here," he said, pointing to his head. "But I've thought about it a lot since. . . . A lot? Hell, I haven't thought about anything else."

"Thought what?"

"That I should have lied. It wasn't worth their lives. Nobody is ever going to forgive me for that, least of all myself. I'm an agnostic, but if I believed in God, I know He wouldn't forgive me for killing my friends. It's unforgivable. Lying is forgivable. I was such a stuffy, snot-nosed little shit, too obsessed with the set of bars on his collar, that I ruined the lives of everybody around me. My loyalty was fucking in the wrong place at the wrong time. The bureaucrats aren't worth it. My men were."

Peach opened his mouth to speak but words wouldn't come.

"Lydia's dead, Peach."

"Jesus Christ."

"We both fucked up, Major." Getts told Peach the story of how he had retreated to his family's summer home, how Lydia had joined him there, how Doc and Grumpy had tapped her phone and followed her. He told Peach about the fight underwater, the explosion that destroyed the Gunnerson and killed Lydia, how he had stabbed Doc and, finally, about Grumpy.

"Maybe I'll have that coffee, after all," Peach said when Getts was through. Getts nodded and went to the door.

"Hey, Corporal," he called to the guard. "Can we get a couple of coffees in here?"

"Yes, sir."

"What exactly did Grumpy say John Barry told him down in Florida?" Getts asked, returning to the room.

"That they wanted Krabac dead, not brought back to Naples. Or anyplace else."

"Can you be more specific? Did John Barry give him his real name? Or who the order came down from?" Getts said.

"Hey, the man wasn't talking to me. You were the one who checked out his authenticity. Colonel Talent verified, you said."

The corporal was back in minutes. He carried a thermos server and two porcelain cups into the room, which he set on the table. "With Commander Bledsoe's compliments, sir. He said this is his own special brew."

"Thanks, Corporal," Bobby said. Peach poured the coffee and added real cream to his cup. As they both sipped at the brew, they realized at the same instant that the coffee had plenty of Irish whiskey in it. It was the best thing Peach had tasted in weeks. It felt like relief to laugh at something again.

"I'm sorry, Getts," he said.

"I'm the one, Peach, who should say the mea culpas."

"The what?"

"Sorry."

They drained their coffees and poured a couple more.

"They set a date for the court-martial yet?" Getts asked.

"No. JAG says they're still working on it but it shouldn't be much longer, now. In a week, maybe two, they'll have the date set. Meantime, they gave me a lawyer. His name is Mark Gentile. I only talked with him once. Seems sharper than shit but I didn't have anything to tell him. Too much going on." Peach really had figured that by this time, the witness against him and the others involved would all be dead. And Bobby knew it.

"I'm not going to testify. They'll have to let you off," he said.

"Then it's gonna be you sitting on the hot seat. Krabac is dead. There's no way to bring that motherfucker back to life and start over."

"You know who Frederick Hazeltine is? Secretary of State?" Bobby said.

"Sure. I know who he is."

"He said that if I'd forget about the operation, if I'd say we were on a training mission, they'd get the case dismissed," Getts said. "They say they've got a written order from a National Security advisor named William Demerit. Who also happens to be dead now."

"So. How do you feel about that?"

Getts took a deep breath. "Well, I don't believe for a second that Demerit would have been responsible, or that he was the one who met us on the boat calling himself Barry. If the secretary wants me to lie, then he must be covering somebody's ass."

"Whose? His own?" Peach said.

"Maybe. Maybe the President's."

"I don't see slippery el Numero Uno stepping up to take the heat on this one," Peach said.

"Whoever it is, he's a big wheel. Maybe this asshole Hazeltine. Maybe even higher. If we can prove that, I can't see them court-martialing you. Or me."

"Think you and I can assault the fucking White House?"

"We might be able to find this guy, John Barry. Then we make him talk to the newspapers."

"My lawyer said he tried it. There is no John Barry, as I think you know," Peach said. But he did like the idea of going into action again.

"Peach, let's find this jerk-off and make him talk. We can't lose anything. If it doesn't work, I'll stand up in front of the world and say I wasn't taking my medication and I invented the whole thing."

"Can you get me out of here?" Peach said.

"For seventy-two hours."

Ten hours later, Getts and Peach were in Miami. Peach was thinking that the local Holiday Inn was just fine by him, but Getts was putting the trip on his plastic, so they headed straight for the Chalet Caribbean, a posh five-star hotel on Bayshore Drive in Miami. Oil paintings in the hallways. Not lithos, but the real deal. Peach didn't ask how much the room was, but he could tell it was a pretty penny, what with the sunken living room, full bar, gauze-like sheer curtains, overstuffed furniture, and two large beds. Peach knocked off a Jim Beam and coke before bed, and they crashed by 0315 hours.

They were up and eating by 0730, feeling ballsy. The air in Florida felt good to Peach, rejuvenating even though the humidity made it seem like you were breathing in water instead of oxygen. But there were palm trees, and no bars on the windows. He was damn glad to be there. They called the Biscayne Yacht Club from the room, but at 0800 hours, either the right people weren't up yet or nobody wanted to talk. They called back at 0900 and did a little better. First, Getts called the dockmaster and asked the girl who answered the phone if they had a Morgan 42 by the name of *Raffish* registered in the harbor. Indeed they did, she said. It was still in C basin, slip 12. The owner?

"Uh, at the owner's request that information can be obtained from Biscayne Yacht Sales. They're listing the boat for sale," the lady said, and gave Getts the phone number.

It's often hard to get personal information over a telephone, which is why the two men went down to the marina and walked right into Biscayne Yacht Sales. The place was a prefabricated wood frame set on mason blocks. On the outside, near the door, were three small wooden plaques with a name on each one. Colin Wycoff, Broker; Liz Benitez, Allen Pratt, Sales. The walls inside looked like white pine, and the place was chock full of maritime kitsch like brass running lights, a brass repeater compass, hanging fish nets, a few stuffed fish, a ship's compass screwed to the wooden plank floor, and paintings of racing sloops, one of a square-rigger entering the port of Boston under full sail. There was also a wall full of photographs of boats currently for sale. There were four desks in the place, which, despite the fact that their clientele was probably loaded, still made the place feel just like a used car sales office.

"Hi. Can I help you?" a man with sun-bleached hair and a heavy coffee mug called out to them from his nearly private office in the rear of the room. He was slender, wore a polo shirt and khaki pants and, of course, deck shoes. He seemed to be somewhere in his middle forties and would have once been called handsome, but his nose was swollen and red from booze and God knows what other things.

"Mr. Wycoff?" Getts said. "We're not customers. We're looking for a man who is a friend of a buddy of ours, John Barry."

The yacht broker gave away nothing that would indicate that he knew who John Barry was. No surprise there. "John Barry?" he said. "I don't think I know him."

"Well, he doesn't live in Miami, but his friend, the man we're looking for, does. He owns a Morgan here in the yacht club," Getts said.

"Ah. What's his name?"

"We don't know. It's embarrassing. We had his name written down in our address book, but we lost it back at our hotel. You know the way hotels are—lose something there and guaranteed, you're never going to see it again. The boat he owns is called the *Raffish*."

The smile on Wycoff's face froze like a dog's asshole in a Dakota winter. "We're the brokers for that boat. It's for sale."

"Yeah, we know that. It's why we're here," Getts said. "We're not looking to buy the boat. We're not trying to snoop around your sales office; we just want to know the man's name who owns it."

Wycoff was shaking his head before Getts was into the third word. "That's confidential information. We don't give out the names of our clients. So if that's all . . ."

Peach stepped around the broker and walked right into his office.

"Hey! That's my office. Out!" Wycoff said.

Peach ignored him and started going through the papers on his desk. He picked up a city telephone book and flung it out of his way, then flipped through Wycoff's rolodex, before opening the middle drawer of his desk.

"Do you understand English, you asshole?" Wycoff said, his whiskey baritone voice rising at least an octave while Peach continued to rustle through papers and pads. Then he found what he was looking for—a master listing of boats for sale. It was a book filled with five-by-seven cards, with a snapshot picture of a boat on each one, along with a written description. Printed at the bottom was the name of the seller, a telephone number, and an address.

The broker made a lunge for the book but Peach moved it out of his way easily. Wycoff then raised his arm and, with coffee already spilling over his shirt, tried to bring the damn cup down on top of Peach's head. Bad move. But before Peach could step forward and wreak some serious havoc on the guy, Getts reached over the man's shoulder and twisted the cup out of his fist, taking care not to dislocate a finger in the process. After that, it didn't take but a minute of flipping through the pages of the book to spot the Morgan. Rather than copy everything down, Peach just pulled the card out of the plastic holder and put it into his pocket. "All set, Bobby," he said.

"You bastards! The police will be on your ass in . . . in . . . no time," he said. Peach just looked at the man, wondering if his own nose would end up looking that way.

"Thanks for your help," Getts said, dropping a $20 bill on the man's desk. Wycoff was frantically dialing the phone as the SEALs walked out the door. As they started the engine on their rental car, Getts looked back at the sales office and saw Wycoff looking wildly out of the window. Getts would have bet he was trying to give the cops their license number. Well, it wouldn't matter. They'd switch them in the hotel parking lot before they left.

The boat belonged to an Arturo Rodriguez. His address was on Buttonwood Street on Key Biscayne. They turned north and got on Highway 1, getting off at the Ricken-backer Causeway. They drove over the ocean for a few miles, and crossed Virginia Key at its southern tip. The road went past Northwest Point, then turned south to the town of Key Biscayne. Though there were public beaches, the town of Key Biscayne was definitely priced out of range of United States Navy personnel. Getts asked directions for Buttonwood at the local Chamber of Commerce, and they arrived there ten minutes later.

Nice street. Nice view of the ocean. And Miami. It must be even more spectacular at night. Mr. Rodriguez's home was laid out on at least four acres of grass and palm trees, encircled by a wall around its perimeter. The wrought iron gate out front was open, so the SEALs helped themselves to the use of the driveway and pulled up in front of the casa. The house was done in what you could call Moroccan architecture—red tile roof, plaster walls, steel sash windows with decorative metalwork on the outside. The thick front door looked like it could stave off Alexander's armies. They rang the doorbell and, just in case, used the heavy iron knocker that hung from the door.

A maid answered. She was young, overweight, and had a pleasant face. She didn't speak much English, so Getts talked to her in Spanish.

"Señor Rodriguez. *Es él casa, por favor*?" he said.

"*Sí, pero él está ocupado. Está esperandolo él?*"

"No, pero nosotros estamos aquí en negocio muy importante. Por favor dígale," Getts said.

"Sus nombres?"

"Robert Getts *y* Glenn Crosley," he said.

"Espera, por favor," she said, and walked off.

The vestibule, as Peach assumed it was called, had a love seat where people could wait for the master of the house. The place was as ornate on the inside as it was on the outside. Lots of art hung on the walls, and the patterned, off-white tile floors were polished so brightly that you could go blind without sunglasses. Lavish draperies of wine, red, and gold cascaded everywhere. "Could we have a unit party here or what, partner?" Peach said to Getts. He looked at his CPO, then looked away. Yeah, he was probably thinking, if we had a team to share it with. Peach bit his tongue as soon as the words left his mouth.

They waited for what seemed like an hour before Rodriguez showed up. He came walking around a corner of the house which, from where the SEALs stood, looked like a library. The man was about five feet, nine inches tall, with shoulders like a Dolphins running back, dressed in Nike sport clothes. He was carrying a Remington 7188 12-gauge, automatic, 8-round shotgun.

Oh, yes, they recognized that little number just like you would recognize an Australian seagoing crocodile if you'd met one once. The 7188, on selective autofire, would empty an 8-round magazine in about two point four seconds. And they knew it would blow the shit out of every living thing inside a radius of thirty yards before you could smile. Peach and Getts were only about ten feet away.

He pointed the shotgun at them and held it with a steady hand. Looking at the man's dark, almost black eyes that never seemed to blink, coupled with the mustache under his nose, Peach thought he looked like a pirate that might have been working these very waters three hundred years ago. "Who the fuck are you?" he said in English with an accent they took to be Cuban. Obviously the man had received a telephone call from his friendly yacht broker, Wycoff.

"Ah, my name is Getts. Bob Getts. This is Glenn Crosley," Getts said. "We apologize for interrupting your day."

Good work, Bobby. Maybe he wouldn't shoot right away, Peach thought.

"I don't know you. I don't *want* to know you. Understand? You the assholes screwing around with my boat salesman?" he said.

"It was the only way we could get your address," Getts said.

"Hey, if I want you to have my address, I send it to you," Rodriguez said. Getts doubted his sincerity. "Now get the hell out of here." He motioned toward the door with the barrel of the Remington.

Peach was ready to go. The man had made his feelings clear. But Getts didn't move. "Señor Rodriguez, you are perfectly right to be angry. My partner and I would not have stolen your address if it were possible for two United States Navy men to do it any other way."

Rodriguez blinked. The working end of the Remington moved downward just slightly as his eyes narrowed. "Who? You are Navy men?"

"Yes, sir," Getts said. "Lieutenant Robert Getts and Chief Petty Officer Glenn Crosley." For a second, Peach thought Getts was going to snap his heels together and salute.

"Show me some ID," Rodriguez said.

The two SEALs reached into their wallets and produced DD cards, each with a picture. They handed them to their "host." Rodriguez didn't just glance at them. He studied them hard, matched the pictures on the laminated cards with the faces in front of him, before he grunted and gave back the wallets. Slowly, he lowered the shotgun. "Well," he said, "I don't want to blow up a couple Navy guys. Jesus, you're welcome into my house, you know? But, man, the way you go about it . . ."

"I apologize again, Mr. Rodriguez, but we're SEALs. I guess it's our training that makes us kind of desperate when we have a problem to deal with."

At the sound of the word "SEALs" Rodriguez's eye-

brows went straight up to the top of his head. Getts had
figured exactly right. Rodriguez, like most expatriate Cubans, was politically to the right of Pat Buchanan and
would happily make sacrifices for the American military,
even though it had let him down in the past.

"SEALs?" Then his voice lowered slightly. "Call me Arturo. You want me? What for? I'm a businessman. You
sure you got the right guy?"

"Just some help, Arturo. Last March you loaned your
boat to a man called John Barry."

Rodriguez was already shaking his head. "No. Wrong
dude. I don't loan out my boat. Never did," he said.

"Not to sail," Getts said, "to meet on. Peach, here, and
I had a meeting with John Barry on your boat. For maybe
a couple of hours. Remember that?"

But Rodriguez was positive. "Nope. Not even for a cup
of coffee. Hey, I want to help you boys out. We got to hang
together, us Cubans and the United States government. I'm
a citizen, you know. Came here when I was seven years
old. Only spoke Spanish, but I made a pretty good living.
You can see, eh? So I owe this country a lot. I would give
my blood for it. But I did not lend no boat to nobody like
you're saying. I would remember."

It probably hit Peach the same time it did Getts. The
broker. He was the guy who loaned the *Raffish* out for a
meeting. The owner never had to know. It could have been
any boat in the marina.

"Ah. I see," Getts said. He stuck out his hand and Rodriguez took it. Peach, too. "I understand now," Getts said.
"We are very grateful to you for helping us with our problem, Arturo. We'll go now."

"But I want to apologize for greeting you with a gun.
Around here," he waved his hand, "we worry about all
kinds of people. Drug runners, you know. They're everywhere. You have to protect yourself. Hey, stay for lunch.
Do you like Cuban food? Maria makes incredible lime
chicken."

"Thank you, no, Arturo. We're in a big hurry, but if you
don't mind, you could make a phone call for us."

Peach thought about the lime chicken as they were driving away from the house. He was thinking that another hour or two off schedule wouldn't have hurt—he was hungry as hell.

They retraced their tracks to Biscayne Yacht Sales. Peach was pretty sure their pal Colin Wycoff would not be so glad to see them again. To their surprise, he was still there when they walked in, sitting in his small, glassed-in room at the rear of the sales office.

Wycoff didn't have a great big smile on his face when they lowered themselves into a couple chairs in his glass cubicle. He suggested they close the door. "Arturo called a few minutes ago. If you had told me who you were the first time around, we wouldn't have had a problem. I don't go for strong-arm stuff," he said, nervously swiveling in his chair.

"Sorry about that," Getts said.

"Yeah," Peach said. "I'm sorry, too, but we're trying to save a terrific young man from spending the rest of his life in prison for a crime he didn't commit." Peach saw Getts roll his eyes.

"Ah," the broker said. "Well, then, that's different. I'm sorry, too."

"So, what we want to find out, really, is something about John Barry," Getts said.

"Arturo says you guys are Navy SEALs."

"Yes. We're trying to stay that way," Peach said.

"Newspapers have been full of Navy SEALs lately. For a month, now. That's you they're talking about, right?"

"Possibly. We haven't been reading newspapers very much."

"Who was that guy you knocked off in Bosnia?" he said.

Getts and Peach just sat and looked silently at Wycoff.

"Well," he said, flipping a hand in the air, "I guess that doesn't matter, does it? What do you want with John Barry?"

"We want to talk with him," Getts said.

The broker kind of screwed up his lips, like he was think-

ing, but he didn't respond. Peach hoped he wouldn't have
to break this fucking guy's arms, but if that's what it took
to make him talk, he was more than prepared to do it. The
broker must have read his mind because he all of a sudden
got cooperative. "Well," he said, "all I know is that he's a
lawyer. For the White House. I met him a couple of times
at fund-raisers. He rents some of our big yachts when elec-
tion time comes around. I don't know him real well."

"He works inside the White House?" Getts said.

"Yeah."

"And John Barry is his real name?"

"That's the one he gave me."

The SEALs thought about that for a minute, then Wycoff
said, "I saw him on television the other night."

"Where?"

"C-SPAN. He was sitting behind a witness table at a
Senate hearing. I was just surfing through the channels, you
know, and there he was."

"Yeah? Which committee?" Getts said.

He shrugged. "Never paid any attention. I punched in
another channel."

Chapter Twenty

The Senate Armed Forces Oversight Committee on Intelligence—an oxymoron if Getts had ever heard one—was in session in the Dirksen Office Building. There were a number of committee hearings going on that day, but Getts figured that John Barry, or whatever his name really was, was not connected with the Agricultural Department or the Education Committee. The military was his connection, and the Armed Forces Intelligence Oversight Committee was the only game in town that week. There was one other possibility. The House Subcommittee on Military Appropriations was in session on the other side of the capitol building, so while Getts did recon at the Oversight Committee, Peach took the Appropriations hearing. Getts approached the hearing room but was stopped by a Capitol Police officer. "Sorry," he said. "The chamber's full."

"I don't want to stay," Getts said. "Just take a look inside. See if someone I know is in there."

"You'll have to wait until the session's over," he said.

"Okay. You don't happen to know a man by the name of John Barry, do you? About five-seven or -eight, scraggly beard, glasses?" Getts said.

"Why?"

"We were in the Navy together. I'm trying to find him."

"Well, there's a lot of people in there, coming in and out all the time. I don't pay much attention unless I know them personally. But I don't know the guy you're talking about."

"Mind if I wait here?" Getts asked.

"Suit yourself. You've got about an hour until they're out."

Getts sat on a hard bench outside the hearing room. His leg still ached but it was getting better every day. At least the stitches were out. He watched people entering and leaving, each passing into the room after being checked off on the officer's list. Must have been classified material being discussed. "See your friend yet?" the officer asked after more than an hour.

"Not yet," Getts said.

"They're almost done in there for today, I'd guess. Sure you got the right room?"

"Not really."

"I don't have his name on my list," he said.

"He might not be on your list."

The two sets of doors opened from the inside, disgorging hundreds of people, most wearing conservative business suits. Getts stood, moving his eyes quickly trying to catch sight of anyone resembling Barry. After a few minutes, the stream of people watered down to a trickle.

"You can go in now, if you want," the policeman said.

"Thanks." Getts walked inside the room to find several dozen people, mostly men, standing around talking in small groups. Others were busy gathering up camera and audio equipment, and making last-minute notes at tables. He looked at all of them thoroughly. No John Barry. Even if he had shaved his beard, Getts thought he would have spotted him. It was a long shot, anyway. He walked slowly out of the room, back into the large hallway.

"This fella must be a close friend," the guard said.

"I owe him a lot," Getts said. "Okay if I come back tomorrow?"

"Sure. Maybe you can get your state senator to put you on the list to go inside," he said, tapping his clipboard.

"Are the hearings secret?" Getts said.

"Confidential," the guard said, nodding his head.

"See you tomorrow." Outside the office building, Getts dialed a discreet number on his cell phone.

"Yeah?" Peach said from the other end.

"Any luck?" he said.

"Nada."

"See you back at the hotel."

By the time Peach got back to the hotel room, Getts was partway down a bottle of scotch, working his way through the "Printers" section of the D.C. yellow pages. Getts figured John Barry had to have his business cards printed somewhere locally, and he had even called the White House printing office. They said they didn't have a record of cards printed for John Barry. So now he was working on commercial printers.

"Try the CIA. Or maybe the DCI, DOD, or DIA," Peach said.

"You think the spooks printed them for him?"

Peach shrugged. "Maybe. He was in the National Command Authority chain, wasn't he?"

Getts was tired of dialing numbers. He closed the phone book and hit the shower. What a waste of time.

"Back again, huh?" the capitol cop said, recognizing Getts the next morning.

"Any chance to get in today?"

"Could with a pass. Did you check with your senator?" he said.

"I couldn't get in to see him," Getts lied.

"Another way of saying they don't want to help you. Well, two hours until noon recess."

"I'll wait," Getts said.

At the noon recess two sets of doors were opened, and Getts missed screening at least half of the people in the hearing room. The lunch break lasted more than two hours. He ate a cold ham sandwich from a vendor and sat on the same hard bench he had occupied that morning. When the afternoon session got started, he got up and walked, trying to keep his circulation going, but never out of sight of the two doors leading into the chamber. He would rather have swum five miles, run ten, and hiked twenty than sit on that damn bench for another hour. He tried to think of something he or Peach could do that would be more efficient. But nothing came to mind. He tried to look inside the hearing room when people opened the door to come and go, but that proved to be an empty exercise. Couldn't see well enough for long enough.

That night, Getts finished all of the commercial printers in the yellow pages of the phone book. Half of them didn't answer because he had called too late, but he left messages for them to call him back if they found the account. None did.

The next day Getts was at the door of the chamber even before the guard. He waited until the guard unlocked the south end door, then the north end. The cop smiled. "Morning."

"Hello." Getts watched everyone who entered. No John Barry. It occurred to him that he could be on someone's staff, and entering the chambers through an inside door. The capitol cop affirmed that it was a possibility. Getts alternately sat and paced the hallway throughout the morning session. By the lunch recess he was seeing faces that looked familiar. But never the right one. The hearing convened again at 1400. He was thinking that there must be a better way to find John Barry when the cop spoke to him in a tone that was almost admiring. "Man, you must want to see your buddy in the worst way."

"Been thinking about him for a long time," Getts said.

"Well, damn, I wish I had someone like that for a friend," the cop said. "I had one, once. Ray Oakes," he said.

"Once?"

The cop nodded. "Got killed. Walking down the street in New York with a bust under his arm. Ray was a sculptor. Guy walked up to him and told him to hand over the bust. Ray wouldn't do it so the guy shot him dead. Right there in broad daylight. Fucking New York. My best friend. Wish he'd have given up the damn bust."

Getts knew how the guard felt.

As the cop turned and slowly walked away from Getts, somebody opened the door and came out. Before the door closed, on sheer impulse, Getts walked in.

He could immediately see from the rear of the room a panel of senators on a raised dais, with a nameplate and a microphone in front of each one, still-camera photographers crouched below. Facing them on the room's main floor was a large witness table. There were television cameras everywhere.

Seated at the witness table were two men, one a civilian, the other a Navy rear admiral. The admiral was familiar to Getts. A Midwestern senator with strawberry blond hair, Mitchell Hammerstead, was questioning the civilian witness. ". . . but we have it right here, Mr. Whirley. I don't know what could be plainer," he said.

"Senator," Whirley said, smooth as silk, "I can't be responsible for the private thoughts of every man in the Agency. You seem to—"

"When an Agency operations officer puts something on paper," Senator Hammerstead said, interrupting Whirley, "on Agency letterhead, that the execution of a head of state of a sovereign nation could be accomplished without implicating the United States, we're talking about something more than the musings of a citizen. We're not dealing with a wandering poet. Do you agree?"

"In the conduct of his job," Whirley said with a continued absence of emotion, "it is the prerogative of an operations officer to consider every possible alternate action pertinent to the task assigned to him. It's game planning. That's all. It doesn't mean we're going to do it."

The senator looked to the admiral sitting next to the civilian. "Do you agree with Mr. Whirley, here, Admiral? That you folks in the intelligence business just talk about assassinations, but you never pull them off?"

Getts recognized Admiral Sturgis. Before the man got into the Intel business, he was an amphibious officer Getts had met at a few parties Sturgis threw at the Creek. He was respected brass. "We're constantly examining options, Senator, but I agree with Mr. Whirley that we don't implement plans simply because we discuss them. Especially since the advent of executive orders to the contrary. The last one, as you know, was EO 12333 signed by President Reagan."

"How does one go about putting into action a political assassination, Mr. Whirley?" the senator asked.

"Well, I guess the best way would be to raise some money and do it on television, sir."

The hearing room erupted in laughter. Reporters made fast notes, and they were laughing, too. Getts was probably the only person in there who didn't think it was funny. "Assassination, at least in peacetime, Senator Hammerstead, have never progressed beyond theory far as I know, sir."

Getts looked very carefully around the room. He didn't see John Barry. "Senator Hammerstead," Senator Bales said to his colleague, "it's gettin' late in the day and if yo' have no objections I'd like to recess till Monday morning. Yo' would still have all yo' time remainin' to pursue your questionin' of this witness, plus the time I took from yo'."

"That's fine with me, Mr. Chairman," Hammerstead said. He took his glasses off and suddenly looked much younger. It made Getts wonder if maybe Barry could slip by him just by shaving off his beard and removing his glasses. He looked carefully around the place again.

"All right, then, this committee stands in recess till nine o'clock Monday mornin'."

Almost like a classroom full of students anxious to be anywhere else, the audience and staff began flooding for exits. Within minutes the room was all but emptied, a venturi effect created by the throng moving out all of the doors. Then, as a door behind the dais opened into the Senate cloakroom, Getts locked eyes with a man standing inside, not more than one hundred feet away. Then the door closed immediately.

Getts trotted toward the west side of the room, ran up three steps to an area where two senators and a few people he thought were staff members remained behind, talking. Before he could get through the cloakroom door, Getts felt a hand on his chest. "Sorry. No spectators back here, sir." It was another capitol cop.

"I saw a man back there I know," Getts said, feeling stupid. "I came a long way to see him."

"Sorry, sir. Nobody gets back there without authorization."

Getts knew he had seen Barry. He had looked right at the son of a bitch, and Barry knew that he saw him. He wouldn't stay in the building long. Getts almost ran out the south door. There were two streets the man could take to leave, First and Constitution Avenue. Getts had quick access to both. He chose the nearest—Constitution. He sprinted directly for a group of people who were waiting for government transportation, taxis and private cars. As he got near the group, Getts saw Barry's balding head, with its meticulously combed over fringe. He was just getting into a cab.

There were two more taxis nearing the knot of people on the corner. Getts pushed his way through men and women, muscling them out of the way. Nobody liked it and some spoke out, but Getts ignored them and got into the backseat of the next cab. "I want that cab up there," he said to the driver, pointing at Barry's taxi. He dropped a handful of cash onto the seat next to him. "Something extra for you if you catch him."

"You jus' grab on to yo' shorts, man. Ain't nobody losin' Tyrone B. LeBogue," he said. Tyrone stomped on the gas pedal, the taxi shuddered, and they tore off like a jackrabbit. Barry's cab was several cars ahead of them. It was 1730, rush hour, and huge lines of cars and buses alternately slowed, stopped, and crawled ahead again. It was like a parking lot.

All Getts wanted to do was get his hands on John Barry. As traffic stopped once again, he jumped out of the taxi, ran through lines of halted cars, and finally reached Barry's cab while it was still trapped among the other vehicles. Getts tried to pull open the doors but they were locked, the windows rolled up tightly. Getts could see the driver was greatly alarmed, and he could see John Barry sitting in the backseat, shifting toward the opposite side of the cab. Traffic ahead began to move again. Getts stepped back from the taxi and delivered a swift karate kick to the rear side window. The glass broke, but did not shatter. He kicked again. This time the window collapsed, but by then the taxi was beginning to move.

Out of the corner of his eye Getts could see a policeman on horseback, galloping toward him along the grassy median of the roadway. Intent on getting to Barry, Getts tried to reach through the passenger window to open the door from the inside, but the cab began to accelerate. He cut and bruised his arm as Barry's taxi sped away. Frustrated, Getts trotted down the line of cars toward Tyrone B. LeBogue's cab, horns honking at the both of them for stopping the now-moving traffic. As he reached for the door, he felt a strong restraining hand on his shoulder. "Hold it right there, fella." The mounted cop was now off his horse and onto Getts.

"I'm after a man up there, Officer. Don't stop me now," he said, pulling away from him. Cops don't like people resisting them in any way, but Getts didn't have time to tell him the whole story.

"Stand right where you are, sir. You're under arrest," he said as he moved toward Getts, his baton already out of his belt.

Getts couldn't take the time to accompany him to the police station. He stepped forward, curled his hand into a fist, and jabbed it into the cop's throat. The blow paralyzed the policeman momentarily, and he fell to his knees, gasping for air and consciousness. Getts removed the handcuffs from his utility belt, snapped them around the cop's wrists, and tossed the keys up the street. By now, the cab carrying John Barry was more than a block away, and traffic was picking up speed. There was no way LeBogue's taxi could make up the time. Getts stepped in front of a couple lines of cars until he got to the side of the road where the policeman's horse stood, patiently grazing on the divider grass, waiting for his rider.

"Whoa, boy," he said, approaching the large, beautiful animal. He didn't know the first thing about horses, not having ridden one since he was ten years old. Even then, it had been a pony. But he collected the reins and, stabbing his foot at a stirrup several times, finally got aboard. The horse was well trained, and very patiently refused to move. Getts tried several giddyaps, clicks, and "come on, boys," but nothing worked. It finally occurred to him that police horses were trained not to respond to anyone's commands save those of their assigned officers. Getts dismounted and, despite the pain in his leg, began running.

He ran toward a complex of business buildings, spotting Barry's taxi pulling toward them. He managed to gain ground despite the pain and shortness of breath, jogging around children flying kites, people throwing Frisbees, and couples strolling in the parkway. A dog began chasing him, barking and snapping at his feet. When he looked up again to spot the taxi, he could see Barry exiting his cab and entering an office building.

Getts turned toward the opposite side of the street, causing traffic to come to an unexpected halt in a hail of honks and curses. He arrived at the front of the building and dashed inside. By the time Getts got there, his prey was no longer in the lobby. Getts assumed he'd taken an elevator. Glancing at the elevator lights, he saw that all of them were above the second floor.

The SEAL scanned the lobby directory, not sure of what he was looking for, then decided he would have to look through the offices in the building, one-by-one if necessary. He decided to start looking from the third floor, and move upward from there. The entire third floor was occupied by an advertising agency.

"Did a man come in here just now?" he said to a receptionist at the main entrance.

"Not in the last few minutes. Is that what you mean . . . ?" she said to Getts's back as he hurried away.

Thinking it would take less time, Getts took the fire stairs. The fourth floor was the home of a law firm, a public relations company, and an import brokerage house. He described Barry to each person who greeted him as he walked into their lobbies. Nobody had seen John Barry or anybody like him.

On the fifth floor was another law firm.

"Afraid I couldn't tell you if the man was here," a

woman in her mid-thirties said. She was a tight-ass lady with pursed lips to match. "This is a law office and we never discuss our clients' business. . . ." Getts didn't wait for the rest of her rap. He walked right by her desk, turned down a hallway, and, hardly breaking stride, opened every door he came to. She came right behind him, screaming in his ear. "Stop that! Do you hear me? I'm going to call the police," she said. Getts just wished she would go to a phone and call whoever the hell she wanted to call and stop that infernal screeching.

A blue-suited member of the firm arrived in the hallway behind her. "Who the hell is that?" he asked her.

"I don't know, Mr. Andover. He just broke in."

"Call building security," Andover said.

"Shall I call the police?" she said, already running back toward her reception area.

"Yeah. Yeah, call them, too." Seeing the look in his eyes, Andover decided he was not about to take personal action in stopping Getts. Getts gently nudged him out of the way as he kept opening doors and searching inside rooms. After he had opened them all, he went to the sixth floor.

The largest office appeared to belong to Merriwether, Bagwell, Schultz and Sachs, another law firm. Getts opened frosted glass doors to find an attractive woman in her twenties sitting behind a desk where she typed and answered phones. Her desk plate said Ms. Spinner. "May I help you?" she said.

"I'm looking for a man . . . might have come in here a few minutes ago. Brown, almost reddish hair, balding, scraggly beard, and he wears glasses. See anybody like that?"

"No," she said. "Not around this office." She smiled, seeming like she wanted to help. "What makes you think he works here?" she said.

"I don't. I saw him come into this building. That's all. Sorry to bother you," Getts said and turned away.

"I'm sorry I couldn't help you find him."

After Getts walked into the outside hallway, the girl picked up her desk phone, and dialed an in-house number.

"Sir? A man was just here looking for you. Yes. Yes, he's gone now."

Getts walked across the street from the office building and simply stared at it. He knew the bastard was in there, someplace. He used his cell phone to call Peach. "Nothing happening here," he said when he heard Getts's voice.

"Yeah, well, I saw him."

"Where?"

"In one of the hearing rooms," Getts said, and told him about chasing Barry to this location. He gave Peach the address and said he would wait for him across the street. Getts's leg ached and his back hurt like a bitch, probably from unconsciously compensating for his leg while running. He knew he had to cover all ways in and out of the building, but it would be some time before Peach arrived. His prayers were answered when he spotted a couple of young black kids hanging on the street. "Hey," Getts called to them. "You guys, come here." The boys weren't yet in their teens, but they certainly weren't intimidated by a ragged looking honky slumped against a wall.

"Yeah? Watcha need?" one of them asked.

"Want to make twenty bucks?" Getts offered.

"Apiece?" the taller one said.

"Yeah, why not?" Getts replied.

"Sure, man."

"Doin' what?" the shorter of the two said.

"Don' matter doin' what," the tall boy said. "You don' want twenty bucks, go home." He turned back to Getts and said "Doin' what?"

Getts described Barry. "Brown hair, almost red, combed over a big bald spot, and wears glasses with steel rims. Know what they look like?" Getts asked.

"Sure, man. We know."

"And he's got a beard. He was wearing a dark suit when he went into that building there, across the street, but when he comes out he might be wearing something else. I need you guys to watch the door to the alley in the back of the building for me."

"You a cop?" the short boy asked.

"A spy," Getts said.

"Spy! Damn, that's all right. Sure, we can handle it, man," the boy said.

"Who we spyin' on?" the tall one said.

Getts was thinking about an answer when the other boy supplied one for him. "Prob'ly another spy. Tha' right?"

"That's right," Getts said. He took a couple of twenties from his wallet, tore them in two and gave each boy a half. "You see the man, come back here right away, then you get the other half. If he doesn't come out, you get 'em anyway."

The taller boy's face lit up with instant joy. "Damn, tha's jus' the way they do it, Leonard. Man, tha's cool."

"How long we gotta stay?"

"It's almost four o'clock now. Watch until six. Okay?" Getts said.

"We ain't got a watch," Leonard said.

"I'll come over to where you are at six. Or my partner will. Take off."

"Wow. You got a partner?"

"Yeah. He's working on the case with me. Get going."

When the young men were out of Getts's earshot, Leonard spoke to his companion. "Spy. Kina shit he think we smokin'?"

"Yeah," the other boy said. "Motherfucker jus' plannin' to take down a seller, bet yo' ass on that."

Chapter Twenty-one

Peach found Getts in a doorway across the street from an office building. "He in there?" Peach asked.

"Haven't seen him leave yet," he said.

"Back doors?"

"Got a couple deputy spies," Getts said, and told Peach about the two kids. They talked for a minute, then Peach started to walk to the rear of the building, when the kids came jogging around to their position. They were young, all right, Peach thought, but they were alert and looked pretty damn responsible.

"We seen him," the tall kid said.

"This is Leonard," Getts said to Peach.

"An' I'm Larue," the short one said.

"Hi, Larue. I'm Peach, Bobby's partner. You saw him?"

"Yeah. Carryin' somethin', too. Coulda been a gun," Leonard said.

"What did he do then?" Getts said.

"Climbs into a nine-eleven, man, an he—"

"Nine-eleven?"

"Porsche," the boy said, making it sound like gauche with a "P."

"Parked on the street or in a lot?" Getts said. If Barry was in the employees' lot, he would have to work there. If he was parked in the street, he might be just passing through.

"Lot," Leonard said. "Nex' to the buildin' he come outta. Got in and drove that way." Leonard pointed south.

Getts handed over the other two halves of the bills.

"Good work, guys. You earned your pay." Peach and Getts had turned away to find a taxi when Leonard spoke again.

"Don'tcha even wan' the license number?"

"Damn," Getts said. "You got the license number, too?"

"Hell, yeah. 634 VON," Leonard said.

The Porsche would be long gone by the time the SEALs could locate some wheels, but Getts had an idea.

Outside a coffee shop in the Brentwood area, there were a couple of police motorcycles parked at a curb. Getts looked through the window and, voilà, a couple uniforms were inside, their helmets off, sopping up an evening meal. Getts walked inside and sat next to one of them and ordered coffee. "Excuse me, Officer," he said. The cop looked at him the way they always do, like they had just been asked for a substantial cash loan. The cop sitting next to him looked Getts over from head to toe.

"Yeah?" he says.

"I, uh, backed into one of those little foreign sport cars when I was parking yesterday. Put a small dent in it. Nothing big, you know. I mean, really a little one. I figure a couple bucks'll cover it, but, you know, I don't want to get into trouble."

"You leave your name on the windshield?" the cop asked, still chewing his dinner.

"That's what I figured to do, then when I got back with a pencil and paper the car was gone. Guy probably never noticed."

"I don't suppose you got the license number?"

"Sure did," Getts said. "Six three four, VON." He handed a slip of paper to the cop. He looked at it for a minute then said, "Well, let's see who this belongs to." The cop stood up from his table and walked outside, his gun, handcuffs, gas canister, and other equipment causing him to walk with his hands and arms out from his body like an overpumped weight lifter. Through the window, Getts saw him talk into his shoulder mike. Getts smiled at the cop still sitting in the booth. He didn't smile back, turning to finish his mashed potatoes and gravy. In a minute the first cop had finished his radio communication, and came back inside. He laid the same piece of paper Getts had given him on the table. Getts could see that a name and address had been written below the plate number.

"This is the fellah you ran into," he said, pushing the paper at him.

"Thanks, Officer," Getts said. "I really appreciate this." As he walked out, he could hear one of the cops laugh and say, "He won't be so grateful when he gets the tab for work on a Porsche."

Getts walked the half block to where Peach was waiting in a rented car. Getts got in. "Well? How'd it go?" Peach said.

Getts read from the paper. "Barry's real name is David Blumfield."

While Peach went to a department store to buy some blue shirts and matching pants, Getts found a chain-operated electronics store. A middle-aged clerk with thick glasses and not much hair waited on him. "I want two white light photoelectric relays that work on one-ten," he said.

"How far to send and receive?" the man said.

"Under twenty feet. The actuator has to move an eighth of an inch," Getts specified. The SEAL watched the man carefully as he put together the materials that he wanted.

"Anything else?" he said.

"Zip wire. Thirty feet."

The man walked to the rear of the store, did some measuring and cutting, and came back with a coil of wire held together with a piece of masking tape. Getts paid the bill and left. After Peach picked him up, they made one more stop at a hardware store, filling a double-strength plastic bag with their purchases.

Getts and Peach rented yet another vehicle, a 1.5-ton Ryder truck that resembled a delivery van. They drove down several alleys in the downtown D.C. business district until they found what they were looking for: a large, empty appliance box. They tossed it into the rear of their Ryder truck and drove to the address supplied to them by the D.C. cop. David Blumfield's home was a few miles north of Chevy Chase in an old but renovated middle-class subdivision. Sixteen fifty-five was one of several recently built town houses on Curlew Avenue. Peach parked the truck directly outside. They were dressed in uniforms that appliance men might wear, each carrying a tool box.

They carried the large cardboard box from the truck, acting as though the appliance was heavy, up the path to the front door, and rang the bell. No answer. They didn't expect one. But they rang again and waited just to make sure. Then they picked up the cardboard box and walked around to the rear of the complex. There was a six-foot privacy wall enclosing a patio connected directly to the house. Lawns were neat, vegetation looked healthy and small, and newly planted oak trees lined each lot.

On the patio in back of Blumfield's property was a gas-operated barbecue grill fueled by a natural gas line originating from within the house through the wall. A sliding glass door gave access to a kitchen area. Near that was an opaque piece of window glass that looked like it led to a utility room, as there looked to be a steam vent at floor level. Peach tried the sliding glass door. "Locked," he said. Getts and Peach could see that a wooden dowel was butted up against the door to prevent it from sliding.

So they looked to the glass window. It was on aluminum rails as well, but it also had electrical conducting tape that ran along the bottom of the pane, attached at one side by wires to a relay box. Although they couldn't see the leads, they knew that they would continue around to a wall unit, where they would enter a junction box built into a central alarm system. Peach opened his tool box and took out a 3/8-inch portable drill.

First, Peach placed a patch of fabric duct tape over an area on the glass, then Getts used a high-temper diamond-tipped drill to make two holes through the tape and the crystalline glass, in two locations, above the electrical tape and the wall leads. They waited several minutes to see if the drill would be heard by neighbors. It wasn't.

Getts spooled out thirty inches of wire, attaching one end to the aluminum duct tape, and the other end onto a terminal of the relay. They used a half tube of liquid solder mixed with fast-drying epoxy to firmly fasten each end. They then used a portable hot air hair dryer plugged into an outside outlet for several minutes to make the conducting glue set. After they completed bridging the alarm gap, the two SEALs used a small pry bar to flatten the aluminum rail frame, and with only minor crunching and distortion, they lifted the window from its place in the wall. Carefully, they placed both tool boxes inside, followed by the bag full of other goodies. Once inside the utility room, they retrieved the loose window and reset it into its former position. Unless someone was looking closely for signs of illegal entry, the damage to the frame wouldn't be seen. Peach and Getts shook hands. "Time for the Winchester One-Step," Getts said.

David Blumfield drove his Porsche into a garage attached to the side of his townhouse. He shut off the engine, snapped off the headlights, and opened the door. Before getting out of the car, he reached onto the passenger seat and took with him his briefcase and a small bag of groceries. He pushed the car door closed with one foot, and walked the few steps to the front door. His key chain was full to capacity—his front door had three separate locks, two of them heavy-duty dead bolts.

Inside, the house was dark. He dropped his keys onto an end table and snapped on a light. He walked through the living room and headed into the kitchen. He left the groceries on a counter, opened the refrigerator door, and took out a bottle of Bombay gin. Before closing the door, he also withdrew a small bottle of dry vermouth. He removed the caps of both bottles and went about the business of building himself a martini on the rocks, including Italian garlic-stuffed green olives. He found a bag of salty taco chips in a cupboard, retraced his steps from the kitchen, and headed toward the den and the comfort of the television and his reclining chair.

Chapter Twenty-two

Before he could find the wall switch for the pot lights recessed into the ceiling, Getts and Peach turned them on. "Stand on that piece of tape," Getts ordered.

"Christ," David Blumfield said, his eyes transfixed on the .45 automatic Getts pointed at him. Peach leaned, relaxed, against a wall. "How did you people get in here? Hey, Getts, don't do anything nuts with that gun. Put it away, will you?"

"Hey, partner, guns are what we do best. So we're going to teach you how to dance the Winchester One-Step. You're going to love it. Step on the tape, Blumfield," Getts said. "Now."

Blumfield looked downward. And to the side. He saw the photoelectric relays set up to form a crossing pattern, their signals converging at the tape at the floor. The four units—two senders, two receivers—were connected with zip wire, and to a mounted Winchester 1300 shotgun. The shotgun was aimed directly at the tape on the floor. Moving with dreamlike slowness, Blumfield stepped into the One-Step circle, right in front of the gun barrel, and stood on the tape. He stared at the electronic apparatus around him. Peach picked up an electrical plug. "Don't move now," he said, and put the plug into a wall outlet.

Immediately, the two senders began to glow around Blumfield.

"Let me tell you how these work, old buddy," Peach said. "If you close the connection by moving out of the range of the photoelectric cells, then that little actuator there, connected to the gun, pulls the trigger. As long as you keep the circuit open, your legs are going to stay attached to your body.''

"Shut them off, for God's sake," Blumfield said.

"We will, but you're going to have to do some writing, first,'' Getts said. He handed Blumfield a clipboard with a writing pad and pen attached to it, keeping his hands high, out of the way of the photoelectric cells. "Be careful, David.''

"You're crazy. You'll go to jail for this," Blumfield said.

"That's exactly what we're trying to avoid,'' Getts said. "You're going to write out the whole story, who gave you the assassination orders to give Mob 4 when we met you on the boat in Miami.'' Getts replaced the .45 in his belt behind his back.

"You're really nuts. I can't do that.''

"Yes, you can," Getts said.

Blumfield licked his dry lips. "You wouldn't kill me.''

Peach said, "Hey, I like your guts. Something special about a man who spits in your fucking eye just before he dies.'' Peach and Getts moved a little farther back from Blumfield's position.

"Shit,'' Blumfield said.

"So, who gave you the order to pass on to us? Must have been somebody high up. Might have been someone in the State Department. Hazeltine? Higher? The President? Did nickel-nuts Spalding send you down there to give us the word?'' Getts said.

"Ask the Navy. You're Navy men,'' Blumfield said.

"We want *you* to tell us. Write it on the pad,'' Getts said.

"I can't.''

"You can,'' Getts said.

"You know what would happen to me if I did that? Nobody would believe me, anyway.''

"Leave that part to us," Getts said. "Start writing.''

"Fuck you,'' the lawyer said.

"You hungry, Peach?'' Getts said.

"Starving. Where do you want to eat?'' Peach said, glancing at his watch.

Getts moved to a sound system Blumfield had in his living room, being careful not to get into the line of fire. He turned on the power, adjusted the volume to a comfortable level. "What kind of music do you like, David? Country western? Rap? No, not rap. Rock? Classical? Classical. You look like a man who appreciates the finer, more complex qualities in life." Getts found a classical music station and left the dial there. "We'll be back in a while, David, after we have dinner. I wouldn't go making a lot of noise because someone might hear you and bust down the door and that would break the circuit. The back door's, wired, too. If anybody but us tries to open it . . . whammmmo!" He turned down the radio volume slightly. "We don't want to bother the neighbors," he said.

As they were walking toward the front door of the town house, Peach said to Blumfield, "Don't faint, and don't try to sit. And don't fall down."

"Getts!" Blumfield yelled as they were closing the door. "Don't leave me here!"

Getts and Peach found an Italian restaurant less than a half mile away. It had a kind of manufactured old-world atmosphere. Empty wine bottles hung from the ceiling, pizza pans and pictures of Italian cityscapes were nailed against the walls, and Venetian music played softly in the background. A waitress asked them if they wanted cocktails. Peach ordered a glass of the house red wine, while Getts went for a beer. They didn't talk much while they waited for the food, and when it got there, Getts picked at his meal.

"You don't want your pasta?" Peach said.

"You want it?" Getts said. Peach had just finished off a half chicken and rice, but then again, Peach was a big guy.

"I'd rather eat it than watch you shove it up your nose," he said. The reference was funny, but it made Getts think of Lydia again. He was feeling depressed again.

Getts watched Peach eat his second meal, then he watched him eat dessert while they each had another drink. They had knocked off the better part of two hours and figured they should probably get back to their old friend Blumfield and see how he was doing.

They let themselves back into the house through the rear kitchen door. They found the lawyer, still standing in one piece. He appeared to be very uncomfortable. "You bastards," he snarled as they walked in.

"Goddamn it, Bobby," Peach said, "I like this guy. I swear if he gives me the finger and says 'fuck you' I'm going to kiss him right on the lips."

"Peach doesn't like many people, Dave. You being a lawyer and all, you're probably used to being hated, but you've certainly worked some magic on Peach. When it comes time for you to die, you won't have to worry about somebody taking care of your shredded fucking remains. Know what I mean?" Getts said.

"Dave," Peach said, "where do you keep the coffee?"

"What?" Blumfield said. He couldn't believe his ears.

"Coffee," Peach said, beginning to look through the cupboards. "Never mind, I found it." He also found filter paper. He spooned out a generous portion of coffee from an open can. "Probably won't be all that good—you should keep ground coffee in the freezer."

"I don't know that it's a proven fact," Getts said to Peach and sank into an easy chair.

"I don't think I've ever had a cup of coffee from a ground can that was worth a shit," he said. He loaded the coffeemaker and turned it on, then joined Getts in the living room, sitting on a sofa well out of the field of scattered buckshot.

"Getts!" Blumfield cried out pathetically.

"Yeah?"

"I can't stand up much longer."

"Knees getting shaky?" Getts said.

"God, yes."

Getts just moved his chair a little closer to where Peach was sitting. "Smell that coffee," he said to Peach.

Peach went into the kitchen, poured a few cups, and called to Blumfield, "Dave, you got any cookies?"

"I'm going to fall, goddamn it!" Blumfield said, his voice quavering.

"Really?" Peach said, sipping his coffee.

"Yes. Really."

Peach turned to Getts. "Want to watch TV?"

Getts shook his head. "Nah, I think I'll just close my eyes." And he did.

"You work in the White House, Dave?" Peach said.

"Yes."

"Hey, do you guys have wild sex parties like they say, or do you just get to watch the boss when he does it?"

"That's enough, Peach," Getts said. "You don't have to insult David, here. He shouldn't have to take that kind of abuse."

"I'm sorry," Peach said. "Bobby's right, Dave. You're a real stand-up guy."

Peach laughed hysterically. Getts closed his eyes again when he heard Blumfield begin to mewl and cry. "All right," he said, "I'll tell you. Shut this thing off."

"Talk first," Getts said.

"We wanted the United Nations to take care of Krabac. He was a dangerous son of a bitch. We figured he'd be better off dead."

"Who's 'we'?" Getts asked.

"The United States," Blumfield said. "The President."

"Billy Spalding, his own self?" Peach said.

"Figures," Getts said. "Go ahead."

"They planned to blame it on Roger Demerit if it ever got found out. Jesus, don't say that I told you. My ass will be grass," Blumfield said.

"What do you think your ass is now, Dave, baby?" Getts said. "Keep talking."

"That's all. Luumba, at the UN, was supposed to handle everything, but he didn't get it done."

"So Spalding gave the order?" Getts said.

"Yes."

"Write it down."

"I can't. I'm going to fall," Blumfield said. Indeed, the man's knees were shaking and it looked like he was going to fall over in exhaustion.

"Then you better write fast," Peach said.

For a period of time, the room was filled with the

scratching sound of pen against paper on the clipboard. "There," he said, finally. "That's the whole story."

Getts read it, then handed it to Peach. "What does Hazeltine have to do with all this?"

"They're pals. Spalding thinks up the projects and Hazeltine makes sure they get carried out," Blumfield said, his lips quivering.

"Write that down, too," Getts said.

"God." Barry wrote quickly and handed the tablet back to Getts. Getts read it over, then handed it to Peach. "Okay?" Getts asked him.

He nodded. "Yeah. Looks fine. Let's take it back to the Creek."

The SEALs started gathering up stuff. "Come on, Dave," Getts said to Blumfield. "You can go with us. The IG will want to ask you a lot of questions."

"I'm not moving anywhere," he said, alarmed.

"David . . . ," Peach said.

"I'm not going. I can't."

"If we leave you here alone, you'll just get a lethal dose of lead poisoning, you know what I mean?" Peach said.

"Then shut this contraption off. Please. Now," he begged.

Getts reached out and shut the circuit off. Blumfield collapsed to his knees, almost sobbing with relief.

"You bastards!" His face was red. He lurched toward Peach, his fists balled ineptly. He swung, making slight contact with Peach's cheek. Peach moved only once, and Blumfield was on the floor clasping his throat. Somehow he managed to scramble to his feet, and headed straight at Getts with his head like a drunken bar fighter. Then he tripped.

"Atta boy, Dave," Peach said. "You'll feel better once you get it out of your system."

The attorney scrambled to his feet. "You guys are the worst—"

"Worse than you assholes in the White House?" Peach interrupted, subduing him.

"Calm down, Dave, you're with the varsity now," Getts said.

They had to more or less drag David out the front door, kicking and screaming because he had much more important things to do. "David, we're only two hundred miles from Little Creek. Ever been there? We can make it in three hours of driving. You can tell the guys down there the same thing you wrote here." Getts patted the paper in his jacket. "Then you're free to go. Is that asking too much?"

"I can't. Jesus, if they knew. If they caught me I'd . . ."

Then the bad news showed up. Two cars full of suits pulled up in front of the house just as the SEALs and Blumfield walked out. They let their suit jackets hang open as they advanced to where the SEALs stood near the front door, making sure they saw their pieces.

One of the cars was a limousine with smoked windows and ambassador's license plates. Nobody had to tell Getts who was in the backseat of that car.

"Mr. Blumfield, I'm Agent Mitchell," one of the suits said. "These are Agents Hecker, Boord, and Ronkowski. Have you made any unauthorized statements to these men, sir?"

"I, uh, I signed . . ."

"Shut up, David," Getts said. "It isn't any of their fucking business what we talked about."

"You signed what, Mr. Blumfield?" Mitchell pressed.

"Well, it was something that . . ."

Getts interrupted again. "Dave, you're a lawyer. Tell this servant of the people to kiss your ass."

Agent Mitchell gave Getts a very harsh look. "Hey, swabbie," he said. "You keep your mouth shut. You're interfering with a government agent in the conduct of an investigation."

"Bullshit. You're a hatchet man for the President and that leech that works for him, Hazeltine." Getts nodded toward the smokey windows.

"Have it your way, wise-ass. . . ."

"You reach inside your coat and come up with a piece,

they'll need DNA to find out who the fuck you were," Peach said, leveling the Winchester 1300 on Mitchell and his buddies.

"You've really torn it now, man. Threatening federal officers with a deadly weapon. You'll get ten years for that." He turned to Blumfield. "Come with us, Mr. Blumfield."

"Don't do it, Dave," Peach said. "Come with us to Little Creek and do the right thing. These guys are pricks."

"But I work for the government," he said.

"That's right. You work for the government, not for Hazeltine and not for the President. For the country. Tell these people to fuck off," Getts said.

"Dave," Peach said, still holding the Winchester on the feds, "you'll have respect for yourself if you come with us. Go with them if you want to, we won't stop you, but if you go with us you'll feel right. You'll be wearing size twelve balls."

Blumfield stared at Peach. He took a deep breath, then stood a bit straighter. Then he looked at Getts, and nodded his head. "Okay, let's go," he said.

Secret Service personnel are well trained in hand-to-hand combat. That's just for openers. They aren't little guys, either. And they know how to shoot weapons. In this case it was mutually understood that it just wouldn't look good for United States Navy SEALs to gun down federal officers, but it was also true that federal officers would have a lot to answer for if they fired on a pair of Navy SEALs.

Having said that, the feds were not about to let someone—anyone—flip them the bird and walk off. So Agent Mitchell, whether he liked the idea or not, stepped in front of the departing Blumfield. Peach hit Mitchell behind the rib cage, right in the kidney, with the butt of his shotgun. Mitchell went down like a poled ox. Ronkowski, the biggest of the feds, caught Peach below the jaw, under the ear, with a fist like concrete.

All fights that get serious, whether between highly disciplined fighters or not, turn into dirty street brawls with people gouging eyes, pulling hair, biting and kicking. Lots of kicking. And it's an exhausting business. Fights like that don't last very long, but if you're in one, you think it's been going on all day.

The fist that landed on Peach's neck sent a galaxy of stars through the back of his eyeballs to the front of his head. As he fell, he managed to remember to roll sideways to avoid the certain kick that was coming from Ronkowski.

Hecker and Boord went for Getts. He threw a fist at Boord's throat, hoping to take him out of the fight quickly. The blow landed an inch from its target, and while it inflicted major pain—and swelling trauma that would eventually cause Boord to be treated at a hospital—it did not put him down. Getts had no time to turn fully before Hecker grasped Getts's left arm and twisted it backward, trying to break it. Getts's instincts and training did not desert him; he relaxed the arm and dropped almost to the ground, rolling backward. This pulled Hecker slightly forward, in a direction he did not anticipate, and while he was off-balance, leaning forward on his toes, Getts performed a "sweep" kick. The kick was aimed at the Achilles' tendon of Hecker's leg, and found its mark. Getts thought he had snapped it or at least paralyzed the fed for some time as the agent dropped to the ground.

Boord was hurt badly, but to the agent's credit he ignored his own pain and went to the ground with Getts. He slammed an open hand onto Getts's face, flattening his nose, and went to the sailor's ear with his fist, striking him repeatedly and viciously. Getts was strong, however, and he head-butted Boord just above the nose. The sound was like two bowling balls colliding on a return rack. Boord's head snapped back and a stifled scream of pain escaped from the fed's mouth. He collapsed near Getts.

Ronkowski's kick made contact with Peach's side, but it wasn't firm enough to break ribs. In one of Peach's favorite and classic martial arts moves, he dropped to the ground toward his antagonist and, now between the fed's legs, delivered a palm-edge strike underneath the big man's testicles. Ronkowski fell to the ground, howling. Peach placed his hands together and swung upward, a massive two-fisted uppercut that nailed the federal officer directly on the point of the chin. The blow made Ronkowski's teeth shoot out of his mouth as if from a popcorn machine.

In the midst of the fray, a tinted window of the ambassador's limousine rolled down and the pasty face of Hazeltine, mouth gaping in disbelief, looked out.

Mitchell, while not fully recovered from his kidney blow, painfully launched himself at Peach, aiming to land a knee to the back of his neck. Mitchell never saw it coming. Getts landed a roundhouse kick on the side of Mitchell's head, catching him just above the ear. Mitchell not only went down, but he would be out for a period that would include two brain scans.

Hecker was still strong and undazed, but he was unable to support himself on both legs. Peach knew the agent had no chance as he moved toward him in a fighting stance, feet apart, one slightly ahead of the other, not crossing his feet as he advanced. The agent threw a futile punch, but was immediately off-balance because of his injured Achilles'. Peach slipped the man's fist and drove an open hand into Hecker's throat. Peach did not put every ounce of energy into the blow, lest he kill the nearly defenseless fed, but he put him out of the conflict. The fed grabbed his throat, sucked mightily for air and crawled, gagging, toward their car.

Getts retrieved the Remington shotgun, flipped off the safety, and blew out all four tires of the agents' vehicle. Then he walked over to where Hazeltine sat, still open-mouthed. "Hello, asshole. Have a nice walk home." Then he blew out three tires on the limousine.

Peach, blood all over his hands and shirt, smiled at David Blumfield. "Hey, Dave, baby, let's stop on the way down to the Creek and soak up some suds. Hell, you got to have some fun in life, huh?"

Epilogue

The expected court-martial of the surviving members of Mob 4, Chief Gunner's Mate Glenn Crosley and Lieutenant Robert Getts, never convened because of lack of evidence of wrongdoing. Chief Gunner's Mate Glenn "Peach" Crosley was given an honorable discharge "at the convenience of the government" and took up residence in Oakland, California.

Lieutenant Robert Getts, United States Navy, was allowed to resign his commission under a cloud of controversy. He returned to Palo Alto, where he applied for and was accepted into Stanford University's Graduate School of Psychology.

President William Spalding finished his second term of office without any public backlash over the death of General Vadim Krabac.

Former Secretary of State Frederick P. Hazeltine heads a Washington, D.C., research foundation and consults with the media on a variety of issues, both foreign and domestic.

Captain James P. Rolland, USN, returned to Little Creek from Europe with a videotape of Colonel Arnold R. Talent's recollection of events concerning Krabac's death, supporting David Blumfield's testimony. Rolland retired the following year, having served thirty-one years of active duty.

David Blumfield left the Washington, D.C., area to practice law in New York City. He is currently a partner in Kaye, Allen, Thiele and Bell. He appears often on television and in print for his views on White House machinations.

The Honorable Unan Luumba served a third term as secretary general of the United Nations and currently lives on Fifth Avenue in New York.